D1739326

The Yarn Woman mystery series

The Yarn Woman
Wailing Wood
The Rusalka Wheel

My sincere thanks
to copy editor Bonnie Lemons
and to the readers of the Yarn Woman mysteries.

Early Morning Press

THE RUSALKA WHEEL

A Yarn Woman Mystery

By Brooks Mencher

Swiftly turn the murmuring wheel!
Night has brought the welcome hour,
When the weary fingers feel
Help, as if from faery power;
Dewy night o'ershades the ground;
Turn the swift wheel round and round!

— *William Wordsworth,*
from Song for the Spinning Wheel, *1812*

Alexei Basara

Early November, 1817, Mielnica Podalska, Old Ukraine

THE FOREST is a wild place where wolves can hide.

But as Alexei Basara made his way along the night-black forest trail, he wasn't worried about wolves. He'd heard no howling. His ears weren't troubled by their snuffling. He wasn't worried about a wolf catching his scent. There were no man-killers stalking him along the side of the trail, or hiding in the underbrush, waiting. At least, not wolves. Shivers of fear shot through him.

Alexei was almost running now, then slowing down, panting, and again breaking into a laborious jog. The frigid air hurt his lungs. He believed the story about wolves stealing little Ivan Kulyk from his crib, though no one actually knew the Kulyk family. The villagers didn't know exactly where the Kulyks lived. No one could describe the two-year-old child, Ivan. Was he curly-haired? Was he dark or fair? Yet everyone told the story as if it were true, as if they knew, as if they'd seen the poor child dragged off by the leg, leaving only a trail of blood. Only one man seemed to truly know what had happened, or that it had happened, but that was enough for Alexei.

The truth about wolves was that sometimes on a moonlit night Alexei might hear a long, lonely howl from deep in the forest at the onset of winter. ... Still, sometimes they would steal into a child's sleeping room ...

Alexei's grandmother, who was Russian, would have called the Kulyk tale bylichla: a wonder tale that circulated among the people as a true story.

Alexei was running again ... at least trying. There had been no howling on this night. And Alexei knew that wolves were afraid of men. He'd heard that and he believed it. But more, wolves were afraid of leshiye, the evil spirits that dead men can become.

The forest may indeed be home to wolves, but it is more a place where the "unclean dead" wander in the moonlight — what Alexei's grandmother called those who had died unnatural deaths. They were restless spirits. The thought terrified him to the point of screaming. His grandmother, never at a loss for words to describe the "other side," called them leshiye, forest demons, plural. A leshii was one of the restless dead. Such ghosts waited in the forest to lead the wanderer astray. Lovelorn maids, despondent and long dead, led young men to their dooms is what his grandmother had said. Everyone knew it. And a man who was evil in life? Evil in death, of course, and double. They had the "the devil's breath," which no man could withstand. Once the evil breath was upon you, either death or eternal idiocy followed ... walking, blithering fools who would be better off dead.

He stumbled, but caught his balance before he could hit the hard ground. The jarring twisted his knee and pain shot through the side of it, inside, in the joint between the bones. It was cold enough now that it could snow again. A thin film of ice had formed at the edges of a rivulet that ran alongside the trail, and the icy edge caught the moon where the trees thinned. Frost dusted the leaves that hung over his path. He was limping. His beard and mustache had frosted from the vapor of his breath.

Alexei looked back at what had been following him. However fast he hobbled, even if he jogged along as best he could on that wicked night, it paced him. Now his knee hurt so badly … he hoped the cold would set in hard and numb it, quickly. He kept looking back over his shoulder at the leshii. His heart … he could barely keep it in his chest. His mind was in such a frenzy that it seemed to buzz between his ears. And he did not remember that the dead had no power to kill by their own hands: Fear was their only weapon. So said his grandmother, but her words drifted away like driven snow, and Alexei was ruled by horror.

If only it could have been a wolf, he thought! A wolf is from the land of the living.

The leshii who trailed him was little more than a silhouette: a tall, gaunt man with a limp so distinctive that Alexei recognized who he had been in life. It was Viktor Levchenko. Viktor had wandered from the village two years before, in the dead of winter in a stumbling, falling, fighting drunk. In life, he'd been an evil man. A cruel man. And in death, he'd been swallowed by the forest. He'd wandered off and died in the winter snow, and his cruelties went with him out of the village, and the village was a far better place without him. When they finally found Viktor's body, his left side was frozen to the ground. They had to wait until spring to get him out, and even then … His face had been frozen to the earth! The unforgiving earth tore at him.

Alexei moaned at the thought.

It's all in how you die, said the Old Believers — drunk, suicide, murder, or even an unexpected death: These were the demons in the forest, alive again in an in-between world, malevolent and jealous of the living, longing for the peace that would come with death.

Alexei, breathing hard, tried again to break into a run. Faster. His knee hurt very badly. His knee didn't move fully. He was forty-two years of age! His heart labored and his poor mind screamed so loud he could hear it. His eyes searched desperately for an escape.

But it was too dark to see. Only the bare trail could be detected through the icy mist of his breath.

Viktor Levchenko was closer now, his shadow stretched and as thin as a fence post. His clothes were so loose they caught the frigid breeze, and flapped. He was like a bat, he was a scarecrow ... he was skeletal, his face so thin. His teeth protruded. Viktor's crippled leg, loose and popping in life, was no longer an impediment but propelled him forward, fast as a wolf, almost gliding.

Then there appeared a second shadow beside him, this one small and wizened. It was crippled and bent over like an animal. It smelled, even at a distance. It was a shadow beside Viktor's shadow. Her white hair was long and ragged and it hung to the ground because she was so bent over. One hand was empty, dangling, maybe paralyzed; the other had a roll of string or yarn that was unwinding as they loped after Alexei. Its very strangeness might have made a drunk man laugh, but not Alexei. He could see it all in the moonlight, even beneath the shadows of the trees. His mind was so frenetic that it fixed on that ball of yarn and he was convinced it was one of his own, from his own house, stolen. He recognized it! In the dark! The tears froze along the sides of his eyes. His thin beard and mustache crackled. Who would even know he was dead? The thread of his life was unwinding, just as his grandmother had warned. Their evil breath would soon be upon him.

The unsettled ghost of Viktor Levchenko pushed Alexei on, deeper into the forest. The crippled hag with the hanging arm shuffled forward at Viktor's side, two legs and an occasional fist on the ground.

Alexei, straining forward, trying to see the path in the dark, recognized nothing now. No tree seemed familiar, and the trail was foreign to him. Why had he decided to walk home from the village? Why had he walked through the standing stones of the old cemetery? Good Lord, why had he done that? He'd been a fool. He had tempted the dead. No one would miss him for days, even weeks.

And why had he opted to take the shortcut along the edge of the forest? The shortcut should have taken half an hour, but now, time was no more. He had veered into the forest, the dark, pushed by the two leshiye. Somehow, he realized he had entered a liminal land, a place between the living and the dead. Only a miracle could save him now.

Alexei was sweating profusely beneath his thick coat. He didn't dare throw it off or he'd meet the same frozen fate as Viktor … except that he hadn't been drinking. He'd only gone to the village dance to hear the tones of the instruments that he himself had made: the fiddles and flutes, the kobzas and banduras. He'd made them all! Didn't that count for something in life?

He stumbled again and this time fell, sprawling on his face and chest. He cut his hand trying to break his fall. He'd bloodied his nose. Scrambling to his feet, he looked back and began to run again. The humped-over creature was beside him, on his left (Alexei's grandmother had once told him that Death always hovers on the left), so bent over it barely rose above his waist. Its white hair covered its face, but her nose stuck out. Most of the hag's yarn now lay along the trail, as if marking the path. But that was Alexei's yarn. The remaining ball was only a few inches in diameter. He knew his death was near.

She smelled horrible. Alexei's life was unwinding, like the yarn. His grandmother had said, "One Fate to spin the thread of life, and a second to wind; the third Fate is the Angel of Death, little Alexei, who unwinds!"

He could hear the hag panting in its effort to keep up with him. It had a raspy, phlegm-clotted inhalation. Viktor, all the while, was only a dozen meters behind him, hobbling and coughing.

Then suddenly, the light became different. The forest canopy had separated and the light of the bright winter moon illuminated the trail and trees. He had come to a small clearing. He could see a creek to his left, as wide as two men are tall, and it flowed so slowly that it seemed not to move at all. But in his memory, there should have been no forest stream — just trees and undergrowth. The rivers all were north, much farther from the village. He must have run deeper into the trees than he had ever ventured before.

He looked back again. Viktor Levchenko had stopped at the edge of the clearing in the middle of the trail, his arms hanging motionless at his sides. The hunched creature was no more than a black blot next to Viktor. It, too, had stopped abruptly. But Alexei could still see Viktor's eyes. They were plaintive. They asked for something, but he couldn't tell what. Viktor was going to kill him … it was in his eyes.

Alexei blinked, and Viktor vanished. He blinked again, this time in disbelief. Both leshiye were gone. Alexei shook his head like a dog who'd been struck. A few brown, frozen oak leaves were all that littered the path. They cast sharp moon shadows on the hard dirt. A light breeze rustled them and dusted them from the trail. Standing there, he could hear his heart still pumping. His ears were pounding with it. Fractions of a minute passed, but Viktor and the hag didn't return. They were somewhere else in the world, but not on Alexei's path any longer.

He turned around, facing once again the frightening forest trail in front of him. There was a bend in the white-black ribbon of water. There was no wind; the breeze had gone as quickly as the unhappy ghosts. It was very quiet. The moonlight touched the edges of the tree trunks and the leaves high up, and glazed the few shallow ripples in the river.

Not knowing what else to do, Alexei stumbled a few meters farther, toward the river bend, mindlessly. It widened. The water deepened and slowed. There was a languid eddy at the curve, and the deep water was black below and moon-white on the surface. He crept closer to the water, careful of his footing along the frozen bank. After escaping the demons — Viktor Levchenko himself! — only a fool would slip now, and fall into the water and drown!

The moon hovered. It was three-quarters full. He wished it could lead him home, but Alexei had little hope of returning home anymore. He had gone too deep into the wood. The thought that he would never get out of the forest settled on him like a melancholy wind. He felt it was not the real Podolian forest at all, but a ghost forest. He was as good as dead.

His lungs hurt. He was so tired. He had icicles in his beard. The rim of his hat: ice. He knew he'd never get out of the forest, but he wished it could have been daytime. He'd never see the sun again.

There was something in the water.

He couldn't tell what had moved, but something had rolled below the surface, disrupting the sheer obsidian face of the river, mounding it, moving it … like a large fish, but larger than he had ever seen. It was nearly as large as a man. By watching the swells, he could follow the creature as it crossed from side to side under the water, but he couldn't see its shadow or its form under the surface. Can moonlight penetrate a river at night?

Suddenly, it breached, throwing strips of black water off itself and into the air, the little streams splashing down onto the surface, destroying the silent moon's mirror. Alexei's heart, already exhausted with fear and running in the dark from demons, froze. There was nowhere he could run, nothing he could do to avoid what was in front of him now. He tried not to scream. Tears streamed down his reddened cheeks, steaming in the air. When he finally screamed, it was little more than the drawn-out moan of a small, dying mammal.

He shivered madly as a shape crawled from the water onto a wide, flat rock on the inner bank of the curve in the stream. Its thin-fingered white hands grasped the side of the stone, and with a well-practiced kick it propelled itself out of the pool and onto the rock. It sat there on its haunch, dripping, its eyes catching the cold light like the wide, wet eyes of a fish.

Alexei blinked and blinked, but he was unable to grasp what his eyes beheld. There before him sat a slender, very pale, very beautiful woman, her long golden hair dripping. She wore nothing.

He tried to swallow. He knew what she was: a river demon. His grandmother had illuminated him on the water devils, and she had a name for this one: Rusalka.

Alexei didn't remember slipping to his knees until the pain from his injury flashed into his consciousness. Knowing his life was forfeit, he turned to run, but the vision kept pulling him back. He wasn't even standing! Entranced, he couldn't pull his eyes away from it. His hips locked and he couldn't get to his feet. Struggling, he fell over. He might as well have been clamped in the teeth of a steel wolf trap. It would have been better to be clamped in the teeth of a starving wolf. Alexei saw himself as Viktor Levchenko, fallen on his side, the left side of his face pressed to the frozen ground, where he would die.

She would drown him. She, the rusalka, one of the restless dead, would finish the job that Viktor Levchenko and the hag had started. Alexei Basara was more frightened of the rusalka than he had been of Viktor's wandering, malevolent spirit. Yet ... after the rusalka held him under, he thought, at least it would be over.

She dove liquidly from the rock, making hardly a ripple in the slow stream. A second later, she climbed gracefully onto the bank where Alexei lay frozen in fear. She stared at him, her hollow blue eyes glimmering in the dark. She studied his soul, evaluating him. Alexei had never seen blue eyes in the moonlight. Her lips voiced words he couldn't hear. He wanted so badly to hear her voice. He could tell she was thinking ... she was weighing her options, making her choices. He knew that she knew everything about him, knew it with a simple look. Then she looked back at the water, smooth again like volcanic glass.

The demon had made a decision. He could tell. He tried to pray, but couldn't remember the words. God had fled. God didn't like the forest. Everyone said God doesn't like the forest, which was why the leshiye could live there.

The rusalka sighed deeply and silently; he could tell that, too. He could feel her loneliness penetrate him. She leaned down to her pool in the forest and blew across the surface. The unexpected action confused him. It bewildered him. Her breath was a mist in the freezing air. Something enormous had happened in that breath, but he had no idea what.

Then she stood, naked, as pale as the belly of a fish, and walked slowly and purposefully toward the trembling Alexei Basara. He began to weep, not for his fate, which was obvious, but from the unmanageable fear of the unknown, which caromed madly and mindlessly through his body.

* * *

ALEXEI BASARA AWOKE in Rusalka's arms. She had wrapped his greatcoat around them both, keeping him warm with the heat of her body on that night, for in a matter of hours the cold set in, and the river froze. The dirt of the trail froze hard.

When he opened his eyes, the thin winter sun had risen. She had her arms around him, and she was sleeping. She was warm, soft. He wished she would never move. The uncontrollable fear of the night before had vanished. The memory of that terrifying forest trail was vague, almost gone. It had been like a dream, and now he found himself, he thought, with a village girl at the edge of the old forest, along a tributary to a tributary to the great River Dniester that flowed, much like life itself, along the northern border of his native Podolia, the southwest forest region of old Ukraine.

He wondered why the girl had been swimming on such a cold winter's night, and how she had gotten there, to the stream. It was so far from the village. He wondered which of the villages she might be from, for there were many. Where were her clothes? It didn't make sense. Neither did his emotions, for his heart felt as if it were on fire. Until that night and in that place, Alexei had never been in love. Now, he could not be released from its grip for even a moment.

He was pressed against her in the coat. Her left shoulder, as she lay on her side, was very white, but it had a mark on it, on the back of her shoulder. In the morning light, it seemed to him to be a birthmark that was purplish red. It was shaped like a fish. He touched it. Her shoulder was cold. In fact, he discovered that her whole body now seemed cold, as if her internal fire had gone out with the rising of the sun.

She woke. She smiled at him. But she didn't say a word. Instead, she glanced at the crook in the river, as if it held not only the vapor of her breath but all the words she would never be able to utter. She held her lips to his for a very long time, breathing softly, her eyes closed. He felt her breathing.

Alexei finally realized that he was not with a village girl. He was sleeping with Rusalka. He swallowed. He wondered if she had traded her voice for a chance at mortality, like the old story. Only wordless promises remained. She had traded her voice for a soul, her water realm for a life with Alexei Basara, a simple Podolian luthier.

They walked back to the village, Mielnica, the old mill town in the heart of Podolia. She could laugh, though she couldn't talk. She wore his outer hemp shirt and his long linen underpants because his coarse wool trousers tore at her skin ... and because his linen under shirt, frankly, smelled like his fear from the night before. They shared the great coat, closely, and walked slowly, one trying not to trip the other. It made her laugh. Perhaps Alexei could borrow some clothes for her, he thought, in Borschev, or in Skala, so that no one would know. He had to get the birthmark on the back of her shoulder covered. People would talk. People would be afraid. To Alexei, the mark was beautiful, and he wondered why he thought that. But it was. He wanted to touch it, to touch her again. But the folk wouldn't like it. Perhaps the two of them would have luck making it invisibly back to his small house. Maybe they would; maybe Alexei Basara's luck had changed that night.

If it had indeed changed, it had changed forever.

Helen Oliver

THREE DAYS AFTER Helen Oliver's thirty-fifth birthday, she discovered a small antique and collectibles shop in an alley in San Francisco's Chinatown near Waverly Place. It was a dead-end alley between Clay and Washington streets.

Her car was at her apartment; she'd taken the bus because parking in Chinatown is a myth. She'd spent hours wandering on and then far off the beaten tourist track. The shop building was brick, like those off Embarcadero, and built in the 1940s. Years of wind-blown trash gathered in corners away from the light, and did its best to rot in the cold and damp.

The alley was dim because it was narrow. The buildings were tall and had few windows. The brick was dark with years and soot. The only light came from above and it was perpetually cold except at noon when the sun was briefly allowed entry.

Helen looked up at the crooked street signs at the corner in an effort to remember where she was. She saw no pop-ups selling cigarettes or candy, no one with a tray of jade animals of the Chinese zodiac, no one selling luggage and spring-loaded knives and small bottles of water. There were no pornographic magazines, nor their unsavory salesmen, tucked into shallow niches at the corners. There was no vender to dispense cheap little umbrellas that could be used once before they flipped inside out. These small booth-shops were a Chinatown mainstay for both locals and tourists, but they needed foot traffic to survive, and there was none at this alley. There were only puddles of rain from the day before. For all anyone knew, this alley might not even have existed ... anyone but Helen Oliver.

Looking across the damp, broken asphalt, she could see only two windows. The one along the right side belonged to a meat curing business where red-glazed, plucked ducks were hung, awaiting orders from restaurants. A smoke-blackened galvanized stovepipe protruded from the wall beyond the window, just higher than a person, and thin wisps of smoke or vapor escaped. The odor was fatty and musky.

A mural of an orange cat had been painted on the weathered brick wall before you got to the glazed red ducks. The cat looked like a giant lubok − a stylized, hand-painted Russian woodcut. Helen immediately loved it. The brilliant orange stood out sharply from the weathered brick and chipped mortar. It was the only mural of its kind in the city, including the alleys of Little Russia. But such an image was not foreign to her. She dallied over it, inspecting it and adoring it. There was little doubt it had been sprayed by a demented Russian, homesick for century-old lubki − and orange tabbies. Helen decided its many swirls, set like tiles, had been sprayed using a stencil. It was very good work, really ... a Russian Banksy who was fond of orange. She took her cellphone out and took a photograph. She had not seen a lubok since her childhood. She missed them, but hadn't realized it until now. She checked her phone for the picture. It wasn't there. She was doing something wrong. She'd never used the camera part before. She tried again, but didn't realize her finger was over the lens.

This was the first shred of Helen's history to present itself that cold summer day, and she would have no record of it. The phone went back into her bag.

The antique-store window was on the left down near the warehouse, which stared up the alley to the intersection at Clay. The window was dark and, by alley standards, large. Beside it was a wood door with one step made of gray, soot-soaked marble. It was cracked. The window, too, had a large crack; it was in the far lower corner. A bead of silicone rubber had been squeezed along it to keep the rain out, and the silicone had discolored into an amber smear. But with the spider webs, which had caught small pigeon feathers and soot, it seemed to adequately hold the glass together. Above the window, hidden in the shadow of an eave, was the sign, Sterling's Fine Antiques & Collectibles. The lettering needed to be repainted. It was hard to read.

It was August 26, a Wednesday, and a typical cold, damp, overcast day in San Francisco. Helen peered into the smoky window and felt that this was going to be her lucky day after all. The orange tabby Iubok was a herald, she decided.

She couldn't see much through the window, even holding her hand against it and keeping her eyes in the shadow. But she felt lucky anyway, and that wasn't a very common feeling for her. Maybe it had something to do with being in Chinatown, with all the happy colors, the sounds, the smells, the crowds. The Chinese have a word for such an enormously lucky day — jiri — and though she had never heard the Mandarin word, she felt in her bones that this could be one of those rare days when one's very destiny can change. To Helen, who had spent her life fleeing from people and politics and tragedy, the thought was wistfully appealing.

She stepped back from the window and observed her reflection. She straightened her back and her skirt. She took off her knit cap and pulled a wisp of blond hair back behind her ear, and pulled the cap back on. Despite all that was available in San Francisco, she'd had difficulty finding a hair stylist she liked and whom she could afford. She'd resorted to one of the chain outfits, which were cheaper, but she really dreamed of having someone do her hair right. Still, Helen had an allure that defied the styling of her hair.

Her features were not typical and in the right light she was striking. Her blue-gray eyes were large and wide set; her hair was fine, flaxen colored, but lacked the correct nutrient-based conditioner, so it was usually ratty looking. She was slender, with almost no bust. Her ears were small and elfin, her skin light and even waxy.

She had no friends, few acquaintances, and, despite her peculiar beauty, no suitors. People, generally, did not like her because they felt uncomfortable around her. She thought that was their problem, not hers.

Despite the maritime cold, Helen had worn a top with straps. Her blouses were all in the hamper and she wasn't going to the laundromat until tomorrow. She wore a soft blue cardigan over the camisole, more or less as a shirt, and then a second sweater over the blue one. She would have worn the blue one even if it had been warm: She had a birthmark on the back of her left shoulder that she preferred to hide, and so she kept it covered. It was reddish purple, dark, and large enough to be embarrassing. It was in the shape of a fish, about four or five inches long. It didn't trouble her personally, but the negative effect it had on others forced her to cover it up, even in this age of screaming body art. Besides, it wasn't a tattoo: Tattoos, she thought, are beautiful, with flowing shapes and gentle coloration in reds and greens, yellows and blues, like a rainbow. Or, they could be brilliant and shocking, say things like "love" and "give" between a person's knuckles. Tattoos exist by choice. In Helen's mind, her birthmark was a curse that she could do nothing about. Her grandmother had called it a "kiss from the gods," and by that she did not mean the Christian God. Helen had doubts about a god like that, one that could do that sort of thing to a person. In defiance, she had a beautiful koi tattooed on her ankle, in bright and beautiful colors.

Helen's nature was meek. When she spoke, her voice was barely audible. She was a shy woman who didn't lunch with her coworkers. She had a problem with her voice and she found gatherings embarrassing.

The doorstep to the antique shop hadn't been swept. Cigarette butts covered the asphalt like fallen leaves. Helen imagined a couple of trees sitting on a bench along the wall of the building at the back, chain-smoking and swapping tree stories. It made her laugh.

It didn't seem like anyone had crossed the threshold for months. There was a trash can to the right. It overflowed. Except for the trash and glazed ducks, the alley seemed to lack evidence of human life. A recent light rain had pocked the shop window with dark little craters of dust that had dried. It looked miserable, and it wouldn't have taken much to wash it, thought Helen. The door had a small glass window and it, too, had small circles of dirt left by rain. There was a red and white "Open" sign in it.

The door was unlocked, which surprised Helen: The shop really was open. Still, she could see that it was rarely visited. She entered quietly, afraid to wake the ghosts that surely inhabited the place. She wanted to take her red heels off, to make no noise, but did not. The shop floor was unswept; dirt sounded like sandpaper when she stepped. The shop lighting was insufficient, and it took a minute for her eyes to adjust.

There was junk everywhere, packed in and up and under to the point of absurdity. How could they sell anything when you couldn't move through the sea of stuff, let alone see the merchandise? Still, under studied examination she found cut-crystal lamps and hanging bronze lights, and from a filthy corner of Cairo were two-toned scarab rings that protruded from slits in a dirty, blue velvet box behind a glass cabinet. In another cabinet, she could see silver toe rings and lapis earrings, and brass and copper bracelets of low quality and considerably worn. On a shelf above were small stone statues of Osiris and Anubis. There was practically a whole shelf of Anubises, and Helen wondered if the plural, in English, was Anubi. For all she knew, the figures could have been authentic. But surely not for the $35 on the yellowed price tags. Real value? She thought they might be worth a dollar and a half, retail. Helen prepared herself for exorbitant prices on, essentially, thrift-store junk.

But it made her smile. This was her lucky day, after all. There was no telling what she might find.

On another shelf were cigarette lighters of green and red plastic and transparent Lucite with colorful beads and tiny bobbles inside, drowned in clear naphtha. There were woven scarves on wooden coat trees, glass boxes, enameled boxes, Russian boxes, nested boxes shaped like little Russian girls with daisies, but she could tell at a glance they were from China or Mexico; there were baskets, blue bottles, cocaine or snuff vials possibly from the Ming Dynasty if they weren't fake, which they were, and an odd assortment of stringed and wind instruments, both broken and unbroken, strung and unstrung.

There was even an old kobza! It was now getting interesting. She hadn't seen a Ukrainian folk kobza, like a lute but with a rounder soundboard, since she was six.

There was used furniture of every kind and from every age and nation. She saw camphor chests from China and cedar chests from Pennsylvania. There were tchotchkes beyond number from the spherical earth's infinity of corners.

Soon, she could see that there were two people in the store besides herself. The shop's proprietors included an angulated, antediluvian crone whose skin loosely covered her unfortunate, twisted bones, and a man in his sixties or seventies or eighties who may have been her son or her husband or her unfortunate lover, and who was her equal in emaciation and ugliness, inside and out. The man was tall and favored one leg when he walked, and his feet hit the floor heel-hard, as if he were in cowboy boots and wasn't used to them. He wore shoes that had once been black.

The crone suffered a debilitating curvature of her spine and could not stand erect. She spent her days staring at the floor, and she had to turn her head to the side to see, for example, a customer. Her white hair hung sideways off her head, and it was long and ill-kept. Bent, she was perhaps four feet tall.

The man, who was her son or lover, could stand erect but had to keep his head turned to the side so a customer such as Helen wouldn't see his left side, which had no teeth top or bottom, and the skin on the left side of his face was scarred at the temple and cheek. The general structure crushed in upon itself like a withered melon, which made his left eye slightly protrude. He blinked long and squintingly. The left corner of his mouth was wet, and he wiped it continually with the back of his hand. He was a two-sided man with one half being moderately acceptable (though pitiful), and the other half, when he happened to accidentally show the opposite profile, as frightening as Dorian Gray's portrait.

Perhaps they were the ghosts she had teasingly mentioned to herself earlier, the ones she didn't want to waken. She tried to laugh at her fear, but she had a lingering feeling that these two store clerks would do everything in their power to hurt her. She sighed. She decided she was overtired. And she was too young to lose her mind.

On the day that Helen entered the antique store for the first time, encountering its peculiar and even grotesque proprietors, she also discovered a spinning wheel that had been stacked high on wooden chairs, dressers, and chests. There were Chinese baskets in the mess, and red tassels, and empty picture frames that stuck out from the pile.

The spinning wheel was essentially unreachable. It was haphazardly balanced, and seemed as if any tremor would send it sliding down the stack and into an aisle that was already so narrow that customers had to walk through it sideways. It wasn't shaped like a spinning wheel that one normally thinks of — the Saxony style has the drive wheel horizontal to the fly. Every illustration she'd ever seen of old Rumpelstiltskin had this kind of wheel. The one before her, however, had the fly above the drive wheel; it was an upright wheel ... though it was resting on its side.

Today there were no customers besides Helen. There may have been no customers for months, from the looks of it. The spinning wheel was so high that it hovered just under the cobwebbed chandeliers, almost touching them. To get close enough to see it, she had to evade lamps and hand-painted flower vases that seemed purposefully situated to catch a person's clothing, fall, break, and require payment for damages. She was careful with her clothing; she was not rich and didn't want to pay for broken goods that might be caught by her sweater or modest tan wool skirt. Her purse was red, medium-size and conservative. She kept it close to her body. A red scarf was tied loosely around her neck, over the sweaters. It did not go well with her skirt or the exact red of her shoes, and she normally would not have worn them together. After all, she did have a second scarf. But this was a sort of holiday for her, and she didn't worry about the clothes.

When Helen's eyes fell on the spinning wheel, an electric shock coursed up her spine. She felt that she somehow knew that wheel. Her heart caught. After a minute, she realized that she had stopped breathing, and she gasped, sucking in the stale air of the shop. The air tasted like dust and had an after-smell that reminded her of the glazed ducks in the shop nearby.

She knew how to spin. She didn't weave, and her knitting was rudimentary. She sewed, but everyone where she came from sewed a little out of necessity. She hadn't spun or knit since childhood. She stared at the wheel and could hardly take her eyes off it. Strangely, she felt like it could hardly take its eyes off her. It seemed that, after many, many years, the spinning wheel had somehow found her. It had been waiting for her, and she wondered for how long. Years. She found that her heart was racing.

But Helen soon regained her reason, and her mind returned to her conservatively dressed body. Her pulse slowed back down. She shook her head and smiled at her own silliness. Yet she remained thoroughly intrigued because the wheel was so much like her grandmother's spinning wheel that the legs could have been turned on the same lathe and the wheel trued by the same skilled artisan's hand. That may have meant nothing in this era of mass production, but the old wheel that she was familiar with was handmade nearly two hundred years ago. Its unique aspects, however, would never be truly visible in the shop's dim light.

From her angle in the aisle, she could almost see the flat side of the drive wheel, but she wasn't tall enough. Her grandmother's wheel had designs there: One of the tales of Rusalka had been incised and painted there when the wheel was built in the early eighteen hundreds. And there had been strange strips of iridescence in her grandmother's wheel, as if mother-of-pearl had been inlaid along the surface in thin lines, paralleling the grain of the wood.

Helen grimaced. She squinted. Surely this could not be that wheel. It would be impossible. But her memory of the old folktales came back to her like a flood. Helen had spent her earliest years listening to her grandmother, her babusya, tell her stories of Rusalka, the faerie spinner, the beautiful flaxen-haired water nymph, while grandmother's wheel went round and round and the flax on the distaff slowly disappeared. The flyer spun, the bobbin filled, and just like that someone would appear at their door to buy it … because her grandmother was a very good spinner. Yet, what she remembered most was the sparkling flash of red, of green, blue, and yellow, created by the inlaid shell. It was not overwhelming, but it was … strange. When she was a child, the flashes of color in the morning sun seemed otherworldly.

She had liked the old folk stories about Rusalka because Helen, too, had light hair and was small. She swam beautifully. In fact, she had been told that she looked like her grandmother when Babusya was a child.

She had not thought about the wheel or the old folktales since the day she and her grandmother left Ukraine when it was still part of the Soviet Union. She had been six years old. In a way, she wanted to forget all about the old times and the old country. But she did not want to forget Babusya.

Helen suddenly felt incredibly alone. She had no family. And since her grandmother had died, she was lonely as well. Lonely, she knew, was different than being alone. She felt the soft anguish in her cells. There wasn't anyone else like her, no one with similar DNA — brothers, sisters, cousins even twice removed. There was no one from an old neighborhood … no one she knew from her childhood, from school. No uncles or aunts. Nobody shared her memories. Even her strife was her own — and her worldly challenges could hardly be considered typical. Her childhood memories were no solace to her, but more akin to the rapid gnawing of many mice. She was torn between wanting to reminisce with someone, anyone, and to forget it all forever.

The spinning wheel brought tears to her eyes.

Despite the troubles she and her grandmother had in the Old Country, the rhythmic pedaling of the wheel was a bright memory, something that made all the rest of it tolerable. And impossibly, here was that spinning wheel again, immediately in front of her! She was sure of it, now, standing there. She felt as if the wheel, like a cat, wanted to follow her home. The cat on the brick wall was a sign, and the wheel was the gift. She would like both to follow her home.

Then she thought it couldn't possibly be the same wheel. How could that happen? Too many years had passed, and also too many thousands of miles. Ukraine was a world away. The spinning wheel was gone.

The single pedal that powered the drive wheel had become detached. She could see that much, even from so far below. But the distaff, in its various segments, appeared intact, and the joints appeared tight. But surely, positioned on its side as it was, there would be added stress. It shouldn't be on its side, she thought. The four legs — and the edge of the drive wheel — seemed smooth and snug, as far as she could tell. Helen couldn't see if the bobbin was there because of the angle and height of pile. Yet, the device could have been completely intact, and she was infatuated. This was her wheel! It had to be. The more she thought about it, the more it had to be. Where had it been? She remembered that it had simply disappeared about the time they left for America. When the apartment burned, the wheel had burned with it. Gone like a ghost. Its departure from her life had greatly upset her grandmother, but the times were so hectic and troubled that their attention was diverted away from its unexplained fate. How could it rise from its own ashes? How could it have come to America? How had it landed in San Francisco? How long had it been here? It had been almost thirty years!

Realistically, she finally realized, it couldn't be the same wheel. But maybe the same person had made it? Stranger things had happened ...

Helen couldn't get to the precariously balanced enigma because of the tangle of countless pieces of furniture, many of which had been recently stained brick-red and heavily varnished, as if someone had tried restoring some of the old stuff without knowing the first thing about how to do it. Most of what hadn't been stained red had been painted sky-blue. Up close, the items smelled of varnish and mineral spirits. Helen laughed to herself: Mineral spirits weren't the only ghosts in this old shop!

You didn't really notice the uniform red stain or the blue paint that much because of the dim lighting inside the shop, most of which came from bronze chandeliers hanging from the joists. There was added light from the far-away alley window, but it didn't add up to much.

She tried to take a quick photograph of the wheel with her cellphone. Then she crept as close to it as she could, leaning over a dresser and peeking from beneath a lampshade, and took a second and third picture using the phone's telephoto setting. She looked at the screen and tapped the button. Nothing. She tried again, once. Finally, it seemed to be working. She felt she had to see the turnings up close ... would they correspond to her memories? She didn't know how to operate the cell camera very well, but kept trying. Some of the photos were accompanied by a small flash of light, and some were not. She wondered why. Still, all the images at this point were being saved. She felt triumphant.

The store's proprietors were in the back area. They might not like her taking photos, she thought. She tried to do it discreetly. She hoped to use natural light because she was afraid of attracting their attention with the flash, but she couldn't control it. She took two more photos holding the phone high above her head, meaning to capture the invisible side of the drive wheel, which was face-up at the top. If it was her grandmother's wheel, she would have images of mythical Rusalka in her watery world, blended with bright opal-like striations. The combination of incised cuts and carved relief would, hopefully, appear in their original soft colors. But when she tried to look at the photos she'd taken, the window light behind her made it impossible for her to see them clearly. At least there were images this time. She took a few more pictures holding the phone over her head. The flash went off twice. With a dozen exposures, she slid the cell into her purse.

A moment later, the proprietors approached her on either end of the narrow aisle in which she stood, hemming her in. They were slow and direct, almost as if being moved through the maze of aisles by magnets under the floorboards.

"I would like to know," said Helen in a soft, slightly accented voice, "how much is the lovely spinning wheel?" She still had difficulty speaking, as she had since childhood. It was not her lack of English vocabulary, it was simply getting her vocal cords to cooperate. When they did, she spoke with a slight Eastern European lilt, and her voice was watery, in the mezzo soprano range but with little projection. Some might have found it as attractive as her soft facial features and expressive blue-gray eyes. Helen's lips were thin, yet their shape and curve were mysterious, and her smile was glamorous without intent.

The thin male proprietor motioned the crone away, as if banishing her to the counter in the back where the cash register could be seen. She obeyed, blinking silently at the ground. She hobbled away, somehow avoiding the arms and legs of chairs and the handles of cups that protruded into the nearly impassible aisles. She was nimble despite her age and malady.

Alone now with Helen, the gaunt man, the tooth-side of his face to his customer, pointed with a crooked finger at the spinning wheel. The chipped end of his fingernail was discolored from nicotine and tar.

"It is," he croaked, "$165."

Helen was momentarily distracted by the man's voice. It seemed familiar, but the face was surely not. She'd never seen the man before.

She had hoped for a lower price, considering the quality of the merchandise in the shop. "May I see it?" she asked, trying to sound less interested than she was. She studied the man quietly, evaluating him with the trained eye of a traveler and survivor: There was something disgusting about him … that is, beyond his physical appearance. He frightened her. But whatever unsavoriness lay behind the grotesque facade, its specifics remained hidden from her. If it had not been for the wheel, she would have had nothing to do with the man or his shop.

He sighed and coughed thickly for several seconds. "If you come back tomorrow, we will have cleared a path to it, and I will bring it down and place it on the floor for you," he said, sighing heavily, as if anticipating the work ahead. "We have so much inventory at the moment. … If that is not inconvenient." There was sugar in his voice, but the raspy aftereffect from smoking reduced its sweetness.

She said it wasn't inconvenient. She would gladly be back tomorrow. A few minutes later, having navigated the aisle to the exit, she departed congenially, closing the door softly behind her. The thin man stood in the aisle facing the door, with his hands slack at his sides. He tried to force a smile, but was only half successful.

Helen walked to the nearest bus stop and began the long route to her apartment. The miles rolled by in jerks and bumps. It rained lightly. She didn't have a seat. It was no problem. She preferred not sitting anyway because the seats were dirty. She had ruined one skirt that way. But standing, she was unable to read her paperback, and she couldn't look at her photos for fear of dropping the phone. So she spent the miles thinking, and she became lost in her thoughts. The furniture of her mind, as the bus accelerated and over-braked its way across the city, consisted only of that spinning wheel. It was as if the poor thing had died and, pale and wan, had been tossed haphazardly upon its bier, waiting only for the gaunt man to flick a stick match onto it and send it to heaven with the smoke of a half-smoked Pall Mall, the stub of which Helen had seen in his shirt pocket. She'd smelled it there, too.

She wouldn't let that happen to the wheel. She would never let that happen.

She thought briefly about the man and his voice. But when she turned her thoughts to him, it seemed as if a cloud surrounded her and dulled her thinking. It was strange. The wizened old woman wasn't familiar at all, not her face, not her voice. Nevertheless, Helen had difficulty thinking about her as well.

She returned the next afternoon as promised, and was filled with hope. She was convinced her luck had changed, that her whole life had changed and that, with the fabulous wheel in her possession, her destiny was on a new and sunlit path. She had looked at the photos; the wheel had to be her grandmother's. The flash on her phone camera had played off the pearl streaks, obscuring portions of several photos in a glare of red, green, and blue. It was more like fire opal than mother-of-pearl. But she couldn't remember completely, it was so long ago. She was at a loss to explain how there could be two such wheels in all the world, for surely there were not.

The shop door was unlocked when she returned, though the shop again looked closed. She shut the door gently behind her, not wanting to wake whatever evil lurked inside. She didn't look forward to seeing the proprietors.

She found that the spinning wheel was in the same position that it had been the day before. The man had done nothing to make it more accessible. Again, she marveled at its similarity to her grandmother's, for it was more than the style of legs and armatures that seemed so familiar. It was the cut of the wood and the wood itself. It was the feel of it. And the opal. … She could hardly wait to run her fingers along the carved and tinted images of elusive Rusalka.

She still couldn't see the sides of the great wheel; only the edge where the drive band looped it to the fly. But as Helen stood a dozen feet in front of it, she sensed that something was different about the arrangement of other pieces of furniture, as if some of the chairs beneath the wheel or around it had been moved and then replaced in not quite the same place. She dismissed the notion as unimportant, and refrained from pulling out her cellphone to see if, by reviewing yesterday's photos, anything had actually been moved.

Then she realized that what she wanted most was to see her grandmother once again spin flax and sing, and tell her the stories of the spinner, the soulless, speechless nymph of Ukrainian legend. There were many traditional Rusalka songs, and her grandmother knew all of them. There were Rusalka dances, and Helen even remembered a few, dimly. Rusalka was a story that had followed her from childhood like the birthmark on her back, and could never vanish.

Acting surprised to see the young woman again, the crone crept across the floor from the office space behind a glass cabinet in the back, swaying slightly left and right as she crabbed her way toward Helen. "Oh, Vic," she said, her voice having the harsh crack of a crow, "come and get this damned thing down!" The man, who was now named Vic, took ten minutes getting through the shop to where the crone and Helen stood, and he dallied another fifteen minutes deciding how, exactly, to begin. It took him at least an hour to get the area cleared and restacked elsewhere. Then it took fifteen minutes more to clear a path from the nearest narrow aisle to the wheel. It seemed to be the only item that hadn't yet been stained red or coated with a thick layer of blue.

Helen could now clearly see the side of the drive wheel. It had the same images as her grandmother's. It was streaked with white opal that tried desperately to catch any light that the dim room offered. She remembered now, and yes, it was opal and not nacre. One of the carvings, painted in oil, was the water nymph amid flowing seaweed.

Knowing for certain now what the wheel really was, she could have cried, but she did not. She tried to hide both her tears and her eagerness.

Vic found a price tag on a string that was tied to one of the uprights. She had not noticed it the day before, but she hadn't been able to get a good look when the wheel was above her head. Vic glanced at it, his crushed face registering surprise. In disbelief, he showed the tag to the crone and mumbled something unintelligible. The old woman gasped but immediately tried to cover up her shock. In very clear script on the very white, new-looking tag, was the price: $675.

The crone shook her head. The man, Vic, shook his head. They looked like eviscerated, featherless birds bobbing over seed ... they were something left over from a Days of the Dead celebration in Fruitvale, the Hispanic district in Oakland across the Bay Bridge. "I must have been thinking of that other wheel, the one we sold a week ago," said Vic. His voice whined and wheezed.

"Two weeks," said the crone angrily. "I was going to adjust the price on this exactly because of that last one. We lost a considerable sum on that sale, Vic, thanks to you." She turned her head as she tried to address him, and this added to her contorted appearance, amplifying the curve in her spine, and the ribs of her back could be seen beneath her shirt and sweater. Her cracking voice was taut, as if straining to get through her neck. "This one is quite old and valuable, and large, you see, and I was going to ask $885. I think, at that price, it would still be a bargain," she said to Vic as if Helen were not there. "She could flip it for a third more! You know she could!"

"But we couldn't charge her that much," whined Vic. "After all, I mistakenly quoted it yesterday, and it's only fair that we stay with the price on the tag. We cannot set the price any higher, even though it would still be very much of a bargain at $885. We must remain committed to the $675 price." He held the new price tag up in his yellowed fingers, as if proving his point.

Helen was crestfallen: "$885?" she said wistfully.

"No, no. It says $675, and we will stay with that, dear, won't we Vic?" said the crone. "Now, my dear, we fully understand if you are no longer interested. After all, that fool did say it was $165, though he was clearly in error. He didn't bother to look. He was thinking about the other wheel, which was in terrible shape and was hardly worth repairing. Yet we lost money! It would have been worth $300 at least. Or even $400 if I had only stained and varnished it before it sold. They are in great demand, as you must know, spinning wheels. But, it's gone for $165. A terrible loss. We lease, dear, and you know how things are these days. Rent just goes up and up."

Helen didn't have $885. She might have had $675, but that might be her entire net worth. She was uncertain what the final price really was. Would they change from $675 to $885 in the next minute? Sensing the younger woman's hesitation, the crone asked, "Would you think of buying it for Christmas? It would make a wonderful present. How would you like to buy it for Christmas? For a friend or for yourself ..."

"Christmas?" asked Helen.

"We will set it aside for you, for a small deposit."

"A small deposit ..."

"For, say, $200 now, we will put it in the back with your name on it, and hold it until Christmas," suggested the crone. "Two hundred and fifty will hold it until, say, two weeks before Christmas. I am sure you will never find another like it, and I've had at least four other customers express interest in buying it in the last week. One of them, a man, will be in tomorrow. He was quite sincere. And very good-looking. He wanted to pay by check last week, only to find that he was without a second identification. I said … dear, let me explain … I said he could pay with what cash he had and return with the rest, that my Vic would put his name on it, and take it to the back … put it on layaway. We'd wait for him to return. But he was an honest man, and he wanted to pay the full price all at once. I expect him tomorrow. I felt you should know."

Helen pondered the impromptu layaway plan as she tarried over the spinning wheel, still unable to inspect it fully because of the dim light inside the store. But she loved it. She was sure a competent furniture maker could easily restore it to its full glory … if it even needed restoration. Really, it just needed a good cleaning and waxing.

"No, no," said Helen, "I would like to buy it. Yes, I think I would like to purchase it. Now."

"We will deliver it," injected Vic. "We deliver at a minimal cost every Thursday, and that would be today. We have a van. It gets very good mileage. Surely you cannot transport something of this size and weight — and fragility — yourself."

Helen was fully capable of transporting it herself if she was careful. She didn't want to leave her wheel in this horrible shop for another minute, and she did not want the wheel to be in a van with that man.

She thought for a moment. She couldn't imagine either of the two shop owners — or clerks or whatever they were — being capable of lifting a cup of coffee. Delivery would, indeed, be convenient, but …

"Oh, no, that won't be necessary," she said. "Do you take Visa?" She would carry it to the bus. It was no longer commuting time, so she could probably get at least one seat toward the back.

The crone twisted her head to speak to Helen. "We don't take credit cards," she said. "We accept cash, or a check if you have a driver's license and telephone and a second identification. We always wait until it clears, but we will put it in the back with your name on it and the check number, until the check clears. You know business, these days. One just can't take chances. We would just put it in the back, with your name, and wait. Five days, they say. For a check to clear. Five business days."

Helen Oliver's heart fell to her knees. She had cash, but only enough for the $200 holding fee. Or was it $250? She didn't have $250. They had said both amounts, she was sure. She dug it from the bottom of her purse, pulling out a small red leather pocketbook with a snap closure. She could get cash from the credit card and then try to pay it off soon, before the high interest added up.

Helen was now dealing with Vic, because the crone had vanished into the back of the store, behind the counter where they kept the cash register. She hadn't seen her leave, and was uncomfortable alone with Vic.

Vic sighed when she said she had only the $200 holding fee. He looked up, trying to spot the crone. Then he looked back down at her, for he was much taller than she was. He whispered, "You can return with the rest before the end of the week. There will be sales tax, for the governor, as well." He forced a smile, but it didn't work. "We don't need to collect it now. We'll make an exception. We know you are a nice person and will be back." The smile had corrupted his face.

She agreed to return with the down payment, plus the sales tax, before the end of the week.

After straining her ears to hear the discussion from her post at the back of the store, the hag slinked back to the middle area where Helen and Vic were closing the deal on the spinning wheel. The old woman had pulled on rubber gloves and had a paintbrush in one hand, having busied herself with the business of staining and varnishing an old chair. The brush had half-dried, brick-red stain in the roots of the bristles. It was the same color as most of the refurbished furniture. As they stood, Helen had no way out of the store, for the proprietors blocked the narrow aisles. She was suddenly very uncomfortable, and looked quickly toward the window, hoping for a way out.

Affectionately, the old woman placed her hand on the younger woman's hand and wrist, much as any auntie would touch her favorite niece. "I am sure you will love your new spinning wheel," she said. Helen knew the old creature was smiling; she couldn't see her face. But there was a hint of something in her voice, when she squeezed out the "s" of spinning wheel. Something of the serpent, something from a B movie.

The rubber glove was wet and cold with solvent, and the sensation on Helen's wrist was unpleasant. It seemed to burn slightly. The unexpected creepiness of the touch sent a chill up her spine.

She smiled briefly. It had been a long afternoon. Things had gone fairly well, but she really didn't feel all that well, physically, at the moment. It was very warm in the tight, airless shop. She had difficulty getting her breath. Yet her feet and hands were now freezing. She found it strange, because she had been so hot before. Now, she felt sick to her stomach. Her forehead was wet with perspiration.

She felt claustrophobic in the store aisle, not least because she was blocked fore and aft by the owners. She gently pulled the hag's hand off her arm, patting it, trying to appear friendly. She was confused, and felt she might have to vomit. She had trouble catching her breath. The solvent was thick and clear on her skin. It had been smeared when she tried to remove the old woman's hand. She carefully eased herself into a nearby chair that Vic had taken down when he'd freed the spinning wheel. Her heart was racing.

Helen was very dizzy. She glanced over at the shop's front door forlornly, knowing she couldn't run there before she would have to vomit. She swallowed, and blinked a few times, trying to clear her eyes. She closed them, but when she did it felt like she was spinning madly.

She tumbled from the chair, barely conscious, and lay on the floor, her legs and arms askew, her eyes open and looking at everything sideways. She was strangely embarrassed, and tried to pull her skirt back down over her thighs, but couldn't manage it. At first, her breathing was like a fish gulping air, but soon she grew quiet. Her newly shallow breath began to vanish. Then Helen grew still. Though her eyes remained partly open, there was no vision.

The hag looked at Vic, sideways, and smiled at the floor. She laughed lightly. Vic began to pull at the body. The sleeve and scarf had pulled slightly off her left shoulder, exposing Helen's birthmark. The old woman was repelled by the sight of it, almost cringing as she squatted over the young woman's body. She snapped off the gloves and with a gnarled hand pulled hard on Helen's blouse, yanking it up out of her skirt as she tried to cover the shoulder. "This thing disgusts me," she mumbled. Then she turned to Vic and said sternly, "You keep your hands off it, Vic. You know what I mean. Just get it out of here."

Vic looked at the contorted body. The hag held her chin and shook it slightly. "It's dead, Vic. You idiot. Go get the furniture roller, and you better hope that damned wheelbarrow is still out at the water where you left it, you fool. Dump the thing, I don't care where. And scatter its stuff, you lazy bastard. Stick it with the rest. And take the shoes. Everyone wants red heels these days. Go get the van, I said!" She had a ball of jute twine, and began winding it around the stilled wrists of Helen Oliver. It was a small ball, and the old hag unraveled and used it all.

Detective Chu

DOC WAS DRAWING A MAP for Detective William Chu in the cafeteria at police headquarters on Vallejo Street, using a ball-point pen he'd plucked from the gutter on Jackson. He'd walked almost all the way across the city, and he was tired.

Doc was upset. And he ached, so he was cross. He always hurt by late afternoon and he didn't like walking if there was a destination involved. He wouldn't have done it if he hadn't had to. He needed a drink to dull the pain. He needed a drink, period.

The pen said Wells Fargo Bank on the side. The "perfectly good" pen had either been run over in the street or excessively gnawed, and Chu, as he watched Doc meticulously draw the map, couldn't tell which. Small beads of thick blue ink were deposited here and there on the paper, testifying to the wrecked condition of the cartridge inside the plastic shell. Doc said it had internal injuries, and laughed nervously. His hand shook a little, like the rest of him. It had rattled him to see what he'd seen.

While Doc was drawing, Chu went to the supply cabinet and brought back a couple of new pens and a pencil. Doc slid them into the pocket of his heavily soiled jacket and continued working with the gnawed specimen. Responding to Chu's quizzical look, he said,

"Look, everyone knows that you have to finish a drawing using the same pen. Or you get jinxed. Something terrible could happen. Something worse. Yeah ... uh, is that coffee you're drinking?"

Drawn from Doc's still-functioning visual memory, the map was accurate. Chu could tell because he knew the dock area on the north end of the city. Doc added notations in perfect draft lettering but with small globs of ink paste every few letters. His hands were cold, sunburned, and bent. They were blistered. His nails were blackened but clipped. Doc tried; Chu had to give the man that much.

It wasn't the idea of walking over somebody's dead body, which is basically what he'd done, that troubled the old man. After all, he'd seen a few bodies during his time in the city. For a moment, he tried to count them but then got back to his map, adding lines here and there, and more notations, a couple of more fish in the bay, and after daubing the pen tip, eyes to the mermaid.

It was more the feeling that accompanied what he'd found earlier that day. It bothered him enough to look up the detective, the one who'd gotten him a room in a residential hotel for a month — he didn't know how long ago, but more than five years, probably — and who'd checked in on him every now and then for the last ten. What other man, let alone cop, would take him for duck soup in Chinatown? And he'd done it more than once. Or sizzling rice soup, his favorite? More than twice. Saint Chu ... it sounded like a sneeze. Doc laughed while he was drawing, but he didn't say why. He mumbled, "Gesundheit!" and giggled.

Doc trusted Chu, but only so far. It was the other cops, and the city people, like Social Services ... who Doc didn't trust at all; they were a bad lot. They had only one reason to get into your business, and that was to ruin your life. Period.

Doc wasn't a doctor. His street name was a simple reduction of dock, because of all the time he'd spent among the piers — the 30s and 40s on the northern shore and the 80s on the east side of the peninsula north of the old coconut processing plant; those were the pier numbers. He'd always been most comfortable near the water, whether in summer cold or winter rain. The years of maritime exposure had taken their toll on his face and his hands. But not his soul, thought Chu. The man's soul was intact. You could feel that. Doc had heart.

After an hour, during which time Doc added embellishments to his map while sipping his coffee, Chu gave Doc $20 in fives and ones, another paper cup of police coffee and a white-bread sandwich of ham (or something between ham and bologna) and American, and walked him to the door of the police department. Doc didn't want a ride, and didn't have anywhere to go, anyway. He'd walk north to the bay, maybe a little west, and call it a day. It was already 8 p.m.; it had taken him almost two hours to draw the map.

On parting, Chu asked, "That mermaid, Doc, did you see someone dump her in the bay? That what happened? You have her there along the side, the waterside."

"What, are you crazy?" said Doc nervously. End of conversation. "Try to keep it together, Chief. Maybe you need a wee drink …"

Then, after watching the old man wander off to the west, and with the map in hand, Chu drove out the Embarcadero and then north up the narrow pier access road called Al Scoma Way, past the seafood restaurant. Pier 47 juts north into the bay at about Leavenworth, and then veers west at a right angle. It's wide, consisting of warehouses on one side and a strip of unused "land" on the other where a previous generation of warehouses had decayed and vanished, leaving a ragged DMZ. Chu stopped about halfway. Knowing what he'd find, he'd already notified the medical examiner and sent a couple of officers to secure the area. Their vehicles plugged the narrow road. Chu left his car in the middle of the lane and set the red and blue rotating light on the dash and flipped it on. He walked along the roadway to a fish-gutting bench and stared up at the waxing gibbous moon, watching the sea mist float beneath its golden, nearly green light. No matter how long you live here, he thought, the piers are eerie at night. He wondered briefly how the moon could be 239,000 miles away when it seemed so near he could touch it, and he questioned how, optically, it could appear as flat as a can lid when it was actually a globe. Then remembered something about "parallax" from his high school physics class. The explanation didn't really help.

He sighed and followed the map. Somehow, Doc had managed to sketch in the topography of the sea floor on either side of the pier, noting the position of some of the old rotted pier pylons that were, to all eyes but Doc's, invisible as they languished through their own private eternity beneath the bay. Doc must have remembered their positions after seeing them poke up from the water during the once-in-a-decade super-low tides. Institutional memory is priceless, thought Chu.

The map might appropriately be called a chart due to its maritime notations of depth, invisible pylons, and submarine shelves, caves, and rocks. Doc had smeared some of the ballpoint ink at the edge of his mermaid, who in turn had wrapped herself around a compass (to allow the reader, Detective Chu, to orient the map correctly). The smear, though, was calculated, and shaded the fish-woman into a three-dimensional being. In the forlorn yellow roadway lights of the pier, she looked sad.

The mermaid was eye-catching in her line-drawn simplicity. The image was about four inches long, so her face actually had character. She was bare and flat-chested. To Chu's untrained eye, she was reminiscent of an illustration in a children's book. Her hair was moving as if caught in the tide, and her arm was out as if she were feeding small fishes that passed by. If he hadn't been standing there while Doc was drawing her, he would have thought the old man had used a live model, not his memory.

The crates and dumpsters on the south side, where the now-vanished warehouses had stood, were positioned exactly as rendered on the paper. And the officers that Chu had sent to secure the site had already located the body precisely where Doc had drawn it.

No cartographer could have done better. The body was buried under crates, old crab traps, and broken orange floats and under wet, wind-blown newspapers and McDonald's hamburger wrappers. To Chu, that sort of memorial was very sad.

He couldn't get to the body easily from the roadway, even in the bright moonlight. It was on the other side of some old steel fencing and past twenty feet of no-man's-land. More, the body was zipped into some sort of dark nylon duffle bag. Chu wondered how on earth old Doc could have found it in the first place. The poor old man must have been horribly surprised when he unzipped it, probably hoping to find something he could use, wear, eat, spend, or sell, Chu thought.

The body in the bag? Man, woman, teen ... he couldn't begin to tell at that distance, and he was in no hurry to find out tonight; it was going to be a long night anyway. He realized it was probably the "mermaid" because the mermaid had every indication of being a definite person, just as the map's fishes could be identified by species. He'd wait and have the information delivered to him by the medical examiner or one of the cops. Why? For Chu, this was a bad time for finding bodies. It was the seventh lunar month, a month set aside on the calendar as a Chinese tribute to "hungry ghosts" — the restless dead. It was for honoring ancestors or parents who had passed away. Food, recitations, incense, and goodwill helped settle their spirits. Fake money called "Hell notes" were burned in their honor, and joss paper was burned. And though the month was dedicated to these spirits, the fourteenth day was always set aside as a sort of epicenter of action, a feast and festival day. A day when spirits became boisterous. That was today, this very night. Chu's mother, who kept track of the traditional lunar events, had warned him of this weeks ago. And as always, she'd been right. Here was the proof. And when he saw her again, she'd say, simply, "There's your proof, William. Pay attention. Not everything is in your police book."

The body was certainly human, and the zipper had burst partly open. Even at twenty feet and in poor light, the detective could see that there was a red, hard-cornered purse sticking halfway out of the bag, as if jammed on top in afterthought.

And there was a red scarf near the foot of the duffle, outside it and maybe three feet closer to the roadway. The medical examiner was hovering over it, and two of the cops were standing nearby doing basically nothing. Chu checked the map again, now using a small flashlight, to see if Doc had noted anything else of importance. Two more police cruisers arrived. They couldn't find anywhere to pull off along the pier road, so they parked in the middle behind Chu. The officers finished stringing yellow plastic police ribbon across the area.

The mist crawled over the broken boards, over the empty steel tar buckets and cans of marine varnish far easier than Chu or any of the other officers could, but eventually a path was widened from the roadway to the duffle, free of splintered planks and rebar and jagged wire fencing. Chunks of cement had been rolled to the side. Chu looked up and wondered why the moon was greenish gold and not silver. Had he ever seen a golden moon before?

Maybe he should have taken a few minutes at the first of the month to honor his ancestors. It would have taken such a little effort, he thought. He caught himself in the middle of a long sigh, and stopped. If he had, though, maybe he wouldn't have found himself accepting, with latex-gloved hands, a woman's bargain-basement purse from the similarly gloved hands of the medical examiner's assistant. He wondered who it had belonged to, and by reflex cast his gaze back to the dark nylon duffle. She was lying inside there, just out of sight. She probably wanted her purse back. Anyone would have.

He shook his head. For the first time in longer than he could remember, Chu felt nervous. He guessed that was the word for it. There was something about the purse and the dead woman. This one had gotten under his skin, and it hadn't even started. There was something wrong, if not with the case, then with him. His trepidation was irrational. He laughed at himself. "You can take the country out of the boy ..." he said to himself, and chuckled again. Superstition does very little to fortify one's professionalism, he thought. He had overcome much to climb his way into his impressive position with the San Francisco department, and the cultural inclinations of his native Chinatown were not the least of what he'd managed to cast off. At forty, give or take, he'd set much of his heritage aside to achieve his goals. He had relinquished ties to several of Chinatown's "families," which were more like political gangs or clans of influence than genealogical connections, and, in his youth, he'd concentrated on athletics and his studies while most of his peers did their best to work within the family systems, importing hard goods, rare teas, and even drugs.

Detective William Chu is a self-made man. But he takes his accomplishments seriously and humbly because nothing came to him without sacrifice. He's good-looking, trim, and in very good shape. He's tall, almost six feet. His round face seems too kindly for his line of work, and his hair is thick enough to give GQ's raft of models a run for their money.

As he stood at the pier on the northeast tip of the peninsula, he would not have minded knowing what rumors were circulating in Chinatown's private political circles about the body that had gotten itself squeezed between the crates and buckets and refuse of Pier 47, just far enough west of Fisherman's Wharf and the glimmering, touristy "30s" to exude an aura of danger and filth.

It was an ideal place to dump a body, he mused, a body-dumper's smorgasbord. You could stash a corpse among boxes and crates; jam it into a rusted cargo container; weigh it down with readily available chunks of cement and rebar and offload it into the bay. Splash, and be done with it. There was a break in the fence, which he could see in the moonlight, and the duffle could have been carried or drug into position. But Chu knew to look for a single wheelbarrow tire track on the other side of the breach in the fence.

He would look in a few minutes. That track would indicate that the perpetrator hadn't the muscle to carry the body. There would be a wheelbarrow track, he was sure of it ... though it could be a pair of thinner tracks from a wheelchair or a cart.

He knew that if it had been done between, say, two and five in the morning, the killer might not have been seen. It struck him at that moment that Doc had probably seen it. After considering it for a moment, he had no doubt. Would Doc be able to describe the car that had been used? Did Doc's mermaid have the face of the girl who owned the purse? He thought, dumped, yes, but not in the bay. On land. Why had Doc drawn her in the water?

But there was only one body, one red purse, and one red scarf, at least so far. Perhaps Doc wasn't the first to stumble onto the remains, or maybe he wasn't the only witness to her demise. Maybe there'd been a "picker" doing his dirty work in the night, like the scores of dark souls who'd followed Napoleon eastward, stealing from the dead and dying as they lay in the war fields. Strange occupation, thought Chu.

He walked to the fence to confirm the use of a wheelbarrow, then walked back to his post on the pier, near a dockside fish-gutting table, complete with running water via a faucet with a short piece of rubber hose attached. The medical examiner's assistant and one of the cops weren't far behind him. They brought him the scarf and purse and then returned to the body and duffle.

Chu checked the label on the scarf. It was probably bought at one of the discount department stores that advertised so heavily on the Bay Area's television stations. Or Macy's; same thing. Newspaper ads touted a perpetual sale there of one sort or another. On any day, you'd see a hundred scarves like it. From Chu's perspective, it would be useless in identifying the body. But he was sure that the purse, even if empty, could offer a number of clues to the crime as well as to the identity of the deceased, and while the medical examiner's crew continued to work on freeing the remains, Chu began checking the purse. He had already gloved up. He spread a sheet of plastic over the old fish bench that overlooked the water, and set the purse on the plastic.

He took each item out carefully, almost solemnly. There was no reason to intimidate her spirit tonight — she'd had a rough enough time of it already, he was sure. He tried to offer her the dignity she deserved.

Inside the purse was a zipping wallet with nothing in it. Chu quickly realized she'd been robbed: There was no cash, not even a penny in the clip-closed coin pocket inside the wallet, and no cards. The implications at this point, however, were uncertain: Chu realized he could be dealing with a knowledgeable criminal network that would, without fear of being found, distribute her stolen cards and the information they held to domestic or international buyers who would use them one or two times and then destroy them or even pass them along to fools greater than themselves. They could be in Oakland by now, east or west. This had probably already occurred because the killer would be trying to beat the bank before the cards could be cut off. The bank accounts of the deceased were probably already drained. He hoped the dead woman hadn't been stupid enough to write her pin number on the back of the card ... not that it would matter anymore.

But something else worried Detective Chu: Foremost in his mind was murder for pleasure, not for gain. The owner of this purse wasn't rich. There'd probably been nothing more than one credit card and a bank card and maybe twenty bucks in that purse.

This day wasn't getting any better.

Strange, he thought: Who would leave a cellphone? Chu pulled it from the purse. It was a smartphone, off-brand, but even so would have brought ten or twenty dollars anywhere in the Bay Area. Chu refrained, for the moment, from turning on the phone and checking the call-in, call-out lists. He dropped it into a plastic evidence sack and set it aside like one might set aside a dessert, saving it for last.

He continued to remove the few remaining items. There was no lipstick, and he found that odd. But there was a smear of it on the lining; it was the cherry-red color that that pop singer was noted for. Chu couldn't remember her name immediately, but it was that color of red, which was very popular. If the deceased had even a hint of style-consciousness, it would imply that she had a light complexion.

There was no address book, though any addresses would naturally be on the phone. There was a plastic ballpoint pen that you could buy a dozen at a time at the drugstore, and faux-designer sunglasses that were large and rose-colored and would have covered much of the woman's face. Again, a drugstore purchase. But they would have fingerprints: He dropped them in a small evidence bag. There was a small hairbrush. Chu noticed fine blond hair in the bristles. The hair was long. He did not extract it, of course. That would be left to the forensics team. They'd run a DNA test on the follicles. He noticed there was nothing metallic in the purse, such as a nail file or small scissors.

Ms. Helen Oliver's driver's license had been left in the purse, though it had been removed from the zipper wallet, probably during the search for credit cards. It was of no use to a thief who didn't have very good connections. He surmised that these thieves wanted nothing incriminating left around their workspace. Already in Chu's mind was a serial thief or worse, a serial killer … someone who did the same deed over and over in the same secret place, following the same formula.

He quietly hoped that the woman had not been physically hurt before dying.

After a few minutes, he had what was left of Helen Oliver: Born August 23, 1980, a San Francisco resident; weight 130 pounds; five-foot-seven, race C, hair light, eyes listed as blue but appearing slightly blue-white in the photo. The address of her apartment was listed. That was a bonus. In the photo, she was pretty — different, somehow, but pretty. Then it hit Chu: The resemblance to the face of Doc's mermaid was striking, and after a few seconds the woman's face became unsettling. Here was the old man's model. Chu sighed. Doc must have seen the killer unload her body, close enough to see the dead woman's face. He might even have witnessed the killing. He set the license on the fish bench, and wondered if Ms. Oliver had large feet or small, though he realized that it had no bearing on the case at all.

Thoughts like this set off an alarm in the detective. He knew he tended to involve himself too deeply in murder cases, taking the individuals and the pursuit of justice far too personally. Wondering about something as inconsequential as a shoe size, even if it were nothing more than a passing thought, was a warning sign to him, mild as it might seem to anyone else. The way to solve cases, he reminded himself, was to analyze the salient facts only, and even those should be scrutinized at an acceptable distance.

He decided that she did not have feet anyway. She had flippers. He smiled and shook his head.

Helen had a strange, haunting face. In the DMV photo, her eyes were light, but they were odd in that they seemed slightly far apart, just as Doc had drawn them. The color seemed milky, but surely that was just the poor quality of the state-rendered photograph. Her cheekbones were high, reminding him of Scandinavians or even those of Siberian or Asian ancestry. She was attractive. He'd bet a hundred-dollar bill that she was a transplant from Eastern or Northern Europe.

He handed the license to one of his lieutenants and asked the officer to run it. You can never tell what might turn up. A criminal record? She could have been a prostitute, although Chu was certain she was not. It was just a feeling. This was a case of an innocent victim … until proven otherwise.

It took a few minutes, and the license was returned to him. The young officer handed it to him and said, "She's a naturalized citizen as of 1992. I've contacted immigration, Homeland, and they'll send the file."

"When?" said Chu.

The officer straightened her hair and said, "It could be weeks, they said. No one knows where the files are, anymore. They said it could be with Immigration and Customs, or in the Homeland database. There's a backlog, and federal agencies have priority over local agencies. That's what they said."

Chu shook his head. He stood silently at the fish-cutting bench. Ms. Oliver's body still hadn't been extracted from the pallets and fencing.

He returned his attention to the purse, and ran his latex-gloved fingers along the lining. As he halfway expected, there was a lump along the side under the patterned nylon. Even without unstitching it, he could tell it was about ten bills thick, folded in half and taped to the side. The amount? Anywhere between ten dollars and a thousand. The thin wad spoke to Chu about both the woman and her thief.

What did the bundle of bills say about the perpetrator? One, that the killer was in a hurry. He or she grabbed the cash and cards, tossed the license and phone, and then dumped the body and clothes and purse far from their "workshop." Two, they had limited expertise in the down-and-dirty aspects of their criminal profession. They knew nothing of the "darknet," he decided, or they'd have taken the license. They didn't know much about their victims. They were amateurs. Chu hated amateurs. Maybe they were young ...

And what did the bills tell him about Helen Oliver? She was thrifty, prepared for difficulties, and her social attitudes were like those of people far older than she was. Chu corrected himself: far older than she *had been*. She was like one of the Silent Generation, perhaps even the War Generation, who had survived the Great Depression. Chu was now fairly certain of her rural Eastern or Northern European roots ... though he might just as easily have suspected Central California, or maybe Oklahoma or rural Texas if not for the naturalization. For sure, though, she did not have an elite background.

Oliver, Chu gathered, was not a rich young, socially active woman. She was the opposite. She did her best to get by and was passable in her appearance. She could have attended an opera without raising eyebrows, but she could not have passed, during the opening gala night, among the city's glamorous elite. Her beauty was natural and not the result of cosmetics or expensive clothing and coiffure. Testing himself, he guessed that the mini-wad of bills in the purse lining would be less than a hundred dollars — an emergency sum for little more than food, or a taxi home, or a pair of slacks or blouse she might unexpectedly stumble across at a department-store sale. It was her cash in case her credit card was declined at the gas station or Safeway or Trader Joe's.

He pulled at the top of the lining, separating it at the stitches. It had been separated there before, and then loosely re-stitched. There was a red and gold foil envelope taped along the side, honoring the Year of the Ram. It made him smile. How could he not like her? He untaped and opened the envelope. He counted the cash: Eighty dollars, including seven tens and two fives. His estimate had been off by one bill. They were old and softened by use before she had managed to collect and hold onto them. He placed them in another plastic evidence bag and zipped it tight. What was likely her life savings was now evidence.

All that was left of Helen Oliver's final day on earth had been reduced to that red purse and a black nylon duffle bag with a red scarf nearby. Chu silently wished that the woman had had the chance to buy herself a sale blouse or maybe a nice lunch with the cash, and not have ended up, sadly, in a sack tossed from a wheelbarrow onto a decaying dock north of Chinatown.

He quickly stopped himself from that line of thinking.

Already, the deceased had become far more human than was acceptable to Chu. But he did not fight the primal urge to bring justice to bear upon this sad case of murder. Unable to have prevented the useless loss of life, he would do his utmost to make someone pay for the evil that he or she had brought into the world.

Maybe she hadn't been murdered, he thought ... but the circumstantial evidence was pretty strong.

He looked up from the bench. The county medical examiner and his crew had finally extracted the body and its zipper bag. Chu set the purse aside and put its contents back inside. The driver's license remained on the bench. He stared off over the rough landscape, trying to imagine what form evil took when it entered the world, and once it was here, whether it ever left. This was not a good day for William Chu: He was already emotionally involved in a case that should have consisted of little more than tracking the paperwork.

The medical examiner approached Chu. By now, several very bright halogen lights on yellow tripods had been placed strategically around the site, and they competed with the light of the moon and the dock lights, and outshined them. It seemed nearly as bright as daylight, but with a blue hue. Chu had only just noticed.

"So, Bill," said Sam Ikawa, the medical examiner, "matter of curiosity ... how long do you think that purse has been there in the bag? Half in, half out. Make a guess." Ikawa was snapping off his gloves as he approached, raising his voice to carry the distance of about twenty feet. He was high-stepping over the junk. It was misting lightly now, and minute droplets could be seen in the auras of the halogens.

Chu blinked. He'd been saving the phone for later. The question needed to be answered now. One of Ikawa's quizzes. Chu pulled the phone from the zip bag that he'd put back into the purse, and, still gloved, he hit the button and slid his forefinger across the screen. It had no security code. He found that interesting but not surprising. He went to the record of outgoing calls. There were neither calls nor texts readily visible. He found that sad, but he had suspected as much. He'd have the techs mine it; there had to be something. He exited the phone log and went to the camera, pulling up the photo and video archive. He had trouble making out the photographs because of the halogen glare and the cheapness of the phone screen, but he could read the date and time in the corner: the day before yesterday.

"Wednesday," Chu told Ikawa. "Two days." Then he handed Ikawa the woman's driver's license.

"Mm. The body's been here for a week, Bill. Not less than five days. And it sure as hell isn't your ..." as he squinted at the card, "... Ms. Oliver."

Chu raised an eyebrow. A sense of relief trickled through him ... no one must know, he thought. "Let's take a look," he said finally, almost giddily. His mind, having immediately accepted the twist in realities, was already turning new theories over. One thing stood out: If the body was not Oliver's, then there was no other conclusion than that he was dealing with a serial killer. Sadly, though, her body had to be in the vicinity, and most likely it had been dropped off the dock and into the water. He was now convinced that Doc had seen it.

The body on Pier 47 was male. He was in his sixties, maybe, or seventies, probably. Six feet tall, maybe two hundred fifty solid pounds. His white dress shirt had slipped off his right shoulder, as if the body had been tipped sideways out of the wheelbarrow. He wore a reasonably nice wool suit. There was a single tire track to the northwest from the suspected wheelbarrow, and the oily footprint from a man's narrow-heeled shoe.

"Got a tattoo on the right deltoid," said Ikawa.

"That's good, I suppose," said Chu.

"Got his hands tied with some kind of twine, wrapped a lot. There's a discolored area of skin on the right wrist ... still, after most of a week. I don't know what it means yet, if anything."

"Interesting, I suppose," said Chu. The thought of the young woman, also bound, did not sit well with him. "Is there anything else in that bag with him?"

"You saw the scarf, from beside it. And you have the purse. There's nothing else. There was nothing zipped in there with him. He doesn't have any shoes."

"Pockets?"

"Zilch."

And there were no other tattoos besides the one. The jacket and shirt had been pulled to the side, and the man wore a sleeveless T-shirt, so the upper arm was visible. The design was simple. It reminded Chu of a sailor's tattoo or one of the American eagles you'd find on a military veteran. But this one wasn't American. It was a shield with a sword in the middle, point downward. On the shield was a red, five-pointed star and in the star was a hammer and sickle. He recognized the lettering, CCCP, as being Russian: It meant United Soviet Socialist Republic. There were three other letters preceding the USSR, but he couldn't read them. He didn't know Russian or the Russian alphabet. But he did know CCCP because his sister had collected stamps when they were kids in Chinatown. The Russian stamps were very dull and depressing. They all said CCCP, and almost all of them had the face of either Lenin or Stalin on them, or a picture of a cement building, or industrial workers. "I need a photo of the tattoo as soon as you can get it," he told Ikawa.

The examiner took out his cellphone, took a photo of the tattoo, and emailed it to Chu. "Done," he said, and laughed.

"I could have done that," said Chu.

"Yeah, but you didn't, Bill. So, what are you thinking? You're thinking, I can tell."

Chu had always been upfront with Ikawa, and Ikawa had never let privileged information slip out. So Chu said, "Well, it worries me that I have a missing woman, probably deceased, who's likely from one of the former Soviet satellites, and where I thought I'd find her body we have some sort of Russian gangster. The last thing I need in my city is the Russian mafia. It could be that's just what I have. But keep a lid on it."

Ikawa nodded.

All the while, the cleanup team had been incredibly active. The body was left in the duffle. Along with the scarf and purse, it had been removed intact and packed neatly in the transport vehicles, bound for the morgue and the forensics lab. Another crew would return in the morning to go over everything again in the daylight. The second crew would be more thorough. Maybe they'd find her, after all. Chu didn't look forward to it. He'd have to schedule the divers.

He kept the smartphone. He walked casually away from the hive of activity on that strange, floating arm of the city, and found himself a darkened corner where the spotlights had already been packed away. He was still gloved up. Whatever had happened to her had happened shortly after she took the photos. He knew he would find her body in another zippered duffle … he just wasn't sure if it would be found on land or on the seabed weighted down with broken blocks of cement. After all, Doc had drawn her in the water.

He flicked on the phone again. There were a dozen images from that Wednesday. They showed stacked furniture in some sort of old shop. It was an antique shop or maybe a furniture thrift store. It didn't look like a garage or storage unit. At the top of the stack appeared to be a spinning wheel of some sort. He could see the edge of the drive wheel and uprights that held it. But in some of the photos there were light refractions that looked like bursts of red and green, probably caused by reflections or overhead lighting; it was a cheap phone. He could see several lit chandeliers along the upper edge of the image. The colored flashes made it difficult to see the wheel. He could make out the turned legs. He knew nothing about spinning wheels, but it was clear to him that the photographer did.

He looked carefully at a photo that caught a little of the outside street through the shop window.

He pulled out his own cellphone and hit the memory key for Ikawa. He said, "Yeah, Sam, William. Listen, I'm going to need that twine on his wrists tomorrow morning, or at least a piece of it."

"Done."

Chu thought, Sam Ikawa always said "done." He said, "To my desk by eight?"

"Done."

It was early in the investigation. Very little added up. Chu looked at his watch, pressing in the knob to get the greenish background light to appear. He never thought of checking the time on his phone. Where had the night gone? It was nearly two in the morning. He put the phone back in the evidence sack and handed it to the last officer on the site — second to the last, actually: One had been posted in a cruiser to watch over the area until morning when the sweepers and divers would come in. He instructed the officer to have prints made of the photos and have them on his desk by eight in the morning. There was no argument. Still at the scene, Chu turned to his cellphone again and tapped in a well-remembered number.

* * *

"YEAH, TEDDY? BILL. YOU BUSY?"

He had called me at work. He always calls me Teddy. And he never refers to himself as "Bill" unless he's alone, probably on some stretch of lonely industrial waterfront. My Chu-only nickname is from Theodore Roosevelt, who, like me, was stocky, square-headed, mustached, and wore wire-rimmed glasses, though mine are only for reading. My real name is Nat Fisher. I said I didn't get off until six that morning (it was now Saturday), and didn't have to work Saturday night. I had an actual weekend, which was a rarity at the Bulletin, where I work as a night-shift crime reporter. I said that whatever he was doing, I was doing. I knew it would be worth my while.

"I'm making an appointment with the Yarn Woman for tomorrow," he said dryly. "Today, I mean. When it's light."

I said he should think again because she wouldn't answer her phone. He was talking about Ruth M, a textile forensics expert whom the department occasionally consults.

He said he knew that, but hoped that Mr. Kasparov would answer his. Mr. Kasparov is her answering service, driver, friend, surrogate uncle, everything. He has known her since she was about ten years old. Uri Kasparov caretakes the Avaluxe, a retired Art Deco theater where the Yarn Woman lives. She has a second-floor flat.

"We can meet at the coffee shop at ten. That won't be too early," said Chu.

I said I'd be there. Then he suggested that if I wasn't doing anything right now, it would be worth my while to head out to Pier 47 where they'd found a rather interesting body and that he would meet me out there to go over some of the details if I could leave now. He said he was still there. I checked the time: 2:30 a.m. My shift was over half an hour ago, but, with a good lead like this, I grabbed my jacket to head up to the north piers.

That worked for William Chu. He said he'd just wait.

The Yarn Woman

"CAN YOU TELL ME ANYTHING about this spinning wheel, Miss M?" asked Detective Chu as we sat toward the back of the coffee shop. "And, do you know where we can find it?" The photos were spread on the table before us. "Clearly," he said, "Helen Oliver was captivated by this spinning wheel. Shortly before her disappearance, perhaps only minutes, we don't know, that wheel was incredibly important to her. There were no other photographs in the phone's memory, not even photos that had been erased. She wasn't much for keeping Kodak moments, and she wasn't much for staying in contact with friends by phone."

Detective Chu had asked to meet us there because it was less than two blocks from his Vallejo Street office at the Central Station. After spending the night and the morning at the piers investigating the body, he was behind in his paperwork and in too much of a hurry to meet anywhere else.

Miss M sat near Chu. She's about five-foot-three and muscular in a linear sort of way, like a swimmer or a cyclist. Her dark chestnut hair is thick, and though it's somewhat long she always wears it up, rolled and pinned in place by knitting needles, chopsticks, and occasionally actual hairpins. Her eyebrows are magnetic, but not as transfixing as her brilliant green eyes. They emanate intelligence, but also betray a gentle eccentricity. She appeared small, seated next to Chu.

Though his inquiry was summarily delivered, William Chu has had a long professional friendship with Ruth. Still, he does not call her by her first name, and she doesn't refer to the detective as William or Bill, as I do. It's a matter of respect.

We were in the heart of North Beach, practically in the shadow of the Peter and Paul Church. I exaggerate: The landmark's a block away. I've liked this San Francisco street corner as long as I can remember. Bill and I used to skip school, flee to the cafe and sip espresso in the afternoon among the rabble of the city. We listened to poets by day, jazz by night.

We were seated at a round table that was too small for four, but had four chairs. It was too small three, though I didn't mind being wedged up close to Ruth. You get used to tight spaces in the city, including the cramped triangular footprint of this cafe. It sits on a wedge sliced out of San Francisco's North Beach pie. I sat with my back to the window. It was dark, overcast and cold, a typical summer day in what the poet George Sterling called "the cool, gray city of love."

"So, Miss M," Chu said, "why was this so interesting to her?" He tapped the photos with his fingers. "Where is this shop? She was, as far as we can tell, not a spinner — and we examined her apartment a couple of hours ago (a small and barren one-bed). At least, not an enthusiastic one ... we found a couple of balls of wound yarn in a box. They looked old. They were colorless. There were some photographs ... she had photographs ... and they were old as well. She was not, Miss M, a textile person. Who was she to have been so attracted to this spinning wheel, then?

"We're dealing with at least two suspicious incidents, Miss M, one being the murder of a Russian male, the second being the disappearance and, I suspect, the killing, of a young woman. It's about that shop, as a location to commit murder. And here, we have a rare antique thrown into the equation. I assume it's a rare antique ...

"Because the bodies ... or possessions ... were dumped in the same place, it stands to reason they were killed in the same place by the same perpetrators. It's a textbook serial killing ... Please don't let that out quite yet ..." He looked directly at me. "... And Ms. Oliver used what were probably the last moments of her life to take snapshots of a spinning wheel that had been tossed onto a bed of old furniture as if it were a funeral pyre!"

He reached for his coffee. He added another sugar.

Ruth moved the photos around on the table, examining each. "I don't know where the shop is, Detective," said Ruth, looking up. "I'm sorry. It appears to be tucked back in an alley. ... I don't know how it could have escaped me, but it has. I'm fond of mysterious little shops." Ruth seemed both sad and surprised.

"The photographs aren't all in focus," she began again. "She doesn't have a steady hand. In one, her finger obscures most of the image, so I agree that she isn't one to take photos with her phone under normal circumstances. She's not used to it. They're hard to hold, you know, and make an exposure." Ruth didn't carry a cellphone herself. "And I see that she keeps her nails fairly short and uses red polish, because the shadow of her finger on the upper left of that photo has a red refraction," she said, pointing. She paused. "Red polish, so, probably red lipstick? Are you sure her name is Oliver?"

Why would she ask that? Ruth's eccentric manner of reasoning was making itself known.

"We're checking her record, Miss M. Her driver's license was found in her discarded purse, and I haven't gotten a federal report as of this morning. It may be on my desk now. We do know she is a naturalized citizen, but that's all. We discovered her purse only last night. And, yes, she used red lipstick."

"And the picture that shows the outside of the shop? In one of them you can see the business across the street, like a restaurant or something."

"Nothing on that yet. We're getting patrol officers on the ground to help identify the business, but San Francisco is a big town when you're looking for about six inches of somebody's storefront window. It could be almost anywhere."

"It almost looks like there are light flashes in a few of the photos, where the red and green are so strong ..."

"Yes, the phone was inexpensive, Miss M. I'm sure the lens isn't the best," said Chu.

She looked at him. "I said 'almost.' It looks more like a reflection of something on the wheel than the refraction of light from above or from a window ..."

Chu grimaced slightly. "Like a bicycle reflector?"

"Like some sort of inlay in the wood ... mother of pearl comes to mind."

Even though many of the photos were out of focus, as Ruth had pointed out, the physical printouts from Helen's smartphone archive were high quality, and while several of them betrayed Miss Oliver's unsteady hand, a few were clear and the objects within them well-defined and reasonably well-focused.

Although the wheel couldn't be seen entirely, Ruth couldn't take her eyes off the photos. "Amazing," she mumbled. Then she took a deep breath and composed herself. "Well, the style of the wheel is typically Ukrainian ... the four angled legs, the table, the fact that it's an upright (that is, not a Saxony) without being a 'castle' style. I would say it's from the very early nineteenth century, maybe 1810 to 1825, and though it has folkish elements, it's heavily influenced by Italian style and English artisanship. When was the last time you saw a table with hand-carved edging like that? Everywhere, everywhere, there's embellishment, carving, coloration ... yet it's tasteful, not overdone. One would expect, perhaps, a floral theme, but it's not. It's marine." She looked up at us, surprise written in her eyes. "That's odd. And it's so intricate. I can't see the face of the drive wheel clearly, but it's unusual ...

"The maker must have traveled extensively. That worldly influence is strong enough to separate it from other Eastern European wheels of the period."

She sat up straight and addressed us directly. "Look, most of the wheels from this time and place were simple. Even crude by today's standards. But this is art. This is unexplainable."

She peered back down at the photos. Then she looked up at me and asked if I'd driven this morning. It was a typical Ruth non sequitur, and caught me off balance. I said I'd parked my car at the newspaper and walked because there's never any parking in North Beach. She looked at Chu. He said, "Walked. Two blocks."

Satisfied, Ruth smiled and was silent.

"It's rare, then?" said Chu, picking up the train of discussion again.

"Oh, very. But more, it's an anomaly. In the greater scheme of things, a piece like this shouldn't exist. First, I suppose, are the turnings. They're atypical, and reflect the English influence I mentioned, as if it were from York, say, of about the same era. That's highly unusual, given the structural design ..."

"What do you mean by 'turnings?'" asked Chu.

"The parts that are shaped on a lathe. Furniture makers before the industrial revolution called themselves 'turners' and their workshops were called turneries. And I would say they were turned in a rural area, not using a machine lathe but a more primitive folk tool of some sort. ... I mean, they're not carved in a duplicating jig. There's a variance from one leg to another, for example, or the uprights. Still, this is the work of a master. Frankly, this wheel compares to some in my own collection, dating from about the same era. And those are museum pieces. This one is completely beyond what I've seen." Then she added, "And I've seen a lot of wheels."

Ruth sipped her coffee, then with a long-handled spoon, stirred up the chocolate of the mocha, which had settled. "I walked, too," she said. "It's a nice morning."

Chu didn't respond, just sipped his coffee and looked for another packet of sugar. Then he thought twice about it and didn't open the packet.

"In any case," she continued, "the turnings would include, here, the legs and uprights, the maidens and the mother-of-all, the spindles or spokes in the great wheel (some of the drive wheel is carved freeform, I mean, I haven't seen anything of this age that's even close), and of course the bobbins, which I don't see in the photos because of the angle." She reached for my notebook, which was on our table, and quickly sketched the parts of the wheel. She labeled the parts she'd just drawn and the turnings she had just mentioned. "These turnings are atypical in that they are very delicate, and the design is light and elegant. One would expect a much heavier wheel with thick turnings from that part of the world at that time — so thick, in fact, that the flat sides of the blanks would still be apparent."

Ruth stopped herself. "I think it's from the Podolian region of Ukraine, near old Bohemia, because of the turning patterns ... the Kingdom of Bohemia would have included the Czech Republic and most of Germany. Podolia had a strong wool and rug industry at the time we're talking about. They raised zackel sheep there, an Eastern European rug-wool breed. Their wool was and still is traded west for weaving kilims in Bulgaria and Serbia, using the Black Sea route. As for the design itself, the carving, I want someone else to look at it ..."

I asked myself, did someone know more than the Yarn Woman about a spinning wheel's so-called embellishments?

Several customers entered the cafe. As the door swung open, I could hear the rain, which had gathered force. A couple left their single umbrella upright near the door and stood for some time at the counter, deciding on their coffees and rolls. They sat near the counter in one of several empty tables and conversed in French. We were right in the slack time, after most people have had their morning coffee but before their midmorning pick-me-up.

Unfortunately, Ruth's information was of little immediate help. Chu said pensively, "Though I'm not familiar with the region, Miss M, it seems that Helen Oliver may have realized what she was looking at. I wish I had the ICE report on her immigration." He looked at his cup; the coffee was gone. He seemed unhappy about that. "Tell me, is it valuable in a monetary sense?"

Ruth looked at me. On cue, I left the table to order a second round of coffees. She said, "To the right buyer, if the buyer is a well-funded museum, absolutely. But I can't tell until I get some information on the designs carved into the drive wheel. The light's poor, the focus is wanting, the angle is bad. She was holding the phone over her head to get them. But I think I know who to ask. I'll need to borrow your prints for a day or so, Detective, depending on her schedule."

"Consider them yours," he said.

"Thank you. But you're right about this person," Ruth said, changing course. "She absolutely knew she'd stumbled upon something very rare and valuable … either that or she had a deeper connection with it. Whatever it was, it stopped her in her tracks."

I sat back down and distributed the cups. I could tell Chu wanted to check his watch, but courteously did not. He had other matters pressing. But Ruth could feel it, and took the cue.

"In summary," she said, "we know it's a Ukrainian wheel made by a trained and well-traveled master artisan. It's from a specific region. We can date it as circa 1820, and define the influences — the turners of York and I would even say the luthiers of Italy because of the flame-grained maple of the treadle. It looks like the back of a violin. There are other musical influences, but I won't burden you with them. Obviously, I would suggest that Helen Oliver has a Ukrainian background. But unless we can identify the shop, all the information in the world on that wheel isn't going to help find her, unless ..."

"There's one other thing," said Chu.

I waited. Ruth waited. She didn't finish her thought.

"The Russian's wrists were bound with cord."

"What kind," she said immediately.

"I don't know. I brought it for you to look at." He drew a plastic zip sack from his jacket pocket and placed it on the table.

"Flax cord," she said. "It could be hemp, but it would have to be very, very good hemp. May I remove it?"

"Here, use these, and don't let it touch the table." He handed her a pair of latex gloves.

"Right." She snapped them on. She was careful. She took a triplet magnifier from her bag and studied the strand. "I'll need to keep this for a day or so as well," she said.

Chu thought about it. "Fine."

"Did you know it was spun with human hair?" she said.

"What?"

"Has human hair in it. I can tell that with just a twelve-power lens. Gray to white, but I'd like to look with my microscope. With that, I can judge the age of both the fiber and the hair. Have you seen anything like this? I haven't, outside of some indigenous art from the weavers of Peru, for example. They used to weave their hair into the weft strands to create shadowed tints. Don't get me wrong, this isn't South American. That was just an example."

"Keep it, but please keep it carefully. It seems to be falling apart, coming unraveled. You know how it is back there." By that, he meant back at headquarters where he was answerable for every undotted "i" or misplaced "t."

"Of course," she said.

"Great. And, let's see. Preliminarily, we believe the dead man on the waterfront was a Russian national who'd visited the U.S. several times a year for the last thirty years," he said.

"That makes an interesting connection to the Ukrainian wheel," said Ruth.

I had begun to stare out the window at the car lights going by. They caught the spattered rain on the window glass. Chu was trying to piece it all together. "I think it might be coincidental," he said.

"Why?" asked Ruth.

"Just a feeling."

Ruth nodded

I was disappointed because Ruth's evaluation, it appeared, was of little direct help. Chu still had no body that might have been Helen Oliver's; Helen Oliver was still missing; there was a dead Russian businessman in the city morgue and a red purse at the lab. A multiple murderer remained at large.

"If we can find the shop," said Chu, "we'll eventually find the killer or killers. If we find the killer, I assure you I'll find Helen Oliver." But Chu looked sad when he uttered the final phrase because we all knew he did not mean her, but her body.

"I will talk with Mr. Kasparov," said Ruth. "He has ways of finding things out. And he has connections with the Ukrainian and Russian communities here in the city. There might be something useful ... he might know someone who knows about the shop if it's connected to the Russian." Mr. Kasparov, a Ukrainian, had fled the Soviet Union in the 1980s after serving several years at one of the gulags for perceived crimes against the mother country. I did not yet know what his misdeeds were.

"Yes," said Chu immediately. "There could be something. There could be. If not, I'm worried that we will have more killings on our hands. We're dealing with a serial killer, Miss M." Chu looked at me. He didn't have to say it a second time — keeping mum — and he didn't. It would all come out soon enough, I was sure. A matter of days.

"The Russian," he said, "had an unusual tattoo. I have a cell-phone photo that I will email to Mr. Kasparov. When you see him, could you ask him to comment on it? It's bugging me." He described it in vague terms, but did not produce the photo for us.

"I would like to see Helen Oliver's apartment," Ruth said.

Chu squinted and rubbed his chin. How might he allow Ruth to go through the personal effects of someone who was obviously kidnapped and probably murdered? The solution was simple. "Fine," he said at last. "I'll get the paperwork for you to sign. Officially, you'll be on the case in your usual consulting capacity. That'll keep the mice from squeaking in the upstairs offices. Come by and I'll give you the keys and address, and we can both sign off on it."

"You're so sweet, Detective. Hopefully, you'll have more information from Mr. Kasparov by then on the tattoo design." She meant it, the sweet part.

"Oh yes," said Chu, "there's one other thing."

She looked at him. "That's the second one-other-thing," she said. "I'm beginning to look forward to these."

"We have run some initial tests on the deceased. The Russian was found to have a considerable amount of the drug scopolamine in his system. Illegally, in large oral doses, it is considered a date-rape drug. Legally, it's an uncommon pharmaceutical, used mostly, I understand, for motion sickness. But the medicinal dosage is nowhere near the amount in the man's body. The dose, we think, may have been lethal."

Ruth frowned. "Poisoned."

"It appears."

"And then bound? Still alive, I assume ..."

"Deceased at the time his wrists were bound."

"That makes very little sense ... unless they tied his arms to make it easier to move the body."

"None of it makes much sense, Miss M. I agree with you that it helped the perpetrator move the body without its limbs flailing around during transport. His feet were also loosely bound ... same reason. He was a big man."

"How was it administered, the drug?" she asked.

"We don't know for sure. It's usually taken internally. Or with seasickness patches. That's how the drug is used today. Transdermal, of course, but the medical examiner — you know Sam Ikawa — said a dose through the skin wouldn't be strong enough to kill. Still, there are red marks on the man's wrist, clearly a reaction to something, and I don't mean the twine. Perhaps it was scopolamine. Ikawa didn't know how to get a lethal dose through the skin, but said he'd look into it. I believe there's a connection, so I'm waiting to hear."

With that, William Chu rose and paid for the coffees. He extended his professional thanks to the Yarn Woman, and then to me, and left for the Central Station, leaving Ruth and me at the table. By now, the gutters on Grant and Columbus were running in rivulets and forming pools along the edges of the intersections.

Turning to me, Ruth said, "I've had enough coffee for the day. You?"

"For now," I said. "I have trouble turning down a free cup."

"Phone?" she said.

She was asking if I had my cellphone in my pocket, and could she use it. I said yes I had it with me, and handed it to her. She studied it briefly as if she'd never seen a smartphone before, and asked me to turn it on. I flipped up the number screen. She nodded and carefully poked a series of digits. Then she stood, walked to the tight corner of the triangular room, and carried on a brief conversation, laughed a little, spoke again and came back, asking me to "hang it up." I pressed the red button to disconnect.

Then she asked me to erase its history. I didn't ask. I just did it.

"I hate those things," she said.

"Me, too."

"They're not good for much."

"I just keep it around. You can watch movies on it or throw it at cement walls."

"Can anyone get it? My phone call? The number?"

I said, "No, because I don't have it backed up in the cloud, and I have an automatic erase if I lose it and someone tries to break my password. And I just erased the call history." I then called my desk number and hung up and cleared the memory again as she watched.

"That's what I like about you," she said.

"What's that?" I asked.

"That you won't back up your phone into the clouds."

"Cloud," I said. She was kidding with me, I think.

She smiled. "What are you doing, for example, right now?" she asked.

"With the phone? Nothing. I just erased its memory."

"No. What are you doing, now, this afternoon? 'Now' now."

"Whatever you want," I said.

"That's great. Would you like to take a drive?"

"Sure." It was a weekend and I didn't have to work.

"Okay. Would you like to drive me to a friend's house in the countryside?"

I said of course.

"I would have asked Mr. Kasparov ..."

"I'd love to," I said.

"She lives a hundred fifty miles north."

"That's okay."

"... outside of Comptche — I guess you could say outside, because there isn't much of an inside — and a little south. I think it's about three hours by the time we find the house. Three and a half. But it's not even noon yet," she added, as if to soften the impact of six or seven hours of driving it, roundtrip.

"Find the house?" I asked.

"She lives off the beaten track," Ruth said.

I said I had new tires.

"She really knows spinning wheels. I have a few questions about the carvings. The incised drawings. And the light blobs on the prints. She might know what we're dealing with here. I have somewhat of an idea, I have my suspicions, but Rosemary, well, it's her area of inquiry ... wheels and the folklore that goes with them. You'll like her. And she's a very good cook."

That made me smile. I said it sounded very interesting.

I noticed that she referred to this person by her first name; usually Ruth is more formal. I decided they must be very good friends.

"Rosemary Monday," she said, catching the edge of my thoughts. It's difficult to have privacy with Ruth in the vicinity. One's thoughts are not really one's own. She caught my next one as well, and added, "The surname is Irish. Monday is a mistaken translation for the son of a servant of Eoin, which is Owen or Owain, which erroneously morphed into Luain: Gaelic for Monday. Monday. It's Irish, the long way around."

I nodded.

"Can you call Mr. Kasparov please and tell him what we're doing? He'll be sad not to see Rosemary, but I know he's busy today. They're old friends."

I did. And he did sound sad to miss out on our excursion. Mr. Kasparov tried to disguise his surprise at our trip. There was something in his voice. But he swallowed a few times and caught up with himself, afterwards coming across on the phone as warmer toward me, less formal, than usual.

He suggested we pack a lunch and take Rosemary Monday some croissants from a bakery that he recommended, and Brie cheese. "There is no proper food outside the city," he said, "until you get to the valley. But you have to travel west to the valley, and one has to like Mexican cuisine, don't you see. You might hope to find decent Italian, but there is no certainty in it. And, you will be driving north, not west!"

We had to walk back to the car, my old Saab. We started down Columbus and veered south on Grant through Chinatown. At California, the south edge of the tourist section of Chinatown, there's an old brick cathedral, St. Mary's. We passed through its shadow and

Ruth looked back up at the tower. When it was built in the 1850s, it was the tallest building in the city. Inscribed just under the clock is "Son, observe the time and fly from evil," a biblical quote. She looked at me, raised her eyebrows, and said, "I get the feeling that we're flying right into it."

We walked the last few blocks to the car. I shoved some coats out of the way so she could sit. We didn't stop off at the Avaluxe, which surprised me. Usually, Ruth likes to pick up a few things before she goes somewhere, or perhaps change her clothes. But today, because we'd met with Chu, she had her most important accessories with her: scientific equipment, some notebooks, and her knitting project of the day or week. Nevertheless, when I thought about leaving straightaway, and matched it with Mr. Kasparov's peculiar dropping of formality after I said that Ruth and I were going to Rosemary Monday's, I began to realize the enormity of the trip. Something about it was very much a part of Ruth and Mr. Kasparov's lives, and it was something that I knew nothing about.

Rosemary Monday

THERE ARE VESTIGES of a century-old cattle industry on the northward route from the city. The land consists of rolling, golden hills with spreading oaks. But the miles on Highway 101 did not go quickly because of the traffic, and since we were in no hurry anyway, we decided to take the scenic route and veered west to the beautifully winding Coast Highway. It turned out to be a lovely afternoon drive with the vast Pacific rolling on our left and an overcast sky with occasional brief showers.

I asked Ruth about Rosemary Monday. "She's a collector of spinning wheels?" I asked.

"She has a few. She's an accomplished spinner, and is knowledgeable about fibers and natural dyes. You'll see her dye garden. But she's a folklorist by training. Recently, she helped Mr. Kasparov locate a few nineteenth century marionette plays with fairytale plots. You have no idea how hard they are to find these days. He's working with one of them right now." The man's hobby is carving string puppets, marionettes, and making them dance. He'd picked up the habit as he fled the USSR south through what was then Yugoslavia, home to widespread marionette theaters.

"Is that how you met, through Mr. Kasparov?"

"No. She was a lifelong friend of Mrs. Reynolds. Then, when I was at Vancouver getting my doctorate, Rosemary was a visiting scholar. She's a Slavic folklorist, and, specifically, her area of research was fiber spinning. We spent a lot of time together then. Our academic areas were different, but we had a lot in common."

"Small world," I said. Mrs. Reynolds adopted Ruth after Ruth's mother died. The women had been friends. Ruth was about ten. Mrs. Reynolds, a concert pianist, was as extraordinarily knowledgeable about textiles, knitting, and all things fibrous as she was about Mendelssohn, Bach, and Chopin.

"Rosemary is eminent in her field," Ruth said. "I think she finally got tired of academia, though, because now she only writes … no lectures, no universities. She's still publishing, while trying to keep people away."

At that point Ruth fell silent, taking in the scenery of low ferns and tall trees, of moss-topped split rails from decaying fences overgrown with brush and wild paintbrush and sweet peas. I felt it was best to probe no further into the life of Rosemary Monday; we would be there shortly anyway. Soon, Ruth pulled out her knitting and picked up the beginning of a dark cap or beret. She was necessarily silent for a while because she hadn't finished casting on.

Three and a half hours after leaving San Francisco, we pulled up to a timber gateway that had no fence, and there was no house we could see. There was a small goat inside the gate, eating ferns. Its short hair was black and white and it wore a brass bell around its neck.

"The doorman," said Ruth. She smiled. "That's Roland, from the French epic." Twenty yards past the gate was the house, but we could only see part of the front as we approached because of the encroaching trees and vegetation. The roof was covered with cedar shakes, and the shakes were overgrown with bright green and copper-brown moss.

"Those are what Rosemary calls 'the people,'" said Ruth. "Roland's job is to keep the underbrush down. He's a hard worker. The rest of Rosemary's goats all produce fiber — pygora, angora, that sort of goat. Because she has goats, she can keep a few angora rabbits. The goats keep the raccoons away from the rabbits."

"It seems like a lot of work, like there would be many chores on this farm," I said.

"Oh, she and her husband manage to keep up with it. They have two grown sons who help."

Ruth knocked on the door. We heard a skittering of claws on the wood floor inside, and the muffled woof of a dog. After half a minute, the door moved inward and standing there was a woman with a cooking pot in her right hand. She set the pan on a nearby table and greeted Ruth with a hug. Ruth introduced me, and Rosemary shook my hand cordially. In a glance, I was sure she had completed a critical evaluation, and I was somewhat uncomfortable under her microscope. Then the two of them fell to talking as if they'd never spent a minute apart. I had the feeling that Rosemary knew of my existence in Ruth's life, though Ruth had never mentioned her to me before today.

I left my jacket near the door. We walked to a wide kitchen. Rosemary brought the pot with her. She had been curdling goat milk for cheese. I didn't understand the process completely, but watched as she strained the curds through cloth, which she then hung to let the whey drip into a bowl.

There were toys in the kitchen, so I assumed there were children around somewhere. I guessed her age at about fifty or fifty-five, though her waist-length hair was a mix of prematurely snow white and striking orange-red. Her face and demeanor were energetic, and her hazel eyes, for lack of words, seemed benevolent. She was striking.

I was wrong about her age, of course. Rosemary is in her seventies, I gathered after much discussion. She wore layers of clothing that began with a long gray linen dress that she had made. Over the linen she wore a knitted orange cardigan that fell in the back to her thighs and over that was an open vest of golden upholstery-type fabric. She had a beaded necklace and a beaded bracelet on her left wrist.

The dog meandered into the kitchen. She was a short, long-haired border collie, and protective. She was the same color as Roland: black and white. She greeted Ruth happily, but positioned herself strategically between me and everyone else in the room, just in case. We had tea from water that had already been heated on an enameled gas stove. It was four in the afternoon.

Ruth left the photos she'd borrowed from Chu on the table in the kitchen and took her bag up the short staircase to a bedroom. Obviously, we were staying the night. The room was small with one double bed. Quilts covered it. The walls were pine and there were two windows that looked out into pine branches. One window had a bird feeder outside. The room had a closet and there were clothes in the closet. I could tell they were Ruth's.

Apparently I did not have my own room.

Afterward, we settled into a small living room that had a wood stove and ducts from a propane furnace. There was a primitively installed, double-paned skylight in the slanted roof, which lit the room brightly. The chairs were old and comfortable. Rosemary said her husband was out in the gardens and would be back shortly.

"We have everything on a drip system," she explained, "but there are still weeds, and the pruning and trimming. And the people. I should say, the goats."

I asked what they grew. She didn't answer right away.

"Herbs, and dye plants," she said finally. "We have woad and Japanese indigo, *Persicaria tinctoria*, which we grow commercially. The ginseng's five years old now. Cultivating woad in California is illegal, but ... And then the usual vegetables: kabucha, pole beans, a few tomatoes, zucchini, and there's an apple tree, plum, and a few others on the east end. It keeps Miguel and the boys busy enough."

Ruth said Miguel was Rosemary's husband, and that "the boys" helped run the ranch. The toys I had seen belonged to Rosemary's grandchildren.

Ruth said she had some photos she wanted her to see. She explained the basics of the case: a missing woman, a dead Russian, the spinning wheel, and an antique shop that was probably the murder site. I brought the photos from the kitchen and handed them to Rosemary. She took them, leaning back into her chair and fishing her reading glasses from one of her upper vest pockets.

She said nothing as she leafed through them, taking considerable time with each one. It wasn't hard to read her expression. She was surprised, maybe even shocked, but you could only read it in her eyes; she didn't utter a word.

She set the prints in her lap and said, "Ruth, did Angelina ever mention the Rusalka Wheel to you?" She was referring to Mrs. Reynolds, who was formerly Angelina Romano. The Romano family controlled the San Francisco waterfront from the 1940s well into the nineties.

After a moment, Ruth said, "She did. That's the point. I wondered if that were possible, that the photos could show the wheel she'd told me bedtime stories about ... but I had nothing to go on. I asked if I could see it once, and I think she tried but for some reason it never worked out. I never saw it."

"Oh, it's real and so is its peculiar history. Angelina spent the better part of a year tracing its roots and assembling the documentation."

"What?"

"It has quite a history, Ruth. But the only images of it are one old engraving and a pencil drawing. Nicolas I of Russia tried to acquire it ... I would say about five years into his rule," said Rosemary. "That's actually documented. It was 1830-ish. The engraving shows the wheel and the czar in one of his castles. Despite his wealth and power, though, he was unsuccessful. The Rusalka Wheel was never his. What's to be said? At times, destiny rules."

Ruth said nothing for a few moments.

Rosemary added, "And there is one crude sketch of the wheel in work compiled by the Czech folklorist Karel Erben, dating from the 1860s. The images are strikingly similar. Whether Erben drew it or if it was drawn by one of his sources is a matter of contention among scholars. This occurred during one of his excursions to the countryside; he was gathering folktales about Rusalka, the nymph."

By the look in her eyes, Ruth knew she'd made the right decision in visiting Rosemary Monday. "I think she should have told me more about it," she said, "I mean, that she'd researched it. I thought her interest in it was more happenstance."

"She probably didn't have the opportunity to discuss it with you once you'd settled in. You were so busy." Rosemary looked directly at me, her eyes piercing, "Ruth was a prodigy, Mr. Fisher. She played piano and flute, and had quite a recital schedule. Too much of one for her age, probably. Angelina, after the adoption, was teaching her to spin and knit as well."

I sensed a discomfort in the room. Rosemary's comment had angered Ruth. "How could I have been so preoccupied that Mrs. Reynolds wouldn't have told me about that spinning wheel in considerable depth?" she asked. There was a brief silence, but the tension in the room didn't dissipate.

"Ruth, you remember those first few months together, you and Angelina?"

"Of course."

"You weren't easy."

"What do you mean?" The air chilled even more.

"Your mother had recently passed away, Ruth, and you had no idea what was going to happen to you. You'd also recently lost your grandfather. You didn't know that Mrs. Reynolds would be there, that she and your mom had already worked it out. Some might have thought you were a little troubled around the edges. It wasn't easy for Angelina, either. I mean, she obviously loved you, but there were a lot of barriers at first. She had arranged her life to be entirely independent. But things changed dramatically. And her performance schedule was a challenge, just to start. She understood that it wouldn't be smooth. ... And, you had a temper."

"Me?" asked Ruth sincerely.

"I think you underestimate the emotional resources it took after losing your family. She always felt you were very brave."

"Hm. I see. You know, she left for several months just after I moved in with her. Mrs. Reynolds did."

"She was investigating the wheel. That was when she went overseas. Poland, Ukraine, I'm not sure anymore. I think her absence upset you."

"It upset me terribly, Rosemary. It was inappropriate. And Mr. Kasparov, too. I'd just met him. And then, poof, they were both gone. I found that very upsetting, and very common. I almost left. Walked out."

"I'm sure you did," said Rosemary compassionately. "She tried to arrange with people to look in on you while you stayed with her family, with Tony. There was Julie. Don't forget Julie." Julie Romano, cousin to Mrs. Reynolds. Tony is Anthony Romano, Angelina's brother, with whom she'd been close.

"They should have said something, you know, about having to go. Or Julie should have said something. Rosemary, I thought it was me. I thought I'd done something to upset everyone."

Rosemary was silent. She didn't know how to respond to a child's pain, especially pain inflicted so long ago. She said, "Well look, Ruthie, she loved you at first sight. That never changed. You were barely four, taking lessons from Angelina, a diva. Then when you were ten, the adoption … I think she would have done anything for your mother, but, I have to say, it was you who she wanted in her life. Still, she was new at intimate relationships. Angelina was, I mean really, she was eccentric. … I know they tried to get back from Europe as soon as they could."

Ruth sat there silent for a minute. "There's no one like Julie," said Ruth simply, though there was something akin to reverence in her voice. "But she had years to tell me about the wheel."

"Later," said Rosemary, "well, I don't really know. I suspect that the opportunity to talk about it never arose. Angelina went from one project to another, always climbing, never looking back. Think about it ... Did she ever reminisce about anything she ever did?"

"No. Never."

"She was always composing something. She just wouldn't slow down," said Rosemary.

"I'll bet she never played an encore, either! Up and off to the next concert." They both laughed. The shadow of abandonment passed like a cloud eaten by the sun, and the temperature of the room returned to normal. "Geez, Rosemary," said Ruth, "you know more about me than I do. Let's change the subject ... I hate old-home days."

"Sure. I'm sorry."

"So," said Ruth, regaining herself, "Mrs. Reynolds was able to substantiate the rumors about its existence, the Rusalka Wheel?"

"In a word, yes. But I haven't thought about the wheel for years. As I said, it took her a year and more, and considerable travel. I think she was away for nearly two months."

"Three months and two weeks. And you believe she actually saw it?"

"She did. She said as much. I have always suspected that she assisted in its appraisal, and helped establish its provenance. That, for me, would account for her not wanting to talk very much about it. My feeling was that she thought the less said about it, the better. The fewer people who knew about it, the better. The fact that she said anything at all tells me how much she must have considered you a confidant."

"She could have said more," said Ruth, still not satisfied. "Well, where was it? Where is it now?"

"You mean where is it if we're not looking at it in these photos?" said Rosemary.

"I see," said Ruth. "Then that *is* the Rusalka Wheel?"

"She never betrayed its location, not even to me," said Rosemary. "The owner or owners were very secretive, and Angelina was a woman of honor. But I've always suspected it was in California, and I would have gone so far as to say the Bay Area."

"I need to know where it is, where the photo was taken."

"I don't know. She never offered the slightest clue. There might be a mention of it in her papers. But I can tell you a little bit more about your photos, because I do think we are looking at the Rusalka Wheel itself. And, I can give you information on just who she was. That might help. Tell me, are you up on the mythology of the nymph, Rusalka? It might help you in your endeavors."

"Not at all," said Ruth quickly. Yet I was sure she was familiar with the mythology of the nymph and was merely getting Rosemary to elaborate.

"Well, would either of you like more tea before I go on and on about the lore of 'the thread of life' and Rusalka's role?" she asked. We heated more water and Rosemary made a fresh pot of black tea.

Then we got down to business.

"Spinning wheels are very prominent in folktales," Rosemary began, breaking the silence that had fallen. "The Grimm brothers collected a number of such stories on their travels in the German Empire. They published their first works in, maybe, 1812. The brothers found themselves dealing with peasant tales of golden spinning wheels, wheels of wood, talking wheels, self-spinning spindles, magical weaving shuttles, wheel-spun hair, and so on. What I call the tradition of the handspun thread, however, dates into prehistory. We're talking about thousands of years, not mere hundreds. And, we're talking about the thread that connects the world of the living to those who have gone on.

"Now, the Rusalka tales were gathered west of Germany, in what was then the Empire of Bohemia. The rusalki were water nymphs. In the oldest Bohemian tales, rusalki, plural, were equivalent to goddesses. They had a role in sunrises and fertility, the animals, the trees and herbs, childbearing, the turning of the seasons, planting and the success of the harvest, and all the rituals that related to those earth elements. Some scholars consider this ancient time to be an age when God was female. All of these elemental worlds were under her or their auspices. According to the Greek historian Herodotus, the nymph cult in Bohemia and Russia, honoring rusalki, was thriving five or six hundred years before Christ."

I now realized what Ruth meant by Rosemary being a folklorist by training. While she talked, the dog slept near her feet. The dog seemed to be used to this.

Rosemary continued. "Capitalized, Rusalka was a specific person. Written in the lower case, rusalka was also the species of nymph. Then, after society became patriarchal," Rosemary continued, "she became seen as a demon, luring poor little men to their pitiful deaths by drowning. This was an enormous change, involving the elimination of the nymph cult, the death of the pagan goddess cults, and the destruction of paganism in general. God became male. Nevertheless, reverence for the old rusalka remained. Bohemian villagers, even in the Christianized world today, leave her offerings at the bases of forest trees: Shirts or other handmade clothing, balls of wool or flax, woven garments or linen cloth ... all of these items are pinned to the trees or set ritually beneath them. They're pleas for fertility — usually the need for a child or the hope for a reasonably successful crop or a decent husband or wife. There are dances and songs, today, in her honor."

Rosemary poured tea in our cups and sat back down.

"Rusalka was a spinner from the beginning. She often spun her long and light-colored hair into the thread, making it supernaturally strong and, in some stories, magical. Another set of tales describes a red thread spun by her that was said to bind the ankles of people destined to become lovers: This idea is ancient, and common to the mythologies of China, Eastern Europe, and many so-called primitive societies." Rosemary smiled, but I don't know if that smile was telling me that she believed such tales, or that she scorned them.

"The point is, the threads Rusalka spun connected the worlds — our world and the world of spirits, or the world of the dead."

After a brief lull, I said, "Where does the Rusalka Wheel come in?" I hoped not to sound impatient. "Was it from one of the old tales? Was it made supernaturally, according to the stories?"

"No, nothing like that," Rosemary said. "It's not supernatural. The wheel that Angelina investigated had a depiction of Rusalka, the water nymph, on the drive wheel, and patterns had been carved into various parts of the wheel. There was, she said, fire opal interlaced with the grain of the wood. When Angelina first glimpsed the wheel, she said the beauty of it left her speechless. I assumed it had been inlaid by a highly trained artisan. But she said it had not. Her research indicated that the wood came from deep in a riverbed, and had actually been partly opalized. Fire opal filled areas in strips, some of which were nearly a centimeter wide. This, then, was the Rusalka Wheel, which the czar himself had tried unsuccessfully to buy."

Then Rosemary said, "Angelina had file after file on it, Ruth, after she returned with Mr. Kasparov from Europe. They've got to be around somewhere."

"Hm. I never knew about those files," said Ruth. "She talked about, you know, Rusalka, but not about having a hand in the actual research ..."

"Well, now you know."

"I'm not sure where they would be," said Ruth. "But I must have them. It's all there. Maybe Tony has them if I don't."

"Here's my point," said Rosemary. "Angelina said she'd found a cache of field notes by several Czech ethnologists or historians, regarding the Rusalka legend, including Karel Erben, a famous collector of Bohemian folklore. It apparently helped establish the wheel's provenance. She had copies of the man's field notes! She also located the municipal records of the region, which listed such things as births, deaths, and baptisms. With that, and with other notes she discovered that had been left in the archive by a poet named Jaroslav Kvapil, she managed to trace the Rusalka Wheel to a particular family. It took her months. You missed her, I know. But she established as historical fact what was thought to be mere legend. Even the engraving of Nicolas and the wheel was considered an artist's fantasy. She needed Mr. Kasparov's help because she was dealing with several languages in the Soviet bloc in the last few years of the union. He's very good with languages, as you know. Mr. Kasparov kept a very, very low profile, needless to say. He grew a very long beard ... to help hide his face."

"I remember that."

"Window-pane glasses and sunglasses."

"That, too."

"So, because of her research, we know there is such a thing as the Rusalka Wheel, and who made it, and why."

"Why?" asked Ruth, summing up in one word my own questions.

"It was a gift from its maker — a man whose birth and marriage Angelina confirmed — to his love, Rusalka, who was also a historic person, verifiable, though it would be impossible to claim that the woman was a nymph, of course. Your Mrs. Reynolds dug up a love story from the first years of the nineteenth century. The wheel was a testament of his love for her. His name was Alexei Basara, and he was born in the seventeen seventies. He was a skilled woodworker. He made lutes. And he made the wheel by hand at the age of forty-something. She found scraps of Basara's history ... that he'd apprenticed in England and traveled through Italy before returning to his homeland, still quite young."

Those were the influences Ruth had mentioned to Chu. Ruth and I had been listening about Rusalka for hours. Rosemary talked for another hour about the various plots in the many Rusalka tales. It seemed to me a complex mythology, though it boiled down to a very simple story line: Rusalka, a nymph, did not have a human soul. She traded her voice for a soul, and was therefore able to fall in love with a handsome young man. There were a multitude of variations. Two notable operas had been written about Rusalka, one by a Russian named Dargomyzhsky, the other by Antonin Dvorak, yet the essence remained the same. Coincidentally, Mr. Kasparov had only recently acquired, with Rosemary's help, the marionette opera based on Dvorak's *Rusalka*.

In the files of Mrs. Reynolds, Ruth and I hoped we could find some direction to pursue that could help us understand this increasingly odd case of murder and kidnapping in San Francisco. At the time, I could see no connection whatever. I was not concerned with the mythology of a faraway land from a distant time. I wanted to know what had happened to Helen Oliver. Her image on the driver's license, which Chu had shown me, haunted me. Yet it did not haunt me as much as it haunted him. I finally decided that if the myth could bear at all on the case, we should explore it in depth.

Ruth showed Rosemary Monday the twine that Chu had given her. It was in a plastic evidence bag. The twine had bound the wrists of the Russian.

"What do you think of this?" asked Ruth. She explained where it came from, and that she'd identified human hair in the twisted hemp.

"That," said Rosemary, "is a classic example of the thread. In this case, the hair is probably part of a spell. How old is it? It's not new."

"I don't know."

"The hair follicles break easily. Maybe the better part of a hundred years?"

"I'm thinking closer to two hundred," said Ruth.

"Well, you should know. But it's not the thread of life, that's for sure. It's the opposite. Good versus evil. This isn't something you would want to keep, if you are inclined at all to believe in that sort of stuff. It's malevolent."

"I'll keep it outside," said Ruth. "I'll put it in Nat's car pretty soon."

Under the circumstances, I didn't want it in the car, but didn't say anything.

Rosemary smiled, but I couldn't tell if she was a believer or not. She said, "Classically, there are three fates who rule yarn spinning. Spinning represents the human life. There is one fate to spin, one to wind, one to unwind at the time of death. Blending fiber with human hair goes back into prehistory, and so do the three fates. Some of our European societies blended the spinner's hair with, usually, flax or silk, as a token of love, or as a keepsake within a family. This sample you have would be the dark side of that tradition."

By now it was early evening in Comptche. Rosemary's husband, Miguel, returned. He was an astounding character, physically. About five feet four or five, he was a barrel-chested, thick-limbed man with almost no neck, though he wore necklaces that had charms strung on them, several with animal hair and claws. His own long gray hair was pulled into a ponytail, and he wore a faded red bandana across his forehead, which he removed when he entered the house. He wore a leather vest that couldn't be buttoned. He greeted us in heavily accented English, hugged Ruth and kissed her cheek, and went to wash up. Rosemary put a pan on the stove, and she and Ruth began chopping vegetables to roast. I was rather useless, but decided that I'd wash the dishes afterward.

The dogs were fed. The goats. The rabbits. Evening settled into night. Their sons and grandchildren had gone to their own homes nearby. Our hosts retired to their downstairs room. Rosemary Monday's final words to us that night were these: "I'm sure that Angelina's files will show you the relationship between the Rusalka Wheel and your blond-haired victim. I don't know, however, if they will tell you where that poor woman is."

We were left in the permeating quiet of the countryside.

Ruth said she was going for a walk at about ten that night. It seemed she wanted solitude, so I didn't go along. She would have asked. I read a book of poetry by Phil Levine, whose Detroit roots were strikingly different from my current surroundings, but whose sentiments fit well anywhere one might find oneself. I was asleep when she returned sometime after two in the morning. I was on top of the covers of the bed in what was clearly Ruth's room, trying not to appear too comfortable and hoping that she thought I'd been awake all along. She was as quiet as a cat when she got back, and didn't wake me until she pushed herself up against me on the bed. She was breathing softly within minutes. I pulled a blanket over us both.

Mrs. Reynolds' Files

WE LEFT COMPTCHE about ten Sunday morning and pulled up to the Avaluxe by about two. By the time we approached the old theater, everything was wet and gray and misted.

We parked north of the theater and ambled first to the Greek coffee shop a few doors from the Avaluxe. It's run by a man with a handlebar mustache, naturally black, which is to say, undyed. His hair is a mix of black and gray, greased and combed straight back. He employs two waiters who also wear mustaches that are almost as magnificent as his, and they look very much like him. There is a hostess whose black eyes betrayed her relationship to the Greek owner as well. She is probably his daughter. We had very strong coffee, seated outside under a wide umbrella that sheltered us from the drizzle. Ruth bought three servings of carrot cake, which were put into a brown cardboard box with a gold sticker holding it closed. She declined a second cup of coffee. The proprietor smiled and wished her a wonderful afternoon.

Soon we were ensconced in her flat, settled onto a small red sofa among skeins and balls of yarn. In front of us was a low round table, and behind us the long windows looked west over the city. Ruth's cat, Methuselah, who was sitting in one of the windows looking down onto rooftops, meowed. Ruth went to find Mrs. Reynolds' records of the Rusalka Wheel. She said that while walking the night before, she remembered where the files probably were, and if she didn't return from apartment No. 7 in an hour, to call Detective Chu. I was pretty sure she was joking.

While I waited, I found myself perusing her collection of vinyl LPs. There, I found Angelina Reynolds. Her work was recorded in the early seventies and into the eighties. The LPs that struck me most were recorded with the Vienna Symphony (Mrs. Reynolds, Ruth said, refused to acknowledge the Vienna Philharmonic because of its history with the National Socialists before and during the second world war). Her name appears on the record jackets as Angelina Reynolds. Ruth had told me she'd adopted that surname and used the honorific Mrs., despite being single, to avoid the flocks of admirers, mostly men, who pursued her. I hoped that the pseudonym helped. After seeing the "stereophonic" album covers, I had to agree that Angelina Romano Reynolds was unforgettably beautiful.

Ruth returned to the flat after about an hour. Her hair was a mess from digging through boxes and shelves of files. But she had triumphed in her search and was very happy. I took the first heavy box from her at the door and toted it to the table near the south-wall bookshelves where we'd been sitting.

She said, "I've avoided looking at her files for years, you know. It's just been too much. What a fool I've been. There's a letter to me about the wheel. I was supposed to have read it years ago." She looked at me with eyes that said, "I have been so stupid ..."

She didn't show me the letter. Continuing, she said, "But it was no wonder she took such an interest in that peculiar spinning wheel ..." She opened the box and started looking at the papers. "Because of her knowledge of the fiber arts, she'd been asked to examine a very unusual wheel that had been abandoned, like an orphan without a note, at some shop owner's door during the night. She kept a diary in scraps here and there, and I was reading some of the entries before I came back with the box," she explained.

"The owners of the wheel were acquainted with Mrs. Reynolds. They contacted her in hopes of establishing its provenance and approximate value. I think it was just business until she actually saw it. Nowhere have I seen a mention of the location, or the names of the individuals, the owners. Part of the arrangement was confidentiality, but she did leave me the letter. And she did tell me about it back then. I just should have pushed the issue a little more."

The inquiry prompted Mrs. Reynolds' extensive investigation into its linage. The more she dug, the more she found. Her search unavoidably led to the folkloric archives of the National Museum in Prague, where she rediscovered the "lost" diaries of Jaroslav Kvapil, the Czech poet and actor who wrote the libretto for Dvorak's opera *Rusalka*. Rosemary had mentioned the opera in her discussion of Rusalka the day before.

From the box on the table, Ruth extracted the original translations, which she told me were the work of Mr. Kasparov and a Dr. Zhirin, a professor of Eastern European history. She said Zhirin had died several years ago, but that, as a child, she had met him.

Soon, Ruth, Methuselah, and I were curled up on the sofa beside the table, following the librettist Kvapil as he traveled Bohemia in search of his Rusalka. Through handwritten notes and copies of old documents, we learned at least part of the history of the mysterious spinning wheel that was, one way or another, connected to the missing woman and the dead Russian. I only wished that Helen Oliver could have been as warm and comfortable as Methuselah and Ruth and I were at that moment. But if Helen Oliver was cold, and if she was miserable, at least it would mean that she was still alive.

Ruth showed me a photocopy of one of Kvapil's letters. Obviously, I couldn't read Czech, but there was a shake to his penmanship that, to me, betrayed his excitement in whatever he was writing about. Ruth said, "He's going to see the family who owned the wheel. I have the rough translation. He's reached the culmination of two years of searching, and he's finally on the verge of meeting her."

"Her? Rusalka?"

"No, but a descendant of the woman. The keeper of the Rusalka Wheel."

Kvapil's Libretto

July 7, 1895, Lemberg, Galicia autonomous province, Austria-Hungary

JAROSLAV KVAPIL STEPPED OFF THE TRAIN at Lemberg, that old city. It was so old that at various points in its long, long life it had been in different countries: the Kingdom of Galicia, the Kingdom of Poland in the sixteen century, the Lithuanian Commonwealth into the eighteenth, Galicia again in the eighteenth, the Austrian Empire until 1867, and the Austro-Hungarian Empire afterward.

Lemberg was a city tall and thick, a city cold and dark and teeming with life and the arts and the lives of 150,000 souls as it approached the dawn of the twentieth century. It was filled with a broad sampling of humanity — nearly a third were Jewish, and there were Ruthenians, Germans, Armenians, Serbs, Poles, and a smattering of Russians. And the arts! The artisans! They worked like ants in the shadows of cathedrals, synagogues, meeting houses, and tenements. Many cultures yielded many names: Lemberg was its German name and its Yiddish name, but in Ukrainian, it was called Lviv (pronounced l'view); in Russian, Lvov (l'vof); in Polish Lwow (l'vuf). Settled by the fifth century and named in the thirteenth for the son of a Ruthenian king, this "city of the lion" was the most important train stop in young Jaroslav Kvapil's life.

Standing outside the third train car and getting his bearings, Jaroslav tipped back his hat and glanced at the familiar fountain in the market square, admired the brightly colored flowers at the edges of the cobbled streets, grasped his light satchel firmly and pushed his glasses up to the top of his nose. He stroked his goatee in thought. His beard was thin, but he was young. Soon it would be as thick as the well-combed hair on his head. Lemberg was a beautiful city, he decided, but he refrained from comparing it to Prague, the center of the known universe.

Today marked his twenty-sixth visit to Lemberg over a span of two years. As always, he wore a suit and had wrapped a scarf around his neck. He would stay longer this time, and for once he would not be visiting the vast municipal archives.

He had an address written on foolscap and folded in his breast pocket. He asked directions of the first passerby, but, because he was speaking Czech, received only a nod and a shrug. Then he tried German, this time with a couple who were on their way across the square. His direction was pointed out for him with a smile. He asked about a lodging house, but they didn't know of one.

Jaroslav headed for the nearby tenements that surrounded Market Square in the heart of the city. Other than a room for the night, he had everything he needed — a change of clothes, his notes, his pen, his shell comb, and his letter. He had an extra pair of glasses. He would meet her in the tenements. He wondered if that was strange. Her name was Yulia Lazarenko. He wondered if she was beautiful. He expected her to be, but his expectations were rooted not in reality but in myth.

At twenty-seven, Jaroslav Kvapil was in the middle of a project that would, though he didn't know it yet, immortalize him. True, he suspected it, but he didn't know it. Walking across the square, he had no idea he was only five years away from a coveted director's position at the National Theater of Prague, and a mere six years from the premiere of the opera *Rusalka,* for which he would write the libretto to Antonin Dvorak's melody. Nonetheless, on this bright summer day in this city of lions, he had no doubts about the brightness of his future. He was, after all his work and all the time he'd spent researching, going to meet *the* Mrs. Lazarenko. He couldn't help but smile as he made his way north through the people in the square.

Jaroslav thought of himself not just as a poet and musician, but as a student of myth and legend. His studies had formed the framework for his libretto. Day and night, he settled into whatever chair was available, leaning over a library table or sitting back in a hard oak seat at the national museum, and, beneath his spectacles, he had devoured the folklore about the rusalki. Among his books — some of them borrowed, some owned by him, and some of the rarest used only on the premises of public or personal libraries — were Andersen's *Little Mermaid;* Pushkin's unfinished poem, *Rusalka; Undine* by the German baron Friedrich de la Motte Fouque; Gerhart Hauptmann's play; and the text of Alexander Sergeyevich Dargomyzhsky's 1856 opera, *Rusalka.*

The opera troubled Jaroslav because it relied on folktales that Jaroslav thought were impure, and were laced with fear, misogyny, and darkness. The Dargomyzhsky opera portrayed the Slavic nymph as one of the restless dead, a woman who, having been betrayed, took her own life — only to find herself reborn as a rusalka. How crass. How untrue to her nature!

Jaroslav's understanding of Rusalka was much different. To him, she was one of Paracelsus' "elementals," a fairy-like creature who sought only human love and a human soul. Don't we all, he thought? With this knowledge, Jaroslav was convinced he could write an incomparable libretto that would plumb the depths of what it was to be truly human. At night, he dreamed of stage sets and how he could bring the underwater world of Rusalka to life before a vast audience. By day, he had already begun to write the libretto. Sometimes, day or night, he would fume at Dargomyzh-sky's tale. The crazy Russian!

Initially, Jaroslav had tried to recruit a composer within his own circle of friends who could set his words to an operatic score. But his timing was bad. All of them were occupied with their own projects. So he occupied himself with research. He had already digested the story collections of many lands — Germany, Bohemia, Scandinavia. But he wondered about the roots of these folktales. His curiosity led him to the archives of the National Museum in Prague.

He had holed up in the museum for only a few months before he stumbled onto the voluminous work of Karel Erben and Erben's fellow historian, Bozena Nemcova. He was shocked, at first, not only at the vastness of Erben's interviews with Bohemian peasants, but at how prevalent the rusalka myth had been, and probably still was, among the people of the Podolian countryside. The nymph certainly got around! And Erben had collected many, many stories in the manner of the Grimm brothers of Germany. Unlike the Grimms, however, Erben didn't want to publish the stories he laboriously recorded; his goal was to use the tales as raw material for his own stories. Erben's stories, in Kvapil's mind, were dark, even gruesome. But the original tales he'd managed to find were bright and alive! They were priceless.

It took Jaroslav days, weeks and eventually months to find Erben's original field notes; there were boxes and shelves filled with his paperwork. Erben's writing was, at times, little more than a scrawl. Yet, it was a treasure trove hidden in the depths of the archive, untouched for the last half-century. The "informants" were anonymous, but with a little more work and a few well-placed bribes, Jaroslav gained access to the list of names attached to the original stories.

His inquiry eventually narrowed to a particular Ukrainian village called Mielnica, which was not far from the River Dniester. It was a land of forests and small farms. He was shocked at first, that country folk actually believed that a rusalka had once lived among them, right there in the village. In the people's collective memory, though, she was apparently as real as any woman, and they all admitted that Rusalka was the most beautiful woman in the village. And yet, it was from these crazy believers, fools that they were, that he realized he could bring his fictional Rusalka to life, and make her presence in his opera one that was believable, passionate, and vibrantly alive.

After untold hours of poring over Erben's notes, Jaroslav had finally fished a name out of the fieldwork, and that name was Alexei Basara, a simple luthier. The story keepers of Podolia had mentioned him time and again to Erben. According to the collected testimony, not only was Alexei Basara a true historical figure, so, too, was his wife. She was, they said, a rusalka. She had adopted the name Tatyana. Jaroslav realized that nymph or not, she was a real person. The couple had lived in Mielnica, they had been officially married, and they had three children together. When they left that village, according to one informant, Alexei and his wife and their three ragged, shoeless children, fled hundreds of kilometers on foot to the teeming city of Lemberg.

Jaroslav was not looking to prove the existence of a mythological creature. Nearly a century had passed since her supposed presence upon the earth. Impossible! Nevertheless, he yearned to see her eyes. Were they the gray-blue that the informants insisted on? He needed to see her through the eyes of the villagers. Because they believed. They believed! And then, he would project her onstage for the eyes of his audience. It was his job to make the audience believe. He understood that whether a person was a Ukrainian peasant or a member of the Prague gentry, that person must see the same woman: A living, breathing Rusalka. And she would be a lyric soprano, of course ... perhaps even Ruzena Maturova of the National Theater!

What a dream. Basically, Jaroslav's research involved only two sources: the National Museum in Prague, home to Erben's research; and the vast municipal archives of Lemberg. The archives included the births, deaths, and marriages that took place throughout that Galician region of Austria, which included many cities, towns, and villages. Armed with one name, Alexei Basara, and the possibility that Basara had, indeed, ended up in Lemberg as the notes of Erben stated, Jaroslav was certain he could trace the man and his line from the 1820s, when Alexei and the so-called water nymph left their backward village, three children in tow. He had been determined to find a descendant, and to look into that man or woman's gray-blue eyes for himself.

In twenty-five visits to the municipal government building over nearly two years, he searched through the blindingly obtuse and practically illegible public records of marriages and births. The ledgers were wide and tall, they were thick and very heavy. Then, eight months ago, he found the 1817 municipal ledger entry for the marriage of Alexei and Tatyana Basara. Listed in German, the official municipal language, was Alexei's trade as a luthier, his age, his parents, the location of his home, and the name of Tatyana, a woman whose linage had not been noted. He found they'd been married after the birth of their first child, which was not uncommon at the time. It was a magnificent moment. Surprised and exhausted, he removed his wire-framed lenses and, with his kerchief, wiped them free of the dust and tears that had gathered and obscured his vision.

He searched next for the children of Alexei and Tatyana, and it took two more months. He would often leave Prague on a Monday afternoon, travel more than eight hundred kilometers by train to Lemberg, and search the ledgers as quickly as he could before going back to Prague on Tuesday night.

But he did find her: Alexei's oldest daughter, Sophiya Basara. The ledgers listed the mother and father of each newly married couple: Sophiya's parents were Alexei and Tatyana. Further investigation revealed that Sophiya had married a man named Ivan Pipenko in 1840 at the age of twenty — fifty-five years ago. Jaroslav then began yet another search: He sought the marriage of anyone surnamed Pipenko who would list Sophiya and Ivan as her or his parents. It was a simple but time-consuming process.

And he eventually found her. She was Anichka Pipenko who became, upon her marriage, Anichka Salenko. Anichka's daughter, Yulia, was born in 1871. Yulia would now be twenty-four years of age. Further exploration of the municipal records showed that Yulia married Dmytro Lazarenko in 1892, only three years ago, and that they resided in Lemberg, as far as Jaroslav could tell. In Lemberg!

He had located a living descendant of the purported rusalka, Tatyana Basara! The search had taken so long. He was emotionally exhausted.

He wrote to Yulia Lazarenko. He was surprised when he received a return post. When the shock wore off, he was elated. He had never had a better day than when he received Yulia Lazarenko's letter. He wrote again, and arranged a visit. He had now been working on his libretto for *Rusalka* for more than twenty-seven months, months that coincided with his archival research. He had burned the first three drafts because his dear Rusalka was merely two-dimensional. And now, he thought, he would meet the family.

Jaroslav was nearly speechless with expectation as he stepped off the train. He walked a few blocks, asked for directions, and hailed a carriage. He would get a good night's sleep, he hoped, and then meet Mrs. Lazarenko.

As he sat in the carriage, he wondered if, perhaps, he had finally lost his mind. He laughed. The driver turned and wondered if he'd picked up a bad fare.

"Do you know of a lodging house in the vicinity?" asked Jaroslav.

Yulia and Dmytro

July 8, 1895, the tenements off Market Square, Lemberg

YULIA LAZARENKO EVALUATED the man at her door. Funny, she thought, he did not look musical. He was smallish, good looking, bespectacled in a scholarly way, and well mannered. He had nice leather shoes that were not very worn, and they had no abrasions at the toes. She noticed that particularly.

Jaroslav Kvapil, standing in the doorway to Mrs. Lazarenko's rooms in the tenement, decided that the woman in front of him looked entirely as one would suspect the descendant of a purported rusalka to look: She was thin, her skin was pale — even waxy — her eyes were wide and slightly too large. They were pale blue with a hint of gray that made them seem eerie. Her hair was long, light blond, and wispy. Her lips were expressive, thin, and pale. She did not look well, by general standards, but she was beautiful in an unearthly way. It was difficult for him to take his eyes off her.

Oddly, Jaroslav wondered if Yulia Lazarenko could speak. If she could, he wondered what her voice sounded like. Was she a soprano? She had to be a soprano. But her voice would have to be thin, for she had no mass with which to project it — her neck was slender; her bosom shallow.

Expecting the visitor, Yulia motioned him inside where her husband was seated in a chair near the only window in what appeared to be the only room, reading a book. He stood immediately and apologized profusely for not answering the door. He was a very handsome man, square of face with thick hair that was prematurely edged with gray, with a mustache and trimmed chin beard of the same color and thickness.

"I am too often drawn into a book!" he told Jaroslav. "I am Dmytro Lazarenko, and this is my wife, Yulia. She has a little trouble speaking; we hope it is not an inconvenience."

"I am Jaroslav Kvapil, who wrote the letter regarding our meeting. Thank you so much for seeing me."

"May we offer you some lemon water or some tea?"

Jaroslav looked around the room, trying not to let his eyes rest on any one spot lest he appear judgmental. He did not stare at Dmytro's shoes, which had leather patches at the instep. There was, indeed, little to judge: The couple had very few earthly possessions and the room was stark. It could use a coat of paint at the least, Jaroslav thought. "Water, please," said Jaroslav, who understood the value of tea.

Dmytro Lazarenko was average height, solidly built but not fat. His hair was just over his collar. It had a slight wave. Yes, handsome, Jaroslav thought, and perhaps a bit rugged.

"And the little sprite over there," said Dmytro happily, "is Hannah. She is three years old this week." Dmytro was very pleased to introduce their little daughter. She was in the corner of the room to the left of the window, and she was playing contentedly in a wooden tub filled with warm water. "It's the only thing that makes her truly happy," said Dmytro. "An hour in the tub and she's an angel for two days!"

Jaroslav smiled sincerely. Little Hannah was indeed a sprite. She looked very much like her mother, and very little like her father. He tried to calculate the number of generations that had passed since Tatyana Basara, but gave up so as not to appear distracted.

Jaroslav's eyes continued their tour of the humble room, and fell upon three objects of unparalleled interest to him. He was so surprised he nearly choked on his lemon water.

There were two stringed instruments on the wall to the right of the window, near the corner, and a third instrument near the same corner on the adjacent wall. The pair consisted of a spruce-topped kobza and a truly elegant bandura whose graceful spruce soundboard was like nothing Jaroslav had ever seen. These magnificent specimens before him were considered folk instruments, but it was clear to Jaroslav's theatrically trained eye that the "folk," in this case, was a heavenly host.

Yulia Lazarenko had been watching the visitor, and when his eyes fell on her instruments, she walked over and took the third one from the wall. It was a violin of delicate design, and she handed it to him. He was surprised because it was not a skrypka, the common folk fiddle of the countryside, but appeared to be a copy of a genuine Italian violin. It was very light. She handed him the bow, which he drew across the strings. The tone was strong, and the timbre sounded as if it were from another, higher world. He had heard only one other violin like it in his life.

Dmytro said, "Well, sir, you're holding my dear wife's prized possession. Her great-grandfather, rest his soul, was an accomplished luthier, and he made all of the strings that you see here on our walls between seventy and eighty years ago. That design," he said, pointing to the violin, "was unusual for its time in this region."

"I am astounded, Mr. Lazarenko. I am speechless." After voicing that, though, Jaroslav was embarrassed that he had so quickly forgotten Yulia's difficulty with speech. He flushed.

But Yulia smiled softly. She left them, walking across the room to lift Hannah from her tub and dry her.

Dmytro cleared his throat. "Tell me, Mr. Kvapil, what a misplaced family of little-known musicians can do for you? Your message was quite unexpected."

"Mr. Lazarenko," said Jaroslav, "I wish to talk with you about the man who made that violin, who would be the grandfather of your wife." Yet Jaroslav was careful not to betray his intimate knowledge of Alexei Basara of Mielnica, and he had purposefully erred in suggesting that Alexei was the grandfather, not the great-grandfather. It would be better, he thought, not to expose his trespass into the municipal record of their lives.

"Indeed," said Dmytro, smiling. "Yulia has distinct memories of her great-grandfather, if I may correct you, which she has shared with me, not in speech, but in pictures and written words and in various understandings between people who are close to one another. Also, we have found that, at times, Yulia can whisper. But I am afraid it is up to Yulia if she wishes to confide such information to you." He looked at his wife, prepared to follow whatever direction she set. Jaroslav realized fully that his day could be over before it had begun. Nevertheless, he felt he had no choice but to bring up the true reason for his visit, and he could not have postponed its introduction much longer.

Yulia gently handed the still-damp Hannah to Dmytro, which made Dmytro laugh, and that made Hannah laugh in turn. Dmytro knew Yulia's answer: She wished to communicate with this stranger. And from a simple flick of her wrist after placing Hannah in his arms, he understood that she wished to show the visitor one last item that had been made by her great-grandfather.

There were two doors in the Lazarenko home. One led into the hallway shared with the other tenants, and the second to a cramped and dark bedroom, which was private.

Jaroslav and Dmytro waited quietly near the window as Yulia went to the other room. She returned after a minute or so with a spinning wheel of such beauty and embodying such superior workmanship that it seemed to glow of its own accord, its nimbus bringing a warm new light into the large but mostly empty room.

Jaroslav, who had been held speechless by the violin and bandura, was now utterly silent in his ecstasy over the spinning wheel, the like of which he had never seen and could never have imagined. Clearly, the room was now better lit because of it, but how, he asked himself, was that possible? He moved slowly across the room to look at it more closely, to simply touch it. Yulia produced a few bobbins of fine thread she had spun that morning as if to prove that the wheel was as remarkable in its practicality as in its beauty.

Jaroslav spent many long minutes studying every inch of the wheel, from the turning of the spindles to the joinery in the table, to the intricate images that had been incised and painted, as if by a Renaissance master, on the drive wheel itself. But it was the substance of the wood that lay beyond the man's ability to explain. Laced within the grain of the wood were strands of glowing mineral, reflecting the window light in brilliant crimson, sun-flash green, blue that was bluer than an inland sea, and yellow like a golden sunflower. More, there were similar strands of red and gold amber also embedded in the grain.

"Utterly impossible," said Jaroslav to himself. "Dazzling, absolutely dazzling, the mineral, the strands of light. How do you explain it? How can it be? And yet, the gentle carving of the figures is even more other-worldly, Mr. Lazarenko."

"We have been told that the wood is laced with opal, sir. Yet our source of that information was also in disbelief. Yulia has indicated," said Dmytro, breaking further into Jaroslav's reverie, "that she wishes to know why you are interested in her great-grandfather, so interested in fact that she said is clear to her that you have traced the family line from him to her to satisfy your personal curiosity. But about what are you curious? We are only a family of musicians, and I spend most of my days teaching music and language at the public school and one day a week at a yeshiva. Truly, Mr. Kvapil, we are not of much interest. If I may be bold, I say that

Yulia is remarkably beautiful, yet I know you were not attracted to that ethereal beauty, for you had never seen her before now and it could not have been a motive for your visit. Please don't be offended. So, in short, I would say that I, too, wish to know why our quiet little family is of such great interest to you."

Almost before Dmytro finished, Jaroslav quickly said, "I have labored for two long years on a libretto, an opera. Mr. Lazarenko, I have found little support among my friends and professional acquaintances for my story ... and yet I cannot let go of the project. It is a story, I will admit, that revolves around the tales told long ago about the wife of Alexei Basara, forebear of your wife. It is a story of Rusalka, however fabricated the history of the matter might be. In my heart, I know it will become the greatest opera in the empire. Every Czech in the land will have new pride because of it. And yet I am missing one single quality, like a single strand of golden hair. I must know more about this mysterious woman, Tatyana Basara, who is the model for Rusalka, who will be played by a mezzo soprano in the opera. Dare I dream that Ruzena Maturova, the diva, will play that role? That is why I am here. Come what may, I feel I have been given no choice."

Dmytro's brow furrowed, but after a few seconds he relaxed and looked at his wife. What harm could there be if they took this stranger into their confidence? Yulia could tell by looking at Jaroslav that he was no scoundrel. Like her and her husband, their visitor was an artist, a musician. Yulia turned to Dmytro and signaled her wishes, and Dmytro in turn related this to Jaroslav.

"My dear wife sets three conditions to welcoming you into our lives, and if you are prepared to agree to them, we may proceed."

"I will agree to anything," said Jaroslav earnestly.

"The conditions are these: This family and the names of all our generations will remain in confidence and will not be uttered or written in any way that would compromise our private lives."

"Agreed," Jaroslav readily said.

"Second, we may at any point refrain from answering questions or continuing our conversation if Yulia feels uncomfortable about the topic."

"Agreed unconditionally."

"And, finally, there can be no mention, in the libretto or in public discourse or otherwise, of Yulia's spinning wheel, her great-grandfather Alexei Basara's greatest creation. It does, in fact, provide us most of our livelihood, for Yulia is an accomplished spinner, and there is little income from music and teaching in this peculiar age."

The last condition stopped Jaroslav in mid-breath. Eliminate the wheel? How could he do that, now that he had seen it?

"But ... why?" choked Jaroslav. "It is a beautiful ... if it is not otherworldly, then, in all honesty ... who could not admit its heavenly grace?"

But Yulia remained firm on her final condition. Void of speech, she could not describe the intimate reasons for her decision. Dmytro did his best to explain − yet not to justify − his wife's position. Dmytro thought for a moment and said, simply, "The thread spun on Yulia's wheel is what connects the generations of her family to her, and, as you surely know from your research into the folktales, the stories of our people, there is a thread that links us to a liminal world − the land between the living and those who have passed. It is crucial and sacred to her beliefs, Mr. Kvapil. Yulia's connection to the other world is stronger than yours or mine. It is her feeling, you see, that whatever is most secret to us should remain in our own hands and not be put about. She showed you the wheel in goodwill, for she evaluated the inner spirit of you just that quickly. I do hope, Mr. Kvapil, that while you may not fully appreciate my wife's position, you may find it in your heart to respect and honor it."

Jaroslav had not been prepared for such a condition. And yet, as he stood there in that tenement room, he slowly realized that by hiding the singular, most defining aspect of the grand mythology that was Rusalka, he was free to write the libretto in any way he wished. There would be no bonds that would hold him to a specific truth, which the wheel would represent. If he set aside the entire body of myth regarding Rusalka's spinning and the linking of the worlds by her thread — a thread that for each person represents birth, life, and, in the final unraveling, death — his wonderful libretto would be free, and it would be transcendent. It would soar. He realized that, freed of the thread, he could take a bit of one rusalka story and mix it with another, and another, and another, and create a great adventure, a remarkable tragedy. He wasn't looking for the true story of Alexei and Tatyana Basara, but was creating his own story, built on the stones and mortar of a hundred folktales. And beneath it all, invisible, Rusalka's sacred thread would still secretly tie it all together.

"Agreed," he finally said, smiling broadly. "Agreed unconditionally. Your secret will be safe with me. I am no fool when it comes to lore, and see no purpose ..."

After Jaroslav had committed himself to discretion in the matter, Yulia seated herself at the wheel, and tried to speak but could not. Dmytro said, "Yulia, whom you must understand now trusts you fully, would like you to observe an unusual event. She is determined to spin, so that you may see the wheel as it turns. I assure you, you will be astounded. I will also tell you that this spinning wheel was made by Alexei Basara as a gift to his beloved. Together, they retrieved the massive maple trunk from the sediment deep in a river which I will not name. They dove deeper and deeper until, under what little light was available, it appeared that they entered a submarine cathedral. The ancient trunk had been submerged so long that precious opal had been deposited layer by layer. They say such deposits are an impossibility, that they would take millions of years, but then, science must seek to answer our questions 'why,' and not detour us from man's preconceived rules of nature.

"But I caution you, Mr. Kvapil, that you have given Yulia your word of silence. She does not suspect lies from people, and is often perhaps too innocent for her own good. I hope you can understand my caution."

"Completely, sir," said Jaroslav. "Completely."

Yulia began spinning the flax that was on the distaff. In only a moment, the wheel reached its perfect pace. But Jaroslav was a man true to his word. Nowhere in his opera, and more, nowhere in his personal notes regarding his travels and the meeting with Yulia Lazarenko, is there even a mention of what he witnessed after Yulia began to spin on the Rusalka Wheel.

Yulia, seeing Jaroslav's disorientation, stopped the wheel with her hand. She was smiling. Jaroslav moved dumbly to a chair and sat down. He sat for several minutes. Dmytro offered him his glass of lemon water, which Jaroslav drank completely.

"Perhaps you would like to walk to Stryiskyi Park?" asked Dmytro, saying nothing more about the incident. "It is not far, and parts of it have been recently beautified and replanted. The Expo was only four years ago. We often go there and visit the swan pond. It is Hannah's favorite outing." He did not indicate that it was difficult to entertain a man of Jaroslav Kvapil's standing in a tenement.

"Of course, of course," said Jaroslav, whose mind was already turning with new ideas for the libretto. But Jaroslav opted to hire a carriage rather than walk, much to the delight of Hannah, who had never ridden in a carriage or seen a horse close enough to touch.

There was one brief moment of concern at the park, and that was when Hannah sprinted for the pond and submerged herself in the reeds along the bank. Jaroslav, fast as he could, threw off his jacket and prepared to leap into the water. But Dmytro held him back, saying, "Please, don't be alarmed! She always does this." Jaroslav, sobered, turned to his host, his eyes voicing questions that couldn't make it to his lips.

"Hannah," said Dmytro, "is overly fond of water. She has been a little duck since only a week or two old. It was difficult to get used to at first, and I still keep my eye on her. She knows to let me see her on the surface every few minutes."

By evening, the carriage brought the Lazarenkos back to their rooms, and Jaroslav Kvapil returned to the inn where he had lodged the night before. Then he returned to Prague. Once again, he destroyed the now-worthless drafts of his opera. He burned the shreds. And then he immersed himself anew in his writing. He wrote thoroughly and smoothly, and in a matter of weeks he had the first draft of his libretto in hand. He made a copy and posted it to a composer who was rumored to be looking for words that might accompany his music. To the stanzas he submitted to this composer, Jaroslav attached a small message.

Several long months after Jaroslav had completed the draft of his libretto and mailed it, a return letter arrived. It was a brief statement from the composer, Antonin Dvorak, who expressed his commitment to Jaroslav's *Rusalka*. If Jaroslav understood the intent of the letter, Mr. Dvorak was suggesting a collaboration in which Jaroslav Kvapil would provide the story and the words, for music created by Dvorak, the Czech master. And the master replied also to Jaroslav's small, handwritten note that had been included in his inquiry. Perhaps the composer was moved by the request. Or perhaps he was only amused. In any case, Dvorak sent a bank note to the tenement address of Yulia and Dmytro Lazarenko, with a personal letter of gratitude signed by Dvorak himself. In Lemberg, that old city, and in its tenements, a sum such as Mr. Dvorak mailed could change lives.

PART II

Helen's Apartment

BY SUNDAY NIGHT, I was sitting at my desk at the Bulletin catching up with a couple of stories that had come over the police band radio. Ruth was at the Avaluxe with her cat, still buried in Mrs. Reynolds' archives. She was convinced that if we could trace the history of the spinning wheel, we would somehow be able to find the killer, and, more importantly, find his victim, Helen Oliver. That didn't make much sense to me. At first, I thought she'd gotten caught up in a search for the Grail. I couldn't blame her for that. In her field, the Rusalka Wheel was indeed a legend come to life. But my doubt in her was brief; she'd never been wrong before. There had to be a connection; I was just blind to it.

Early Monday morning, I got a call from Mr. Kasparov as I drove back to my apartment in Oakland. I pulled over and answered. I asked him how he was doing. "The Miss," he said, would soon be on her way to the police station to sign on as an official consultant in the case and pick up the key to the missing woman's apartment. Did I want to meet her and check out Miss Oliver's home as part of The Miss's personal investigation? I said, of course. I asked, however, what Ruth hoped to find there. Mr. Kasparov said he didn't know, but he was sure it would be relevant and why didn't I understand that. He added that Ruth had photos to share with him, Mr. Kasparov, but he had been short of time because he was conducting an investigation of his own. He had not yet seen her photos, given to her by Detective Chu. But he would borrow them shortly. We planned to meet in the next few days.

I hadn't yet gotten to the Bay Bridge. I asked him what time Ruth and I should meet, and where. He suggested we meet shortly before noon at the Avaluxe. I looked at my watch. It was six-thirty in the morning, and the light of dawn was in my eyes as I headed to the East Bay. If I could sleep until eleven, I could get a little more than four hours' worth. That worked for me.

But during those four hours, I didn't sleep. I stared at the ceiling trying to piece together what I knew about the spinning wheel until suddenly it hit me that we were no longer simply solving a crime. We were tracing the wheel. Miss Oliver was a short chapter in its long life, albeit the most recent. It seemed as if the wheel were a person who had lived through many wars, including the world wars, had resided in many nations, and which had a long and complex life of its own. Many feet had rhythmically pushed the treadle of the Rusalka Wheel, and many hands, probably very lovely hands, had fed wool and hemp and flax and who knows what else into the orifice and flyer.

The wheel, I decided, held the history of humankind during the period of its life, nearly two hundred years. By reading the history of the wheel, would I — or we — be able to solve the mystery in its final chapter? I think this is where Ruth was going.

Reclining, I held my arm above my eyes and looked at my watch. It was after ten, about time to go. I did not feel rested, but coffee is a cure for that. I decided to use my old steel dripper and have a cup of Vietnamese-style mud, drop-by-dropping it into a cup whose bottom was filled with condensed, sweetened milk. Sometimes I disgust myself.

We met at the Avaluxe. I was greeted briefly by Mr. Kasparov, who was soon off on his own mission and wouldn't be going with Ruth and me. Methuselah hurried from his food bowl in the kitchen, which is just off the lobby on the south side, to stand near Mr.

Kasparov at the door. Then, I think that he, Methuselah, forgot what he had come over for. But no one has ever greeted me like my friends at the Avaluxe, not even when I was young, except for Mrs. Chu.

Soon, Ruth and I were driving south in the Saab to Helen's recently abandoned home.

In a way, I suppose, San Francisco and old Lemberg have something in common. In both cities, there is a blending of cultures and ethnicities, and it's not always smooth. More, the artisan and fine arts communities are as much at home in San Francisco as they had been in Lemberg. Whether Lviv, Lvov, Lwow, Lemberg or San Francisco, there are city corners where the poor reside. Helen Oliver's apartment, for example, was halfway down the peninsula's east side where Islais Creek cuts sharply west from the bay. The landscape is industrial tending toward scorched, and it's been that way since the mid-1800s. The dirt's mostly toxic from such extended use. Warships were kept there during World War II, and up until the mid-'70s it was home to the nation's largest coconut pulping plant, which stank. The creek's name comes from the Native American word for the cherries that used to grow in the area. They grow there no more because of the heavy metals. There's an old crane five stories tall left over from the coconut heyday, surrounded by the water of the inlet. To the south is a water pollution plant and then Hunter's Point. Her apartment is around there.

It was in an older brick building in disrepair. Helen was obviously of San Francisco's struggling working class, and I felt a certain camaraderie upon seeing her lifestyle so closely. Yet I was sure this invasion would not have been welcomed, and I felt awkward being there.

"Look," said Ruth, "you can wait outside if you'd like. But keep in mind that a breach of privacy will mean nothing if we can find her, if she's alive. And if she's not alive it would no longer matter to her, probably." This was the scientific face of Ruth M.

We'd been asked to glove up, and we did. I felt like a second story man, but lacked the black stocking cap of the trade. After we entered, Ruth put the key that Chu had given her back in her bag. I think it was the first time we'd gone somewhere together on a case where she didn't have to pick the locks to get in. She's very good at that. I mentioned it, and Ruth said, "How romantic." I knew she wasn't kidding me.

Helen's one-bedroom apartment was small. It wasn't exactly bare, but somehow temporary, the kind of transiency that lasts for years. I expected to see a wide-screen TV with a game console, entertainment center, speakers, and a computer system with current CDs and a streaming connection to the Net, many clothes, lots of kitchen stuff, and so on. My expectations were too high.

We turned our attention to the small room. There was a mirror on the wall, an old one in poor shape whose dark oak frame was damaged and whose silvering on the back had chipped and tarnished in places. It was low enough on the wall to confirm Helen's height as listed on her driver's license: about five-seven. There was also a long, narrow mirror on the door of the only closet. It looked as if she needed no more closet space. The mirror had a wave in it. She'd probably bought it at a discount store. The orange price tag was still in the bottom left corner, only half scraped off.

There was a wooden table with three chairs in the kitchen nook, a two-burner gas stove with an oven large enough to bake a chicken but too small for a turkey, a half-size fridge, and a deep sink over which the faucet dripped. There was a rust stain in the sink, indicating the age and disrepair of the plumbing. The counter was tile, chipped, in faded yellow. There was a small window over the sink that looked onto the alley. It wasn't much of a view, but these days in San Francisco, any window is a good window. It had cute yellow curtains that one could almost see through. Ruth looked at them and told me that Helen had made them herself. The kitchen, though in disrepair (we were clearly walking amid the tailings of a slum landlord), was very clean.

I looked in the refrigerator and found half a dozen Greek yogurts, some celery, a bottle of soda water, and not much else. There was a half-can of cat food with a plastic lid and a half-bottle of wine that was desperately inexpensive. I checked the cat food and it was still usable. The freezer had some organic TV dinners and a couple of lime popsicles. Somehow, the popsicles struck me as my most intimate look into the woman's private life.

I checked the kitchen windowsill outside. That's where she fed the cat, who must have been making its other rounds during Ruth's and my visit. I put a little cat food in its bowl and put the can back in the refrigerator. I set out fresh water in a small bowl.

The bathroom was immaculately clean. The living room was small, of course, and she had a small flat-screen TV, the kind that are maybe $120 at Best Buy. She had a streaming stick in the control box. Books she had in plenty, in shelves and on the floor in small stacks. But again, the clutter and even the book piles were organized.

Most of the books were in English, but not all. Several were printed in Cyrillic, in large type. There were a few public library books of this kind.

I began to feel uncomfortable again, peering into Miss Oliver's personal life. I walked amid the remains of a dead woman. And it was almost as if I had known her. I wanted to do something for her, but not only did I not know what, I didn't know why I was feeling that way about a person I didn't know. I knew she was something special ... whatever that means.

I looked briefly in Helen's bedroom, the only other room in the apartment, but didn't go in. I let Ruth take that on. But my cursory glance took in a nicely made bed with common blankets and linens, nothing special. The dresser was small and it had little ceramic figurines on it. They were mostly forest animals, like rabbits and deer. There wasn't a makeup table or mirror. All her clothes were put away in either the closet or the dresser. A robe hung neatly on the back of the bedroom door; I could see it through the crack. She had three pillows on a double bed. She had four pairs of shoes, all with two-inch heels, on the closet floor; two were red, one ivory and one black. All of them had scratches where they'd been abraded by cement. There was a chair by the bed and a trunk or chest on the right side which served as a night table.

Ruth went directly to the chest. I sat down in the living room to scrape together some notes, trying to see if anything stood out as interesting. It's hard to judge the world until you write down its description, at least for me.

After an hour, I began to wonder what Ruth had found that was so interesting among the personal effects in the bedroom. Maybe I'd been wrong to stay out of Helen's private sanctum. But Ruth, having unpacked and repacked the poor girl's trunk, returned to the living room and sat down on a small sofa beside me. She sighed. I felt as if we'd walked into a tragic tale and I wasn't sure I wanted to read the next chapter.

She set out the treasures she'd taken from the bedroom. One was a cedar box about the size of a cigar box, and the other was a packet of letters. She opened the box. Inside were seven balls of yarn. The box had a strange feeling to it. I am not the intuitive type, but clearly the yarn balls were something extraordinary — in the sense of otherworldly. It was actually a little creepy, after having listened to Rosemary Monday's explanation of life's thread. I wanted to touch them, but my hand hesitated. I hadn't experienced that before. I was worried about dropping one, only to have it unravel.

"It's flax," said Ruth, picking up one ball. At first glance they appeared to be the same color and the same size. But the more we looked at them, nestled against one another in that box, the more the differences became apparent. Each ball had a slightly different tint, as if its shadow had a drop of color added, spreading thinly through it. One seemed to hint at green, another at orange. But when you looked at each ball separately, they appeared to be about the same.

Ruth, fascinated at the oddity, was silent. She picked up one of the balls and picked at the end until she unraveled a few inches. Of course, she had her portable microscope with her; it's always with her. She put the thread under the objective lens. I believe it was thick enough to be considered yarn. She stared into it, using the attached battery-lamp.

"Lace-weight," Ruth said, clarifying it for me. But it was not clear.

"It's spun flax of very high quality," she said. "Water retted in a river, not a pond, I'm sure. Oh, so carefully. This is, you could call it, a connoisseur's ball of S-spun flax. Linen. It's very old. But it's been spun with human hair. Just a minute." She pulled about a yard off the ball and ran it slowly under the microscope's lens. She untwisted it as she went, allowing the individual fibers to separate.

"It's very long, blond hair. One strand is, I'd say, over two feet long and there's one about a yard. That's long hair for anyone. But then, after we look at all of them, there is going to be a slight difference in each of the balls. I mean, because each one has a slight difference in color. Which would be the hair. This one seems a slightly brownish blond. But that one," she said, picking up a second ball, "has a sap-green cast to it. Let's take a look ..."

She put the new strand under her scope and untwisted the fibers. "Wow," she said. "It's very fragile. The hair follicle's breaking, just from working out the twist. This one's very old. I can't check further until I get it into the rubbery state — a little heat and humidity will do it. But it is slightly green. And that one," she said, pointing, "is clearly orange. One of these seven women had red hair, a beautiful soft strawberry. I'm going to have to look at these at home, not here. I'll have to humidify the balls so I don't break any more strands."

"How old, do you suppose," I asked.

"This one? Let's say it's the oldest, so, a pretty good guess would be ... almost two hundred years."

I was astounded. "Why is it stored in a box? Shouldn't it be in a glass case or something?" I asked.

"I don't know. At least they're away from the light. That's why there's any color left at all. I think Miss Oliver is a woman of mystery. There's just one thing after the other after another."

She carefully set the box aside. "I have to take it with us. I've never seen anything like it. I don't know what it means, but it was certainly important to her. I'm also going to borrow a handful of her photographs, just family photos I think, and these letters ..." She picked up the envelopes. There was a red cord that had once been wrapped around them both directions and tied with a small bow. Now, it simply lay on top. "That's the work of the police," she said. Ruth said the cord was flax, like the yarn balls. "Love letters," she said quietly, holding up a packet of envelopes that were yellow with age. They had to be far older than Helen Oliver. Whose love story? "And there's more," she added.

We sat down and she put the stack of paperwork between us.

"What we have, I mean, in a way, this is off topic. But it's a missing link in the history of the spinning wheel. She has letters between who I assume to be, maybe, her great-grandmother, and a Polish man, making arrangements to flee the city of Soviet-controlled Lemberg, which was at that time apparently called Lvov, just as the Nazi troops were arriving in 1941, according to the letters' dates. That was the time of the great German thrust into Russia and the satellites. The operation was called Barbarossa. The great-grandmother is named Hannah, and her Polish friend or companion is a man named Marek. I read some of them in the bedroom. I can't tell yet whether they managed to escape; I'll have to dedicate some time to the letters. It's not easy. Marek's writing is abominable and his command of the language, abysmal.

"I'm guessing that it's the same Hannah we found in Mrs. Reynold's files, the little baby of Yulia Lazarenko. I mean, my God, we're stumbling onto the unwritten history of one of the great mysteries of the world — the Rusalka Wheel. It's beginning to come together. And it's starting to look very much like Miss Helen Oliver is intimately involved in its history. I just don't know how to link it all together yet. But I'm beginning to suspect that the killers are also part of this saga, somehow."

She looked up at me, the letters still in her hand. I took them from her gently and started looking through them. I realized that I couldn't read them. They were in French.

"What would they do that for?" I asked stupidly. Ruth, however, withheld a barb that I would have expected from anyone else.

"Well," she said, "Looks like about forty-six years have passed since Mr. Kvapil visited Yulia Lazarenko, according to Mrs. Reynolds' records. Hannah, who we know was Yulia's daughter, is about fifty at the time of these letters. She wrote most of them. She was Ukrainian, and Marek Bukoski was Polish. I assume that French was a language common to both ... how they could communicate most easily. Mr. Bukoski has far less command of the language, from what I can see, but it was enough to get by. There are some later letters laced with what looks like Ukrainian that I can have Mr. Kasparov take a look at. I don't know Ukrainian or Russian ... well, only a little Russian."

I held the letters in my lap. Ruth picked them up, and began telling me the story of how Hannah Lazarenko and Marek Bukoski escaped the violence at Lvov in 1941, and what happened to the Rusalka Wheel at that time. It was a story without an ending, though, for we couldn't tell what happened after they left the old city. Perhaps they met their fates on the outskirts of town.

Ruth rose and locked the door of Helen's apartment. It was midafternoon and she had sequestered us from all disturbance. Before us now was the tale of Hannah and Marek and the Rusalka Wheel. Ruth picked up the story of Hannah Lazarenko and her spinning wheel just as the German troops, after days of shelling the Soviet Ukrainian city, were approaching Lvov on foot.

Bullets for a Bandura

June 28, 1941, Lvov, Lvov Oblast, Ukrainian Soviet Socialist Republic

HANNAH LAZARENKO WOKE at 1 a.m. She no longer had a clock. She simply knew what time it had to be. There was not a sound; the entire building and all who remained in it were dead silent. But the lull in the distant shelling seemed more deafening than the artillery fire itself. Her ears rang. Wrapped in a blanket, she walked barefoot to the great room. It was now mostly empty. There was only a table in the middle, and the wood floor was dusty.

No one had come or gone for six days since the German invasion. The building seemed abandoned; the tenements seemed to sleep. Everyone hid. No one moved. Operation Barbarossa had not yet reached Lemberg, which had been known for the last year or so, since its Soviet patriation, as Lvov. But the unstoppable German army was marching eastward, and there were only a few days left until the troops would inevitably arrive.

Hannah stood in the hollow, darkened room. Her spinning wheel was no longer in its corner. That made no sense at all to her. It had been there a few hours before. The door was still bolted and barred; no thief could have entered. The windows were boarded over and impenetrable. Slabs of light at the window tops seeped through by day, but there wasn't enough room between the boards for a thief to get an arm or hand through. And no one could have climbed three tall stories of brick wall. No one could have taken the Rusalka Wheel. Yet it had vanished.

Soon, she and her daughter, Klara, now fifteen, would be gone, slipping silently through the alleys of old Lemberg like small gray mice. A car would take them as far as Ternopil, where they would board an eastbound train, riding as far as they could toward Kiev before the trains were stopped. After that, their journey would most likely be on foot, with the Germans close behind, and with no friend among the Ukrainians. Hannah found it strange, not knowing if they were fleeing the Germans or the Ukrainians. Now she knew how the Jews felt, hated by all, grist for others' survival.

She hadn't sold or traded the wheel. Although she realized it would be impossible to take it with them, she didn't have the heart to let it go. She could have used the money; it would have bought food, if not time. Her life had revolved around the Rusalka Wheel, but it had apparently decided to leave Lvov before she did. Maybe it was easier this way, though more confusing. Hannah couldn't understand how it could be missing: Had it remained, she wouldn't have known whether to burn it or leave it in the hands of enemies, the hands of men who could not possibly understand that wheel. It had a magic of its own, a life of its own. But perhaps it had already fallen into the hands of the Russians, or the Ukrainians, or the traders and traitors that black-marketed the very hours of the day until the German army arrived.

Somehow, Hannah knew it hadn't been taken. It had simply vanished. Poof.

She had no friends left. After all her time in the city, there was no longer anyone she could say she was close to, other than her daughter. There was the old Jew who lived in one of the basement apartments who obsessively brewed raisin wine in old corked bottles for the religious gatherings of his people — she liked him. She had bought him raisins occasionally when she had money and he did not. But she didn't know him well. The Jews were the worst off of all. Most of them had already been purged. Old Isaac had fled months ago. Probably, she and Klara should have done so as well. Isaac was funny, when in the mood. He knew dances that seemed happy. And then there was the lumbering giant who lived down there too, Marek Bukoski. Marek was a hairy, round-faced Pole with a thick beard that he tried to shave into submission every day, unsuccessfully. It used to be black, but now it was flecked with gray and white. He'd sold his razor and strop and stopped shaving about a week ago. His teeth were large and white; he often smiled, as if immune to tragedy. She loved his smile, but was uncomfortable with her growing need to see it. His forearms were as thick as anyone else's leg.

The bandura was still on the wall, for now. The kobza, like the bandura and the spinning wheel, had been made by the hands of her great-great-grandfather. The kobza was already on its way ... somewhere. It was part of a larger deal that would soon include the bandura. The kobza had been like a down payment. She'd had no choice. Hannah was dying inside, relinquishing such treasures.

In a few hours, there would be a knock at the door. According to the agreement, Hannah would scratch at the wood door jamb. The man at the door would then knock again and scuff his shoe on the threshold. Only then would she open the door. He would take the bandura.

The artillery fire had become audible four days ago, vague and distant at first. It moved closer, growing louder day by day, betraying the progress of the German troops. The Soviets were being routed. She had much to fear from the Germans, as did everybody, but she had just as much to fear from the Russians and Ukrainians. The people, she knew, would adopt the Germans as their leaders, and woe to those who deviated from the ways of the people. Woe to the Jews, the Poles, and to Hannah.

The visitor would come tomorrow morning, and Hannah and Klara would depart when it got dark — with the Pole, Marek Bukoski. It took her a moment to frame the timing: Tomorrow was actually today, and the visitor was only a few hours away.

She sighed, still standing in the barren room. Then she went back to bed, crawling in beside Klara, who moved over for her. Klara, unlike the rest of the apartment, was warm, and Hannah pushed herself closer.

The knock came shortly before 5 a.m. It could barely be heard. Hannah scratched at the jamb and listened for the second knock and the scuffing. She pulled back the sliding bolts and carefully cracked the door. Outside was the same small man with the rat-like face who had taken away her kobza two days ago. He could have weighed no more than forty-five kilos. His fingers were long and thin, they were curled, relaxed at his sides. He had gnarled knuckles, like a rat. His nails were chipped and black underneath. To Hannah, they were claws. He was sweating and his light, thin hair was matted at his temples. He had no visible ability to grow a beard, and his hair went across his ears from his temple without dipping down into even short sideburns. His teeth were small, brown, and so crooked they seemed like saw teeth.

He slid inside. Hannah removed the bandura from the wall and placed it gently on the table. She was amazed that somehow, in all the chaos of war, and amid the fear created by a steadily encroaching enemy, there was someone who would profit, who would take the opportunity to expand his wealth at the expense of the most desperate.

The small man smiled as best he could, mouth closed. All his teeth seemed to be in the front of his mouth, making his lips protrude when he tried to smile. He pulled a small, heavy box from beneath his greatcoat. Hannah studied the top, and saw the 7-comma-62 designation. That was the correct caliber. The writing on the box was Russian. Hannah, as instructed, opened the box and examined the shells. She removed several, checking the firing pins.

She did not know what she was doing or what she was supposed to look for. It was just a show. She nodded and put the bullets back in the box. She hoped it would be what Marek needed for his revolver, the kind of handgun used by the Russian and Polish armies for the past forty years. She had no idea where he'd gotten it; in broken French, he'd said the Belgian pistol was "dependable, I think."

The black market was everywhere if you had the money or the goods to trade. Marek had gotten the gun, but he needed bullets.

That should have been the end of it: exchanging one item for the other. The visitor now had the kobza and the bandura, both. But the man, his voice peculiarly sharp, said, "My buyer is interested in the spinning wheel."

"There is no spinning wheel," said Hannah tersely.

"What do you mean, there is no spinning wheel?" asked the man, angry and disbelieving. "You had it two days ago. A few hours. Have you sold it? You sold it!"

"As you see," said Hannah, "there is no wheel. I have not sold it." She gestured to the corner where the wheel had stood. She was frightened. He was a small man, but he was like a ferret facing a larger animal: It was still no contest because the cruel little mammals are so bloodthirsty.

"You sold it," he said again accusingly.

What if she did? But Hannah realized the danger of getting into an argument with the man.

"No," she said, "It has been taken."

"My buyer will be disappointed."

"It was never part of our discussion."

"I described it to him. He asked me this, I answered this. He asked me that, I answered that. To him, the picture of the wheel was complete. He expressed his wish to acquire it; the offer is cash — Russian, Polish, German marks, whatever you wish. I would suggest marks at this point. Or, payment in arms." He pulled a Tokarev, the military semi-automatic handgun that was replacing the outdated Nagant revolver, from his coat. Hannah sensed its value, vaguely. He then placed two boxes of shells on the table along with the clip. She did not know what a clip was for.

"I cannot produce what I cannot find," said Hannah. She was nervous. Should she say the apartment had been broken into?

The man was puzzled. Surely, this woman knew what it meant to say no. She wasn't new to this, to survival.

He carefully slid the clip into the handgun and pointed it at Hannah. She did not like looking into the black barrel. He stuffed the boxes of shells back into his coat and then with his left hand grasped the bandura, nestling it carefully under his arm. He said nothing, but the look in his eyes indicated that, perhaps, his buyer would be satisfied with just the bandura if there were no expense in revolver bullets.

He backed out of the room.

What could she have done? Nothing. She sighed. Now she had nothing — no kobza, no bandura, no 7,62 shells for Marek's gun. There was no spinning wheel. But she had Klara. And she had two sweaters, two canvas over-jackets, boots, a canteen, and about twelve hours before she and her daughter would meet Marek Bukoski at the outskirts of the tenements near the fountain in the square. He would be disappointed about the shells. He needed them for their journey. And she needed him. She didn't know Marek well enough to predict his reaction. He could be irate. She could only hope he would accept the situation. Surely he was honorable. Then, she wondered if it was even possible to be honorable anymore. She admitted to herself that in some other situation, at some other time in some other world, she might have been attracted to him.

Bukoski was a strange man, but Hannah liked him. She wondered what it would have been like to lean into him, he was so big. Her needs were as much emotional, she realized, as physical. He rarely spoke, but when he did it was usually about his younger brother, whom he admired utterly. Marek was older by several years, and smaller. Ulryk Bukoski, the bigger little brother, was a household name in Poland: He was called the Badger, or Mr. Badger, Pan Borsuk, an Olympic wrestler who, if the Olympics hadn't been cancelled last year, would certainly have brought Poland the gold medal. Now, he was somewhere outside Kharkov, 1,600 kilometers east on the other side of Ukraine. Like so many displaced Poles in these horrible times, and with nowhere to go, he'd simply wandered east. The whole countryside was one of wandering souls, nearly senseless with loss. There were thousands upon tens of thousands. But Marek was determined to find him. Hannah and Klara would go as far as they could toward Kharkov, and then, who knew? There were no plans. Maybe Kiev, maybe not.

Hannah wondered what Marek would do when she told him she'd been swindled out of the bullets. What could he do, leave her and Klara in Lemberg? Lvov, she corrected herself. She and Klara would leave anyway.

The women's hair was pulled up under knit caps. Both were blond. They looked very much alike. Their hair was uncut: If caught, they couldn't afford to be mistaken for escaped Russian or German or Jewish inmates with chopped hair.

At the fall of night, Hannah and Klara slipped the door bolts and, bare-footed, padded silently through the building's hallways to the street. The floor squeaked; they walked closer to the walls where the floor was more firm. Once out, they jammed on their socks and boots and laced them loosely so there was some give in the ankles, and shouldered their small bags. Really, they had almost nothing. Klara had a can of fish and Hannah some dried bread and a jar of water.

Marek Bukoski was standing in the shadow of a tall brick building at the edge of the tenements, near the fountain just as he'd said. Hannah's heart lightened. There was no water in the fountain. It was here that Jaroslav Kvapil disembarked the train in his quest to meet Hannah's mother.

So far, she thought, Marek had been honorable, a man of his word. In whispers, she told him of the deal that had gone bad. He smiled and shrugged, and said, "I am sorry about your bandura," but he added that it, the bandura, would be fine. She wondered how he could say that.

Then, Marek handed her his revolver. She didn't want it. He said that he had two guns now, the Nagant and a Tokarev. The new one, he said, was semi-automatic. He smiled, teeth very visible in the ambient light. The old one, she knew, was merely a revolver; it was slower. Marek said he had ammunition for both. She asked how he had gotten the second gun as well as bullets for the revolver, and he said something in Polish, but afterward explained, in very rough French, that he had given her bandura to a teacher he knew, and that it had as good a chance of surviving the German occupation as the teacher did.

This confused her at first. Then, Hannah realized that Marek must have been waiting in the hallway for the small, rodent-like man to leave her apartment. All along, she realized, she had been safe because of Marek. Briefly, she wondered about his age. She was younger, or maybe the same. Maybe older. It was a strange thought, and it didn't matter. She impetuously kissed him hard on the lips.

Responding to Hannah's revulsion toward the revolver, Marek proposed a simple arithmetic: Two guns should not be in possession of one person during such troubled times. Hannah, who was not ignorant of the mathematics of survival, finally agreed, and took the revolver.

She realized that Marek was not stupid, but Hannah wondered if, together, they would be smart enough to cross 1,600 kilometers of unfriendly ground. It was open season on anyone who was not Ukrainian or German.

The drive in the car the night of June 28th went slowly. When the car stopped, they crawled out, Marek first. As they boarded the train, Hannah's thoughts seemed to fly everywhere … to the lover she had never married but who had given her Klara, to the great-great-grandfather she never knew but who had made the kobza, the bandura, and the wheel, and to the great-great-grandmother who was a myth even to her own family. She thought about her mother, Yulia, who had been mute from birth.

The rhythmic movement of the train lulled Hannah to sleep, but before closing her eyes, she tangled her right arm with Klara's left. They would never be separated, especially in sleep. She would never have thought of closing her eyes had Marek not been sitting, open-eyed, beard-bristled, and armed, across from her and Klara. Hannah's left hand was buried in her coat and sweater, her fingers wrapped around the loaded revolver.

On June 30, the Germans captured Lvov. That same day, the liberating Nazis announced that the patriotic Ukrainians would do well to attack any Soviets or Jews in their midst. They did so, and chaos and murder ensued. The Gypsies were as good as dead. The seek-and-destroy dictate was echoed by the occupying Germans as they marched north and east through Ukraine, a land in which racial tensions had silently — and at times not silently — always festered. Violence poured eastward on the heels of Hannah and Klara Lazarenko.

Chu's Case Expands

I DROVE RUTH FROM HELEN'S apartment back to the Avaluxe late Monday afternoon and then went to work, spending most of my shift following developments in the case. On Tuesday I met with William Chu for our "old friends" lunch. Ruth was still poring over Mrs. Reynolds files, and Mr. Kasparov was off that morning on a mission of his own.

Chu and I have had lunch about once a month, sometimes more often, since college. This time, however, it was more of a business lunch than usual, at our mutual inclination: Every time I called Chu, the line was busy because he was trying to call me. Practically overnight, the case of Helen Oliver had unfortunately expanded. More bodies had been discovered, and we were dealing with confirmed serial killings now. News teams from the major networks, alerted to the SFPD's discovery, were already stomping over the north piers to find a suitable background for their video reports.

We met at the Jade Palace in Chinatown, which is run by a cousin of William's named Chu Li Yuan but who goes by Lawrence. Lawrence had decorated the Palace with soft yellow curtains over the windows and baby blue for the walls. He and his wife have seven children, which, I was thinking, made Detective Chu a serial uncle.

Chu confirmed the information I'd already gathered, dutifully offered a few quotes for the record, and with my reporting business completed, our personal conversation followed.

Over lunch, he said that by Monday, as Ruth and I unearthed Helen's clutch of letters, they'd discovered the bodies of two more victims. One was found on Sunday and one on Monday by officers who'd been scouring the area after the red purse had been found in the company of the deceased Russian. The bodies totaled three now, but Chu said that the possible number of victims, some of whom might still be alive based on the forensic evidence, was eight and very likely more.

The dumping ground had been the north waterfront. None had been murdered there; either the body or that person's possessions had merely been tossed into the marine trash. The area in question extended west nearly to Maritime Park, east most of the way to Fisherman's Wharf, and inland past Beach Street. The acreage, with its industrial storage, warehouses, piers, boat slips, aging and abandoned vessels, and crumbling breakwaters, appeared to be an area of convenience for the killer. The deaths had occurred, Chu said, between two and four weeks ago.

The Bay Area is no stranger to macabre killings, and we — news reporters — have adopted the FBI's definitions. For example, a mass murder involves no fewer than four deaths in one location. A spree killer slays two or more in two or more places, and he takes no time to collect his thoughts or cool down between killings. And then there is the serial killer who, according to the FBI, kills no fewer than three people at various locations, but takes a little time between the killings, perhaps to reflect or calm down or plan the next murder. And, no one's officially a murderer until they're convicted in the first or second degree by a court. Until then, they're just persons of interest, suspects, alleged killers, or just plain killers.

We were dealing with a serial killer. For some reason this strain of pestilence is fond of San Francisco. Since 1969 there have been the cases of Karl Warner (three victims); the Zodiac Killer (five known victims but up to thirty-seven possible killings); the Doodler (fourteen slayings); the Trailside Killer (five victims, maybe more); and the Carsons (twelve killings), a husband-and-wife partnership. And there are others.

The current "Pier Killer" was not really unusual for the City by the Bay.

Chu and I sat quietly at our table at the Jade Palace, wondering what might have happened to the rest of the bodies. As we talked about the unfound dead, I hoped no one was listening because it was horrible lunch conversation. Chu said that a few things did stand out: None of the victims had been left with cash — not even coins. Only one of the bodies had shoes, and those were very worn and apparently valueless to the killer. No shoes had been found with the discarded possessions — the briefcases, scarves, purses, gloves, hats, and even hairnets. There was not one piece of jewelry: Chu joked that the perpetrator was an oversized crow or magpie infatuated with shining objects, high heels, and money. I didn't laugh; neither did he.

I asked how he could tell that the objects belonged to the victims and weren't just everyday trash.

"Teddy, look," he said, "this is what we do. We know what's related and what's not. It's our business."

I said something like, "Oh, yeah."

Chu was no longer able to keep the situation out of the public eye. The national news channels had grown dissatisfied with the innocuous feeds from their local affiliates. They were sending in their national correspondents, the men with baritone voices and the women who were as much glamourous actors as newscasters. ABC was sending its anchor for its usual frenzied, end-of-the-world report: San Francisco had another serial killer! Armageddon by the Bay. Chu, the officer in charge, had been relatively forthcoming about the case because he couldn't do anything about the information somehow getting out. Someone in his department had even leaked the nationality and identity of the Russian.

Mr. Kasparov had identified the tattoo for Chu. It was a KGB symbol from the early 1980s. The body had been identified as a Russian businessman involved in shipping. A former government official who'd gone first into security and then into private industry with the collapse of the Soviet Union. He was based in Moscow and had been visiting the city on business. He'd bought gifts for friends in Russia, which the police had collected from the hotel where he was staying. "Which," said Chu, "was why he was probably in that antique store. Shopping." But none of the man's gifts appeared to come from such a store. He'd bought a lot of chocolate made in the city, and little license plates and San Francisco snow-globes (no snow, just multi-colored glitter), and cable-car key chains.

By the time the press misconstrued the facts about the Russian, there was little doubt among the gullible that San Francisco was facing a massive human-trafficking and murder network operated by the Russian mafia and secret police that specialized in young light-haired women from Eastern Europe, like Helen Oliver. The media circus had begun.

In Chu's mind, the photographs from Helen's smartphone, which had escaped the leak only because Chu kept the phone and the prints in his locked desk drawer, grew in significance: They were the only clue anyone had as to where the killings might have taken place. He said he'd been trying to locate the shop with a small crew of trusted police officers assigned to knock on doors beginning on the north tip of the city and working south. Because of manpower problems, they'd barely begun their search.

"Soon, is all I can say," he said.

I asked how the known deaths occurred. He said all the deaths were heart-related, such as heart attack, possibly drug-induced, but all the data weren't yet in. He found it curious that the deaths weren't outright murders. "Like with a knife or gun?" I asked. He nodded.

"And then there's Doc," said Chu, signaling the waiter for another pot of tea.

"Doc?" I asked. I said that I knew a Doc, that he was one of the city's longtime homeless.

"The homeless man who drew me the map in the first place. We used it to find the Russian, which is where the purse turned up. He's maybe in his seventies. I've known him for a number of years. A good guy, really."

It sounded like the same Doc I knew.

With that, Chu pulled a folded piece of copier paper from his jacket pocket and handed it to me across the table. I was impressed with the artwork. But I had known that Doc could draw, and this was clearly the same man. The map itself was clear and, I assumed, accurate. There were ink smears from being folded. The embellishments stood out. Doc had managed to convincingly portray the underwater basin surrounding the piers, and had added several identifiable fish species (identifiable even in miniature, even by me) and a mermaid in a particular underwater niche that I felt certain existed — the niche existed, but probably not the topless mermaid.

"He's been living on the street off and on for thirty years," he said. It was obvious that he considered Doc a friend. It was in the delivery, not the words themselves.

"So what about Doc at this point?" I asked.

"He walked back into the police station after that first visit — not his favorite place, as you might imagine. The second time in three days. He wanted to talk about a person who apparently does not live on the street but who was wandering around Pier 47 in a mindless fashion."

I noted that this sort of thing was an everyday occurrence. Why had it piqued Doc's interest? Why had it piqued Chu's?

"She was a light-haired woman in her thirties," he said, "and then he insisted we drive out there ..."

"Helen Oliver," I broke in.

"That's what occurred to me, of course. He said she might be 'the one.' But he wouldn't commit to a positive ID ... I think he's afraid of the police, when it comes down to it. I have no doubt he knows who she is. But the trust isn't there. Anyway, he said he couldn't look after her anymore, that he was seventy-six and could barely look after himself under the circumstances, and from what I could gather, he tried to get Adult Social Services out there, but they wouldn't listen, or they were too busy, or something. The police are Doc's last resort. I'm pretty sure he'd been looking after her for several days, and I'm also convinced it must be Miss Oliver. He feels he's turning people in, you see. He won't do it unless there's no other option. I thought I'd go out there with Doc and try to find her. Hopefully she would still be there, especially if she was in the kind of condition he said she was." He had another sip of tea. Then he delivered the summary: "The female in question, Doc said, had a red mark on her wrist and one on her neck. So did the Russian. ... I don't know what it means yet. I talked to Sam about it. Ikawa, the medical examiner. Before I came here. He said it's statistically significant. He now feels it's possible that one could get a high enough dose of scopolamine through the skin to incapacitate the victim. It's complex. He had looked into it, as promised, and said he was going to call Miss M ... I imagine they're on the phone as we speak. She was particularly interested in it.

"Anyway, Ikawa, it's his busy season ..." Chu laughed. I wasn't quite sure what he meant, but I gathered that any collection of serial murders would be a busy season for a metropolitan medical examiner. "So, for now, we're operating under the theory that there's a link between the skin rash and scopolamine poisoning."

"But you didn't see her, the woman who could be Miss Oliver," I said.

"No. We drove out there and searched for a while, but never spotted her. We talked further, and I got a description pretty close to Oliver's: thirties, as I said; five-six or seven maybe; weight on the thin side; long hair, blond, messy; tattoos on her ankles and the red splotch on the neck and the wrist. I don't know if Oliver has tattoos. That's about it."

"You know what it sounds like …" I said.

"Sounds to me like a couple of victims might have gotten away, wandering around the city like zombies," said Chu. "But that's the optimist coming out in me. And yet, it sounds like Oliver could still be alive. I also believe that could be the effect of scopolamine."

"What evades me," I said, "is what all this has to do with an antique spinning wheel."

"Speaking of which, how's Miss M? Did she go to the apartment? I need the keys back." She'd given them to me to return, and I placed them on the table.

"I take it Miss Oliver wasn't at home," said Chu. It sounded like he was joking around, sort of a morbid professional humor. But I knew he wasn't kidding. I knew if I could say, yes, we found her, he would feel like a new person. Unfortunately, I had to say no.

Stepen Andreyev

"URI, WHY ON THIS PLANET do you think I would like to recognize where this furnishing shop is?" said Stepen Andreyev. "Run away from it! Flee it like a ghost! It is that much trouble, I say!"

Mr. Kasparov rotated the prints on the table so they faced him once again. He glanced at his watch; it was about 10 a.m. His little tin calendar, which clipped onto the band like they used to forty years ago, indicated Tuesday. He smiled wide, his eyes narrowing, his teeth protruding. "But Stepen, you know these things! You have a good memory. You have institutional knowledge! You see, I have it on the best authority that my little spinning wheel," he pointed with a thick index finger, tapping the photo, "is from Ukraine. If it is from Ukraine, it seems very likely that it was imported by someone you know, and if that is so, then it has ended up in a shop whose location and owner you probably also know!"

"Uri, call me Steve. I am American! Have a hamburger! They are very good here."

The name "Steve" didn't fit Stepen Andreyev, thought Mr. Kasparov. They were sitting at a diner on Divisadero at Fulton because Stepen didn't like the cafes in Little Russia. For one thing, he would be recognized too easily. Like Mr. Kasparov, he'd defected from the Soviet Union during the 1980s, though their motives were entirely different. Mr. Kasparov, with a shoot-on-site order hovering over his head for anti-social behavior dating to 1976, sought political freedom; Stepen sought free trade and the money that accompanied it. He currently traded in two things: merchandise and information. The information went directly back to the Kremlin and the pay was reasonable, but nothing to brag about. The merchandise came from various nations into the Port of Oakland as well as San Francisco's Pier 80. Stepen's specialties were importing Honda automobile engines on the one hand, and planting outmoded audio pickup sensors in the foyers and meeting rooms of various hotels during business conferences and conventions, on the other. He usually posed as part of a janitorial crew that set up for and then cleaned up after the gatherings. It was a nice way of life, and he liked the weather in the Bay Area, where it is always cool, and perfect for buying a new sweater like the one he wore today: a Hugo Boss with a high collar and zipper front. His espionage work was not political; it was economic. He was very modern.

"I do not want to call you Steve," said Mr. Kasparov. "You are Stepen."

"Then call me Al," said Stepen.

"Why?" asked Mr. Kasparov.

"It is a song, Uri! *Call me Al*, by a very famous American song writer. Uri, it was joke, I am kidding you!"

Mr. Kasparov never felt comfortable with Stepen Andreyev. There was no telling what the trader would do for money, and true friendship with such a man was an impossibility. Cordiality was another matter, however, and both Mr. Kasparov and Stepen Andreyev could be very accommodating at need.

"I would perhaps like to buy it, the spinning wheel, for a friend of mine who collects," said Mr. Kasparov.

"It is worthless, Uri! Look at it! Very unphotogenic! You want a nice little wheel, I get you a new one. I take a week, maybe, I find you a fine example. You want one from Norway? I get it! Want one from France? I get it! Name it, I find it, I sell to you at a good price, everyone is happy, your friend collects a fine wheel, fully operational! That one? That you find on top of Mount Trashpile? It is trash! Worthless! Wobble, wobble, wobble when it spins! If it spins at all! I buy it for three dollars and sell for five and call it profit on trash!"

"It is quite old ..."

"My father was old! Uri, those two parts look funny like that." Stepen was poking one of the photos with his finger. "You want the real thing! I get it for you." He was referring to the wheel in the photograph being an upright, as opposed to Saxony. "They build it sideways!"

"I think the age of this one ..." began Mr. Kasparov.

"... My mother was quite old, too, my dear Uri. Would I sell my mother? Don't answer that!" Stepen laughed until he wheezed. He coughed to clear his throat, which mussed his thin gray and dirt-black hair.

"There are patterns in the wheel, as you might see if you would pay attention to detail, Stepen," said Mr. Kasparov. He pointed to the colored, painted image of a water nymph, her flaxen hair caressing her shoulders. It wasn't clear, but with concentration one could discern the main figure. His finger also brushed the red glow that shimmered off the opal.

"I don't see nothing, Uri. Call me Steve. Like Steve Young, retired Super Bowl winner. A very large hero. Steve, it is very friendly. I am a trader, and I am friendly, Uri. You may wish to have a rocking chair, or canned fish. I can find that. But I do not particularly want to find your spinning wheel." Stepen leaned back in his seat. His plate was a crisis of salt and ketchup, and some of the French fry stubs had crept off the back side of his white plate onto the table. And he'd left the lettuce and pink tomato slice from the hamburger because, he said, it was old. "You are not telling me everything, and that is what I suspect."

Mr. Kasparov thought the lettuce was not old, and he thought that Stepen was more of a traitor than a trader. Not a traitor to Russia or the U.S., but to common humanity. He tried not to smile at his own silent pun.

"But what do you think of the wheel? The carving, the painting on the wheel?" said Mr. Kasparov. "Have you ever seen anything like it?"

"Honestly? No, I have not seen such a thing before, Uri. But I still say I buy it for three and sell it for five."

"It is a wheel fit for Rusalka."

"Rusalka? Oh, yes," said Stepen slowly, trying to pull up memories that went too far back for easy access. "My mother told me such stories. Rusalka this and Rusalka that, and the spirits found their way into little balls of yarn, Uri! What the hell do I care about the stories that are old!?" He found himself almost shouting, and lowered his voice. No one in the restaurant paid any attention. "I care nothing about them! Silly people would leave their clothing in the trees for her, for Rusalka! Or pray for a baby! No, I tell you, that is in my memory! In the spring, after the melt, clothing tacked into the trees! Yarn! Balls of yarn, for chrisakes! Little people with barely enough clothing for the winter pin up their shirt on the tree for God's sake! What, are you crazy?"

"Your mother?"

"My dear mother ..." said Stepen. He sighed. "She was a good storyteller. I have seen the opera, you know. The opera of Rusalka. In Moscow, and I was very young and very well dressed. The opera of Rusalka, I must tell you, is not like the stories my dear mother told me about Rusalka! Her stories were very old. Many generations. Rusalka would spin at night, she said, and by day she would lure men to their death! Watch out for her, Uri! She will get you!" He laughed again, and wheezed. "Let us stand outside in the sun for a bit," he said, and rose to leave. "It is cold in here." It was not cold in there, thought Mr. Kasparov.

Once outside, Stepen pulled a crushed package of cigarettes from his pants pocket. They were Chinese cigarettes, the cheapest that a man could buy and still spend money, and the worst-smelling. One had to have an iron throat to inhale the so-called smoke from the things. He had a chrome Zippo that was so old the cloth of his pocket had worn the lighter's corners down to the brass base metal. But the thing still functioned as well as the day he'd un-packed it at the Port of Los Angeles many years ago — along with a case of them and a truckload of American cigarettes.

"It is crowded in there," he said, inhaling. "People listen. I have not lived so long with people in my face to believe that they are not listening to my mouth chatter on and on."

"What are you talking about, Stepen?" asked Mr. Kasparov, who couldn't quite follow the intent behind the man's English.

"The walls have ears, Uri, that is what they say here. And the ceilings have eyes," said Stepen. Indeed, the cafe had a three-hundred-sixty-degree-view security camera mounted on the ceiling. Mr. Kasparov spotted it when he entered. It looked like a black half-globe about three inches in diameter, not the kind of thing that you'd notice. But he doubted it was used to dig Russian informers out of San Francisco's multi-ethnic woodwork.

Outside the diner, they walked south to the corner of Fulton, and veered left into Alamo Square Park where they sat on a bench that looked south over the exposed bones of the city. Stepen lit an-other cigarette and inhaled deeply, happy to use his old lighter yet again. He loved the sound of the top flipping open and metallically snapping closed. It lent an air of seriousness to their conversation. Zippos had always been hard to get in Russia, and they worked bet-ter than the old Soviet lighters, which looked like miniature blow torches. He coughed and hacked for a few seconds, then continued with the cigarette.

"I think you do not want to buy that damned Ukrainian spin-ning wheel, my friend," said Stepen, his voice low and like gravel in his throat. "It is just not for you."

131

"Unfortunately, it is something I must find," said Mr. Kasparov. The two were now talking around issues that each understood as supremely important. It was like communicating in the old days. "There is an oddity involved ..."

"What is this oddity?"

"There is a deceased Russian who may be connected."

"I am so glad you are sensible enough not to say so while we dined, Uri. Even the coffee waiter has ears."

"A large man, broad-shouldered ... I have been told he has a tattoo, which was described to me. It is the KGB symbol, on his shoulder, right side." He purposefully didn't admit that Chu had sent him the image in a smartphone message.

"The mark? You should have told me."

"I did tell you, Stepen. I just told you."

"Ah. Unfortunate that you have to find this spinning wheel, you say?" said Stepen. "You have no idea how unfortunate, now that I know of your Russian friend. But as long as you understand that the stars in the sky will not hide you, I will try to help. But I say again, it is no frivolous acquisition you are discussing to me."

"No. But it is of importance."

"What is a life, anyway, Uri? Expendable, as we both know." The comment made Mr. Kasparov a bit more uneasy. Stepen was referring to the time they had spent together in the work prison, which was where they had met long years and many lifetimes ago.

"I understand, Stepen. But a life is, at times, something one must trade, or at least use to bluff."

Stepen laughed and patted Mr. Kasparov on the back, congratulating him thoroughly for his quick wit. "And bluff! And bluff," he said, coughing from laughing. He offered Mr. Kasparov a cigarette from the crushed pack that he pulled from his trouser pocket. His pants fit loosely and it was easy for him to extract the pack, though he had to lean somewhat to his right as he sat on the bench.

"Your Rusalka spinning wheel is located at a shop that I easily recognize, Uri. It is an old store that was run by a pair of old gay men. But I cannot remember where it is. Chinatown is a mysterious city, my friend, and it has many alleys."

"This is not helpful, Stepen."

"I am helpful, Uri. Do not think poor of me! I give you a name, you talk to him, he tells you the address, you go there and visit! You wear a fake mustache to throw them off! Simple! Do not be disgusted with me for my lack of memory! It is a big world! But I tell you this, I know for fact that people of that store are bad news. Everyone says so. I listen, I hear these things. They are dangerous people, Uri ... you keep in mind my warning. This is new information. A week old is all."

Mr. Kasparov sighed noticeably. "Well then, may I offer you a cigarette?" asked Mr. Kasparov. He drew a pack of American cigarettes from his jacket pocket. The pack was open, and the top of the crush-proof box was askew. One could see into it if one wished. There were no cigarettes in it. There was a wad of green bills.

Stepen Andreyev took the pack. "You need not have removed the cigarettes, Uri! We are friends!"

But Mr. Kasparov took a zip-lock plastic bag from his side jacket pocket, and stacked neatly in it were the cigarettes. He handed it to Stepen, smiling.

"Always with the joke, Uri, always you are kidding around me! But I like that. It is like home. So, as you say, this little curio shop is in that Chinatown alley ..." and he told Mr. Kasparov the name of the alley and the name of the shop, and not, after all, the name of a second party whom he said would provide that information. Payday is always good for business, thought Mr. Kasparov. He did not write the address down; his memory was sound. They sat smiling for another quarter-hour, enjoying the sun while it lasted. There were clouds on the horizon and rain might even set in by evening. The fog also threatened landfall, and already the breeze had picked up.

Finally, both men stood, silent. They did not shake hands, and uttered no words of goodbye. Each turned and walked off slowly in a different direction.

About ten feet apart, Stepen stopped and turned. "Uri," he said, not loud. Mr. Kasparov stopped and turned around. "How about that Putin! Divorced his wife, and still in office!"

Mr. Kasparov nodded. The divorce was some time ago … a year? At least, maybe two.

"Vladimir Vladimirovich. Divorced his Lyudmila! Those Russians! They are crazy! So much they could learn from old Ukraine!" said Stepen. Then he turned and continued walking.

"Perhaps she left him," said Mr. Kasparov absently.

Captured

AFTER HE'D LEFT STEPEN ANDREYEV at the park, Mr. Kasparov went through the bus routes in his mind before choosing the quickest way, bound for, at least to begin with, Tin How Temple and Double Dragon Massage on Waverly alley. He tried to call Detective Chu but the line was busy. He tried a second time; it was still busy.

He looked up at the sky. The fog was coming in from the west, and though he couldn't see it yet, he could feel the frigid air that preceded its march across the land. The sky was hazy. He sighed. But he had found it. He was rather pleased with himself. The cost was minimal.

Transit took a little more than an hour. The storefront was brick in perpetual shadow, the door was stained brown, weathered, and the single large window was filthy and had cobwebs in the corners, inside and out. There were dried flies on the narrow inside sills, and it was fairly dark. The only interior light was cast by numerous small, early twentieth century home chandeliers hanging from a high ceiling. The wattage was probably purposefully low to save on electricity. The sign in the door said "Closed."

As he peered in the window, Mr. Kasparov saw a person who looked much like a ragged bird. She was bent over nearly to the floor. She wore a wig, and the tightly curled hair was an unnatural shade of coppery brown. Broken white hair protruded from the wig at the back. He felt bad about her back, and it triggered memories about conditions in the gulag. He blinked them out of his mind.

She had, of course, spotted him looking in the window of the shop. "Come in, come in," she said, her voice creaking. "We are open for business. Vic!" she shouted, "you forgot the sign again!" Then she turned back to her customer. "You may find something of interest! Yes, come in, look around, take your time. Looking for something for Christmas? Oh, yes, there will be something. There will be something! ... I am sorry about the lighting ... we've had trouble with the electric company. A man is coming out ..."

Mr. Kasparov entered. There were umbrellas and yardsticks stacked against the wall at the entry, and a few type drawers from the days of letterpress printing. They were empty and dirty and were leaning against the umbrellas. Dust was not merely apparent, it grew in balls much like fungus, and the passing of legs and feet along the extraordinarily narrow aisles blew them under chairs and dressers and cabinets, and they moved as if they were mice.

There was a man who was working or standing farther into the shop. He was somewhat tall, but he was skeletal and his skin was like parchment. His cheeks were sunken, but his head was bulbous, as if blown up with a tire pump. His skin even appeared to be burned in places, but Mr. Kasparov knew it had to be the play of light. This must be Vic, he thought. The man was mostly bald, and his teeth, brown from tobacco or tea, were long, narrow and cracked. He appeared to be toothless on the left side, and that half of his face was sunken. He, too, seemed birdlike, though he was not handicapped like the woman. They could have been the same age, or the woman could have been thirty years older than the man. Mr. Kasparov was not sure about their ages.

"Welcome," said the man. "I am Vic. Please, look around, look around! You will find something!"

"Thank you," mumbled Mr. Kasparov. He began navigating the aisles, and it was challenging. Chair legs and table corners protruded from the stacks of dark, dusty furniture, and it was hard not to get caught on them. Other things such as pictures in frames were stacked against the stacks, and he couldn't help but hit a few with his shoe. He worked his way sideways, carefully, and had the situation been different he might have enjoyed the possibility of finding something rare and unique.

That was not to be the case, however. After a few minutes, he spotted the Rusalka Wheel. It was just as he'd seen it in the photographs, piled on top of chests and chairs, lying on its side, the amazing opal-striated maple drive wheel set between the delicately turned uprights. What he had seen in the photos had taken his breath away, because even in the dim light, despite the poor angle of the photo, and even considering the poor quality of the photograph, Mr. Kasparov was sure he recognized the wheel.

Now that it was before him, that certainty was set in cement. He had seen that wheel before, though it had been during his childhood. It had been during the war. It was an impossibility, of course, seeing it now in some San Francisco antique store, half the way around the earth and some seventy years later. Yet his memory was sound. This was the wheel. He couldn't stop his heart from pounding, couldn't keep his memories from flooding back.

Though it was barely a glance, he was sure. He blinked a couple of times. His had not been an easy childhood, and until he stood in front of that wheel, his memories seemed scarce and out of reach. Now, however, they seemed like yesterday.

Mr. Kasparov was extremely careful not to look at the wheel with more than a passing glance. He was not new at this. Instead, he occupied himself by leafing through a few musty books with stained pages and broken bindings. He examined a brass balance that was missing all but one of its brass gram weights, but couldn't see the price tag.

"I am looking for a device on which to wind balls of wool yarn," said Mr. Kasparov. "It is a gift for my niece, and, I'm afraid, I know little about the craft. But she did mention a contraption that apparently winds yarn into balls." He shrugged and lifted his eyebrows. "Or possibly, I don't know, a basket in which she could put her yarn. Something that was, for example, 'vintage?'"

"Yes, yes," said Vic. He made a habit of addressing Mr. Kasparov from his right side. "We have several nice baskets, please follow me." They edged their way through the mess to where there were indeed several baskets stacked on top of other junk and just out of reach.

"What is the price on that basket … can you see? … up on the left. It looks appropriate."

"Yes," said Vic. "That basket is quite old, and it is from Europe. It is $65."

"I would like to see it," said Mr. Kasparov.

Vic seemed momentarily confused. He looked at the basket, then at the incredible journey one would have to take to get through the furniture even to touch it. He said, "Sir, if you wish, I will retrieve it by making a path directly to it. But I must ask you to return tomorrow, for I do not have the time today to unstack and reposition … well, I'm sure you understand."

Mr. Kasparov appeared to be downcast at the idea of having to return tomorrow. It was, he thought, an unusual ploy by the skeletal man. Why would he do this? What was the advantage? His mind played through various scenarios quickly, as if he were involved in a game of chess. Yet he could see no advantage. It could possibly have to do with a condition problem, perhaps a break in the wicker of the basket, or could involve needed cleaning to make a sale.

"Perhaps," said Mr. Kasparov, "I could return in an hour, even two. I have traveled across the city by bus, as you can imagine, which is no easy task for one my age. May I give you an hour? I could go for a much-needed cup of coffee."

Vic thought for a moment. Clearly, he was put out. He was agitated. The old crone, who had been listening to the entire conversation, shuffled up one of the side aisles and planted herself between Mr. Kasparov and Vic. "Perhaps our friend has an idea," she said, her voice squawking through her mouth as if her words were bird legs. She was entirely bent to the ground and had to turn her wigged head to the side so she could gain eye contact with, first, Vic, and then, turning her entire body, Mr. Kasparov.

Mr. Kasparov left. He pulled his cellphone from his pocket and saw that the signal was low. He looked around for signs of electronic interference and found little more than a few transformers atop phone poles. Still, he couldn't connect with either Chu or me. He sighed and shrugged at these whims of fate and returned to the shop about an hour and a half after he had left it. He could see that the area had indeed been cleared out, and there was now relatively easy access to the basket, which was still in place. Mr. Kasparov met Vic and the hag once again. It was dark in that area because the chandeliers were now completely off.

Mr. Kasparov made his way to the basket and lifted it from the rest of the flotsam. He turned it around, upside down, inspecting it. The white price tag, which was on a dustless yellow string, dangled below it. He checked the price. Handwritten in fresh black ink was $148. Though he was surprised, Mr. Kasparov was careful not to show his shock. He walked back to Vic and showed him the tag.

"Oh my," said Vic. "I had no idea ..."

"Vic," said the crone, "we had changed the prices over a month ago. What did you tell this nice man the price was?"

"I had said $65."

"But, Vic, that basket is worth at least $200! I needed to raise the price ... the last one we let go for far too little. We lost money on that transaction, sir," she said to Mr. Kasparov, twisting herself around to address him, "I assure you. But, oh Vic, you are such a pathetic man. Sir, I apologize. And we will stand firm on the price you see on the tag, and we simply will not raise it to what we had planned on, which was $210. I am sure you will be getting a very good value for your money."

But Mr. Kasparov hesitated. He could now see how it all worked. He wondered if they had worked the same game on Miss Oliver, who must have shown an interest in the old Ukrainian wheel. He wondered, briefly, what had attracted her interest in it. Had the dead Russian also been looking at that same wheel? Perhaps he, like Mr. Kasparov, was merely looking at something else.

"I am afraid that is beyond my basket budget," said Mr. Kasparov.

But the crone immediately suggested he put it aside for Christmas. "It will make a wonderful gift. It is one of a kind. I can hold it for you for, say, $150?" The entire incident was distracting; Mr. Kasparov pondered that notion.

He graciously declined the layaway plan. The crone vanished amid the aisles and he was left with Vic, who stood like a dolt near the pile that had held the basket. He scratched his scalp. "Please, look around," he finally said, not giving up on a sale of some sort, even if less than $200. "Or come back anytime. There is always something unique in our collection. Call if you wish any help ..."

Mr. Kasparov worked his way slowly back to the door, only to find Vic already stuck in the aisle, blocking it. Vic was rearranging some of the merchandise. Behind him, Mr. Kasparov could hear the old crone toppling a chair or something as she navigated her way toward them. She had obviously returned to her work of restoring some piece of vintage furniture, for she was wearing latex gloves and had a brush in one hand. The brush had old red stain in the stiff bristles.

"Sir," she said, "you really must come back. I am sure we have something that will please you." She put her hand on the top of his, a friendly gesture.

Mr. Kasparov was surprised. She had paint thinner or some other chemical on her hands, and the touch was quite cold as the fluid very rapidly evaporated. He wanted out of there. For a moment, Mr. Kasparov nearly panicked. He could feel the walls creeping closer to him, the aisles growing ever thinner and pressing in on him. The chandeliers were dripping down onto him as if they were melting.

He looked up, looked longingly at the door. It was far, far way. He was nauseous, and his breathing was labored. A moment passed, and he heard the smack of human flesh on a wooden floor. He almost didn't realize it was his.

Mr. Kasparov thought nothing now. His mind had gone blank and black. Oddly, he could smell the dust on the floor, though he didn't fully realize that he was smelling anything. He was trying to remember where he'd seen that spinning wheel. And then Kasparov Uri Kasparov heard a distant, soft voice that somehow penetrated his conscious, and it said, whispering in his ear so as not to startle him, "Uri, wake up Uri, the sap is running!"

Forest of Nowhere

Late April, 1946, outskirts of Kharkov, Kharkov Oblast, northern Ukraine

"URI, THE SAP IS RUNNING!" Marina Kasparov leaned over her young son and pushed gently at his shoulder. He sat up and kicked the age-gnawed blanket down and slapped his shoulders, punching up the matted fibers of his green wool coat, made from the same material as his blanket, and sewn crudely with coarse, hand-spun thread. Marina already had the fire lit, and he could hear the popping of thin birch branches in the makeshift sheet-steel stove. The smell of wood smoke permeated the previously abandoned train car they lived in. The cut-can stovepipe snaked from the hot tin belly to the steel wall and out through a roughly cut hole. The pipe was as hot as the stove.

"And it is your birthday!" she said, which was a miracle itself in such dark times, though she didn't dare utter the thought for fear of attracting an Angel of Death — not *the* angel, because in these times there was not just one such angel. There were many. They packed like the dogs of the war-torn countryside. She wondered if she should change his name to hide him from angels. She could call him Alter, "old man," which was the most common subterfuge, and never utter the name Uri again. Or was it too late for that? He was five today. Probably today. Using Alter should have been done years ago. Now, they could easily find him. After all, they were angels.

She hated them. They had taken everyone except her child.

The train car was one of several in the birch woods more than a hundred kilometers outside Kharkov, in the Soviet west. The days remained mostly at or above freezing, and the nights were forest-dark and frigid. Marina's breath blended with the moonlit birch bark, white set over black, and vanished amid icicle stars. A skiff of snow covered the ground and the pale birches stood naked and thin and silent, like a poem, and, to the boy, Uri Kasparov, they seemed to stand benevolently above that artillery-shattered earth, watching the soil and trying, with their roots maybe, to hold it together.

His mother, Marina, had already wired a hundred scavenged glass bottles to the clipped-off birch branches, using copper wire they'd unspooled from a discarded electric motor. The factories had been moved to the Urals when the German army approached. Marina had collected and cleaned scores of glass bottles over the past year, and half were already decorating the leafless winter branches of thin birch trees like glistening crystal ornaments. A farrier's hoof-nipper that Uri had found near the creek last spring now lay neatly on the stool near the stove, and there was a little bark still on the tool's teeth from Marina's night's work. She had been out while Uri slept, and her cheeks were red.

She was smiling. She was beautiful. Marina was wrapped in rags and wool from her neck to her ankles, and a perpetual pair of bicycle spokes were nestled in her thick hair. The unwound ends of a ball of wool string that she'd spun on the peculiar wheel she'd found last year poked out from a patch-pocket in her rag skirt. Pan Borsuk, the Pole who inhabited an old freight car half a kilometer southeast, had found the spokes and laboriously sharpened them for her with sandstone and water until they were sharp enough to knit with, but not too sharp to split her handspun yarn. He had also put a new edge on the rusted nippers. Pan Borsuk had been living in the forest longer than she and Uri, and they saw one another every day. It was a safety precaution he'd devised and was readily accepted by Marina.

There were other "neighbors" as well: Vasily Belov, the icon painter (he had once been quite famous); a Ukrainian family of five, three kilometers west; and many others; the Gypsies were gone except for two brothers who had survived but their minds had not. Deeper in the woods were bootleggers, who made birch-syrup liquor in wood-fired, steel-tank stills. Marina saw very little of them. There were a few other Jews who had survived the bullets, but they were difficult for Marina to talk with despite their common Yiddish. The trauma had overwhelmed them all. Their eyes were dark and hollow.

Marina pushed a hot mug of bitter foraged tea toward Uri and he drank it, smiling, because Uri always smiled. Part of him understood the difficulty of their situation, and yet, it seemed to Marina, another part, maybe the stronger part, glowed even in the chaos. "After you warm up, you scrape away the fire pit and get the fuel, and I'll go get the big pot," she said.

They weren't uncomfortable, physically. Marina had found or stolen, depending how you looked at it, enough furnishings to fill most of the old freight car, and she'd fixed scavenged blankets inside to insulate its rusting steel walls. The stove was operational and there was no telling when she might run across a better one. Their clothing? Satisfactory. And she had found a spinning wheel. There was food, but not ample. They foraged, they traded, they prowled. They'd lived in the train car.

But what about Marina's spinning wheel? She discovered it on the second night after their return from the Urals. It was downhill fifty meters from the train car and then up a ravine another twenty meters, at the edge of a small spring pond that provided her and Uri with clear water. The water flowed in a ribbon down to the river far to the south, toward Kharkov. Marina dipped water out with a tin bucket. Most of the year, it was frigid. They bathed beside it anyway.

The wheel was enmeshed in weeds and vines that had grown over it, holding it firmly to a tall ash at the rim of the pond. At first, she couldn't tell what it was. A brown blanket covered it. It could have been anything, even a person. Someone who'd died, or been killed. It had to have been there for some time, she decided, based on the enwrapping vines, for they were thick-stemmed. Eventually her curiosity won, and she crept up and pulled back what she could of the blanket; the vines fought her, as if protecting what they held.

Her surprise at seeing the spinning wheel was comparable to her confusion. Still, its appearance wasn't entirely out of place. There were other artifacts of civilization scattered here and there in the wood. There were even a few old cars, though most of the junk included tubs and chairs. There was a broken piano in a ditch; it was missing some of the white keys. There were even a few tools here and there, if one was lucky. Some of the furniture would have been valuable a few years ago: a fine chair, for example, or perhaps a round table or a poplar chest. Now, only the rusty shovels and hoes had any value.

The spinning wheel reminded her of the stories she'd heard as a child and adolescent about the water nymph, Rusalka. At night, Rusalka spun, and the stories about her were abundant in the region. When Marina was very little, maybe Uri's age, village women balanced balls of yarn in tree branches as offerings to her, because the rusalki were known to leave their pools in the spring and inhabit the forest, especially along the trails. They often pleaded with her for favors. ... If they had no children, then they prayed for children. The Christians, however, feared her like a demon, and said she tempted men.

The image of Rusalka on that spinning wheel, Marina thought, was the most beautiful artwork she had ever seen, and that included Vasily Belov's icons. It had been carved first, and then painted. She looked so real. She looked alive.

Marina returned to the spring nearly every day, and finally worked the wheel free of its living cage. The vines were hard to cut. She asked herself how the wheel could have survived the weather. It had been rained on, snowed on, and subjected to the searing heat of the summer sun and the cracking ice of winter. Yet the wheel was intact, its wood unsplit. There were thin strips of white that flowed within the grain of the wood, and when the light was right, usually very early in the morning, the sun would set the white aflame in brilliant red, blue, and green. Marina didn't understand how such a thing could be, but she often rose early simply to see the colored light beneath the sharp morning sun.

The carving and tinting of the water nymph and the fishes on the great wheel were strangely untouched by age and weather. They were beautiful, their yellows, deep blues and greens, the reds, were still brilliant; the wood was smooth. She wanted very much to believe that the wheel actually belonged to the nymph engraved on the drive wheel. She wanted to believe that Rusalka inhabited her spring. For Marina, fantasy was never very far away. It was like hope.

Uncertain what to do, she carried the wheel back to the freight car. She oiled and waxed it, trying to catch up with the aging. She studied the opal, but did not know what it was or what to make of it. She tried to spin wool from scavenged quilt batting, and managed to make thread for crude sewing as well as a little yarn for knitting. Then last summer, midsummer, Marina and Uri explored an old barn about five kilometers from their train car. It was too far to roam safely, but they'd lost track of time and distance. Uri climbed a wood ladder to the loft, and though he found no tools, he discovered three hemp sacks stuffed with fleeces. They'd been abandoned, but had suffered damage only at the edges. It took them twice as long to return to their home as it had taken to get to the barn because of the load.

Marina carded the wool as best she could with two wood combs that Pan Borsuk had carved. The Pole helped, and Uri found it amusing to watch the big man try to manipulate the combs. Then, Marina spun outside the freight car because inside there wasn't enough light. She spun and she spun, her hands, finally, gaining a hint of softness from the lanolin.

She made use of the evening sun, sitting with her yarn and needles just inside the wide sliding door, trying to knit a sweater for her child. But she didn't know much about knitting. The sweater was more like a small blanket, and it grew slowly. She decided it was a shawl. Later, she thought it was a scarf. Finally, it was a blanket again for a person's shoulders or lap.

Why didn't they live in one of the abandoned homes of a nearby village? Because scavengers there were looking for something, anything, to steal, to sell, eat, or to trade for food or for their lives. They were fine right where they were, for now.

"Are any of the bottles full yet?" Uri asked, hunching over as he sat in the bed, intruding on his mother's daydreams and fears.

"Some from yesterday," she said. "They're down near the creek, but you wait for me. Understand?"

He nodded.

Soon, the kindling and firewood were set beneath the old iron pot, the same one they used the first time. Once the preparations were ready, Marina and Uri left the train car and the unlit fire, and they made their way downhill and southeast to the creek bed where she'd tapped the birch trees the day before. They were farther than those she tapped during the night. Mother and son were very quiet, as always, though Uri had no easy time of it in his boots — they were small for boots, but he was still a child. The straw and paper helped, but it didn't keep him from stumbling on the creek stones as he tried to balance himself in the thick horsehide monstrosities.

If he was to be a wrestler, he decided, then he must learn balance.

Uri spotted the first bottle, hanging like a fat, sun-violet icicle on a low-lying branch. Marina had tapped that one just for him, and the bottle was half full. He pulled it down. Uri was short, even for his age, but he was thickly built. He had a toad-like frame that others might have made fun of, the way boys do, under other circumstances. But there were no other boys. Actually, Marina wished he was fat, but he wasn't. He was thick-boned, built like a five-year-old brick with a block head (but cute, very cute), and a nose too large for his face. Not a fat nose, just long and narrow. She wished she was fat herself; her bones showed.

Uri held the bottle up to his eye and smiled, sniffing it. They sat on the bank and shared the icy birch sap, its sweetness in stark contrast to the life that surrounded them. They drank it all, then wired it back up to the nipped-off end of the branch, and began gathering up the rest of the bottles, carefully pushing carved greenwood plugs into each to keep the precious sugar-sap from pouring out. This was Marina's tree-tapping area, and it was largely respected by the samogon makers, the moonshiners, who worked farther north, deeper into the forest.

They gathered the bottles and carried them carefully uphill in a bucket to the train car and the pot outside. They hauled in spurts: The sap bottles were heavy. Marina listened for activity around them but heard nothing. Then she heard some commotion to the north — nothing serious. Less than a kilometer in that direction, Belov the icon painter had taken up residence in a goat shed. She'd modeled for him several times but received a few copper kopeks only once. What could she do with those anyway? But she would not remove her shirt for him; why should she? Mary never did. Belov considered asking Marina if the boy could model for the Christ child, as Marina had for Mary, but he never actually suggested it — it was Uri's nose.

Marina did not particularly like Belov, and avoided the area of his goat shed.

Pan Borsuk lived to the southeast, and he took care of things very well. He was a big, big man, a wrestler whose Olympic dreams had faded with the onset of German hostilities and he, like so many thousands of Poles, had set out on the infinite migrations that defined their chaotic time. He had, for no apparent reason, assigned himself to look after Marina Kasparov, who was just a girl, really, and her child, and took it upon himself to instruct young Uri in Greco-Roman grappling, which, in his mind, was the world's finest art.

Marina and Uri poured bottle after bottle into the pot and prepared to spend the day tending the fire as the thin sap was reduced to syrup. She'd get one or two bottles of pure syrup from a hundred and twenty bottles of sap, but a single clear bottle was so prized that when she sold it, they could live for more than a month. Yet for every bottle she traded, Marina and Uri kept a half-bottle, maybe only a quarter-bottle, not simply to sweeten their life, but to use medicinally. It was a purifier, a vitamin, it was food, a fever reducer, and a smile generator. It was far too valuable to sell an entire year's production.

Uri kept the fire going through the day while his mother slept. She slept very little at night, but never explained to him the need to remain awake. Yet Uri was often awake, feigning sleep, and she gazed at him, his perpetual smile confounding and delighting her. She napped an hour at a time during the day, but Uri was sure she kept one eye open. Both her eyes were shallow, with dark circles beneath, but, it seemed to him, so were everyone else's he had ever seen, even Pan Borsuk's, and he was the greatest Pole in all Ukraine. Sometimes at night she would spin wool in the dark, manipulating the beautiful wheel under the soft glow of an oil wick, near the stove, and Uri, pretending to sleep, would simply listen to it whir, listen to the steady, rhythmic press of the treadle. It was like the universe, he told himself.

Marina woke in the late afternoon and brought in more fuel for the fire. "Uri," she said, "tell me how old you are today if you multiply by 10."

"Fifty."

"And last year?"

"Less. Forty."

"Seven minus four?"

"Three. But I'm five. Five is very good today."

"It's your birthday, Uri. But first, you have to read me the newspaper story in the corner." She handed him an old, yellowed newspaper printed in Cyrillic, and he read a brief Russian account of something about a polar expedition.

They studied math, reading, writing, and survival, but mostly survival.

It was barely past noon, in the forest far north of Kharkov, which had once been Ukraine's capital. The relocation of the seat of government followed closely on the heels of Stalin's first Five Year Plan, which brought the famine, called the Holodomor, to most of Ukraine. Then, as if the earth could take endless blows, Germany's invasion added an even darker pall to the land, and the Drobitski Yar, the ravine, the trench, began to fill with bodies. Which was worse, she wondered, the Red Army that enforced Josef Stalin's starvation policy, or the Nazis and their rain of bullets? It didn't matter.

Soon, there was a crude network of survivors within the forest, but little trust among them. Why had they returned from the mountains? There was no reason to the massive migrations of the time; everything was chaos. The crisscrossing paths of humans brought Marina and Uri Kasparov first to the forest, then to the Urals, and then back to the birch-tree forest sometime after Pan Borsuk drifted east from Poland after months and years of wandering and hiding.

But … it was Uri's birthday! His gift had been wrapped in a rag and tied with a spun-wool ribbon in a frayed bow, and it was beautiful to the boy as it lay on the stool. His mother was now 20, and though her smile was youthful, her face wore the tired lines and shadows of the time. Though Uri was born at the end of the worst of times, his very presence made Marina happy, and that gaiety amid such evil was magnified by the boy's bizarre, even absurd, aura of satisfaction and innocent curiosity. He smiled before she'd tied off the umbilical cord, and even now his grin made her survival possible.

There was a flat sweet cake in a tin on the stove beside the gift, and syrup to drizzle over it. It was wonderful. And Uri knew what was coming; not the present, but the promise his mother had made last year. She'd promised, and this was the day — he felt like he'd been waiting forever.

They sat in silence for some time, and then Marina said, "Your father's name was Yuri."

"But my name is Uri," he noted, his voice serious.

"Yours is Uri. His, Yuri. You're named after your father, but you are not him. You see?" This was her promise to him, this discussion of his father, whom he had never seen and never would see.

"Yes. What was his other name?" There was barely a pause between her statement and his question.

Marina studied the boy, her dark eyes registering a range of emotions. Some moments passed before she said, "I don't know."

Uri found that acceptable.

"But," she said, "I named you Kasparov twice to make up for it." Now it was her turn to smile. "Kasparov Uri Kasparov. That's our surname. So there are three of us in the world!"

That, too, was acceptable. He laughed. His upper teeth protruded somewhat, even at that age, and it made him smile like he had sour candy in his mouth ... not that he could have known what sour candy was.

"He was a Kobzar," she said. "A Kobzar is a minstrel." The Kobzars, with their ballads of Cossack battles and heroics, had been purged by Stalin long ago. Hundreds were buried in the yar.

"Yuri's bandura had a birch top, and he could play it wonderfully. You'll have musical talent, Uri, I am sure."

He felt that his fingers would be too thick to work the delicate fret board of the kobza, the Ukrainian lute, or the bandura, the harp. He shrugged. They didn't have one anyway.

"I was at the Dzerzhinsky Commune when we met, when I met your father, Yuri, Uri. There were a lot of children then, living alone in the city, in the ghetto, the countryside. Thousands and thousands and thousands. They took me from the ghetto to the colony and I worked there all day long making electric drills and, later, little cameras. We made Russian Leicas! I was there since I was five or maybe six, I'm not sure. I was your age!

"Your father was an assistant at the tank factory on the other side of Kharkov. They were making the bystrokhodny tank, the 'fast tank,' for the war. He was very, very smart, Uri. That is why you are good at arithmetic."

Uri nodded. She wondered if he understood.

"You could be a good engineer," she said. "And the next thing I knew, my Yuri was gone and you were here with me."

"Why don't you have any brothers and sisters?" he asked quietly.

"Any what?"

"Or any parents. Or something … a little brother."

She shrugged. It was a conversation for some other time. Everyone was buried in the yar, which was a mass grave first for Stalin and later for Hitler.

"I feel lonely," he said softly.

What had she done? This was his birthday. She forced a smile, "We'll have to make do, that's all. Let's have some cake!"

They did. Uri unwrapped his gift. The handle was beautifully carved white birch, about four inches long. The scabbard was about the same length and fitted neatly over the blade, tubular like the handle, and carved. When Uri pulled them apart, the blade was exposed — flat on the back, bellied near the front, and thick with a chisel-like edge. "It's for carving our little birch figures," she said. "Pan Borsuk ground the blade and I made the handle and scabbard and pinned them."

It was beautiful. He slid the iron blade back into the wood scabbard. He put it in his pocket. He'd never let it out of his possession.

The day, despite the discussion, was lovely. The afternoon remained, and Uri decided to check the bottles.

"And you are going where?" asked Marina.

"To the spring," said Uri.

"Fine."

Marina let him go. What could she do? She wanted a strong son, not even one who would ask permission. Not a boy who was afraid. She began brewing tea from gathered herbs.

As Uri made his way through the tall grass downslope, Pan Borsuk, the wrestler, carefully threaded the undergrowth and approached the train car from the opposite direction. Marina waved. She was happy to see him. He greeted her and asked about the gift. Yes, she had given it to Uri. Pan Borsuk nodded proudly.

He sat, carefully, outside the freight car near the door, where he could keep his eyes on the grounds. He watched the short, wide Uri Kasparov crawl down the hillside like a sure-clawed crab. The spring was just to the west, up a perpendicular ravine and in a small meadow just out of sight.

Young Uri carefully worked his way through the trees. Then the trees cleared. Near the spring, he heard light voices. He crouched and waited silently. He thought about going back and getting Pan Borsuk. But he knew they were not the voices of men. He slowly crawled his way through the grass to the spring. He was very quiet.

Finally, he could see where the voices were coming from. Their hair was long and whitish, their skin as white as their hair. They were thin and naked, and, he was close enough to tell, their wide-set eyes were as blue as the sky. A chill crawled up his back and he shivered.

They looked just like the woman on the spinning wheel, and Uri decided they'd come back for the wheel his mother had taken from the spring. Were they angry that it wasn't there at the spring pond anymore? Did they think his mother had stolen it?

He didn't know what to do. He carefully set down his water pail and waited, watching, entranced. He couldn't see their clothing, which lay in a heap in the nearby trees. He couldn't tell if they were soaking, lolling, washing, or waiting to venture from their watery world into the forest, where, he knew from the stories, they would climb up in the trees and stay there all spring and summer. That water was cold, he knew.

Not knowing what else to do, Uri Kasparov decided to walk up and greet them. He moved toward them, waving hello, as if he were merely going about his business of gathering sap bottles.

They saw him immediately, and slunk into the tall grass. As Uri walked closer, he realized that they were thin, not as one thinks of slender and beautiful, but as one might think of emaciated. Their long hair was not brushed, but matted in some places, and ill-kept. It was nearly white from the sun. The rusalki, he thought, were as much victims of the war as himself.

"I am Kasparov Uri Kasparov," he said, "and I have come for water and sap."

"Go away," said the older one, "so that we can get dressed."

"Oh, yes." And Uri turned and walked a few paces away. He remained looking in the other direction until they said he could turn back around.

And when he turned back, he was smiling. He liked them. Their clothes were rags. They were journey-worn, and their eyes and cheeks were shallow. Nevertheless, they tried to smile back at the child ... God only knew where he'd come from or who he was with. The older woman whistled softly, to which Uri responded defensively, crouching and moving into the underbrush that separated them.

A big man appeared amid the trees to the right. Uri was shocked. He looked just like Pan Borsuk! Maybe he was a few centimeters shorter, perhaps a little less in weight. And older, with gray streaks in his hair and beard. But he had the same face, the same eyes. Uri choked in surprise.

Marek Bukoski eyed the boy carefully, and put his pistol back in his pocket. He even smiled. There was something about the child that emanated genuine happiness, and amid all this! Marek waved to the boy.

"You look just like Pan Borsuk," said Uri, this time in Polish. He'd greeted the women in Ukrainian.

It was Marek's turn to be shocked. He choked at the sound of his brother's name.

"What do you mean by that, that I am like Mr. Badger, boy?" asked Marek.

"You look like my friend."

Marek thought for a moment. "If I look like your friend, that is because I am Marek Bukoski, the brother of Pan Borsuk, whose name is Ulryk Bukoski, and who is the famous Olympic wrestler. Is that who you mean when you say Pan Borsuk?"

Uri was confused, and thought for a moment. "I have to go," he said. And with that he dropped the few sap bottles he'd gathered and ran back to the freight car where Marina and Pan Borsuk were drinking tea, sitting in two scavenged chairs outside the box.

The wrestler, realizing there was trouble, got to his feet immediately. He motioned for Marina to get in the freight car. He grabbed a thick, short piece of iron bar. "What is wrong, Uri, quickly," he said.

Uri, breathless, said, "There is your brother and two rusalki at the spring, Pan Borsuk!"

"Uri, Uri," he said, "are you hurt?"

"Marek Bukoski has a gun, but he put it away."

Pan Borsuk was stunned. How could Uri have known his brother's name? Ulryk didn't even know if Marek was still alive. He had not heard from his brother for many years. But, never one to shy away from the unknown, or from danger, Pan Borsuk began walking down the slope that led to spring. Hope filled his heart. Uri followed.

* * *

THE REACTION OF HANNAH LAZARENKO and her daugh-
ter, Klara, when they saw the Rusalka Wheel in the freight-car
home of Marina Kasparov was no different than the astonishment
on the parts of Marek and Ulryk when they saw each other for the
first time after so many troubled years. There was no shortage of
tears. Happiness descended on Marina's steel-walled home in the
forest, and, however brief it might eventually be, she inhaled it like
the wind that came down from the Urals. The brothers, for days,
hardly left each other's side, and the mere presence of Hannah and
Klara brought out Marina's long-buried need for companionship.

Those few bright spring days, cold and wet in the morning,
cold and bright in the afternoon, were etched in Uri Kasparov's
memory. A week passed blissfully, and part of a second week.
Room was made in the train car, beds were make-shifted for all, and
between foraging and trading with neighbors, there was enough to
eat.

But surrounding the festivities, there was the chaotic aftermath
of war. It was never far away.

And, though not equally pressing, there was the mystery of the
Rusalka Wheel. One day, about a week after their arrival (they had
spent years traversing the countryside of Ukraine, living briefly
here, perhaps longer there), Hannah could no longer set aside her
fascination with finding her spinning wheel in Marina Kasparov's
home. One morning, she simply asked Marina if she might move
the wheel outside where she could see it. Of course, had been Marina's reply.

Hannah ran her hands along every element of the wheel, and
there was no doubt it was her great-great-grandfather's creation, the
same wheel that vanished the night of June 28, 1941, from her rooms

in Lvov. There was no doubt at all. She listened to the tale of its discovery at the spring, and urged Marina to tell it over and over again, as if the retelling would make it more possible.

But it was not possible. Its presence defied reason and nature, and the impossibility was compounded by the wheel's perfect condition after years exposed to the elements as the vines slowly grew around it, sealing it to the tree at the edge of the spring pool. And more, it was anguishing for Hannah to see the Rusalka Wheel in another's possession, even if that person was Marina Kasparov, even if that place was the middle of the Forest of Nowhere, practically as far from Lvov as one could get and still be in Soviet Ukraine.

Marina, who was not insensitive to the woman's plight, and realizing beyond a doubt that the wheel was truly Hannah's, simply gave it back. How could she ignore the history in that wheel? Behind it all was the hand of Alexei Basara, who had made an immortal gift to his beloved Rusalka, and Marina believed that. Not to believe, under the circumstances of her life, would have been to die.

* * *

AFTER ANOTHER FEW DAYS, it became clear to all they should leave the wood. The Bukoski brothers decided to lead Hannah and Klara, Marina and Uri, to Moscow. Could the journey be any more difficult than the trek from Lvov to Kharkov? It could not. The war was over.

"Uri," said Pan Borsuk one day. The boy had walked over to the badger-man's train car. Ulryk was sitting on a wood stump. Uri tried to touch the big man's shoulder but withdrew his hand halfway. Pan Borsuk was cleaning up a few things, preparing to leave.

"Uri," he said again. "We will all leave here pretty soon. We will go to Moscow, you, your mother and the others. And Marek. We will take your mother to Moscow."

Uri nodded.

"I have this," said Pan Borsuk, holding out something small that had been wrapped in an old newspaper and birch bark. "For your mother and you. We must get to Moscow, and there is the name of a friend in this," he said, holding out the parcel and shaking it softly so Uri would take it. Uri did and shoved it deeply into his trouser pocket.

"Something could happen along the way. You never know," Pan Borsuk continued. He swept one big arm laterally, so as to encompass all the land that was before him.

Uri looked around him. He realized that his friend was suggesting that the path to Moscow could be dangerous, and that he, Pan Borsuk, might be separated from the rest of them. Pan Borsuk was preparing for that possibility.

"Never take from the dead, my Uri," he said. "Avoid that."

"Dybbuks," said the boy.

"Eh?" groaned the man.

"Dybbuks." Wandering ghosts, in Yiddish.

He shrugged. "Or the dead will follow you … all the way to Moscow. Bad luck will follow you. You will leave them alone. Understand?"

The boy nodded.

"There's some money in that," he said, fluttering his fingers in the direction of Uri's bulging trouser pocket. "Russian money. I want you to keep that for me. You will be our treasurer. There is not much, but some. A few rubles. It will give us some time. And there is a name there on the paper. If we are separated, you can trust him. He is a Russian wrestler. He is a champion. He is a like a brother to me, like my Marek … we should all be brothers; then this would never happen." He looked over the grounds, his wide face drawn, his eyes very dark beneath thick brows.

"You will remember all the wrestling I have taught you, Uri. You will be great. You will go to the Olympics. You will go to the Olympics, Uri!" Even if he had not been sitting in a Ukrainian forest, Ulryk's days and hopes of Greco-Roman grandeur were long over. Too many years had passed.

"Uri," he said after a long pause, a pause so extended that the boy began listening to the breeze in the leafless trees. "You should go now. Get the rest of them ready. Tell the others we are leaving."

Pan Borsuk rustled in his clothing and pulled out a silver medal. He handed it to the boy, but said nothing. Uri couldn't read the Polish — he could understand the spoken word and speak it himself, but he'd never seen it written. When he held the medal just right, so it caught the sunlight, he could see the wrestlers in the center. It was Pan Borsuk's greatest achievement, his memory of the Polish national finals. But even then, the times had grown grim: Germany invaded his Poland. The Olympics were cancelled. After the Polish competition, the Badger had posted a grim note to his brother and began his long journey, a meandering and directionless path that ended in a birch forest far from home. He called it the Forest of Nowhere.

Uri Kasparov stood silently for a few minutes, not knowing what to do, trying to feel whatever it was a five-year-old was supposed to feel, and he didn't know. Then, finally, the big man broke into the boy's reverie.

"You must have a heart of iron, Uri. Do you understand? Like your knife. Iron works for you, it bends for you, becomes sharp for you. It is better than steel, for it has a soul. And when it is in your heart, your core … you cannot be defeated."

Uri turned and left. He had work to do. He couldn't see well, though the thin light of dawn seemed to be coughing itself up into Uri's world. There was light, but he couldn't see. He wiped his nose and eyes with the cuff of his coat, and he walked slowly back to his own freight car. He tried to summon up a smile and almost made it.

Marina was sitting in the gap of the sliding steel door, her feet touching a wood slat box that served as their step up into the freight car. Hannah and Klara had gone to get water. Marina's face was red, he thought, from the cold morning air. Her eyes were reddened

— winter will do that, in the morning. But really, he knew she had been crying again. Uri handed her the papered bundle from his pocket. She inspected it and handed it back.

"You must have an iron heart," he told his mother. He waited a minute as if pondering his new knowledge. "But what if the other ones have an iron heart, too?"

Her eyes closed slowly, then opened slowly. Were other women's five-year-olds like her son? Were they all so old inside their heads? Was he a product of this horrible age, or was he just an old soul? Alter would not have been a bad name, after all. Old man. She gazed at him for a moment, and then said, "Noit brecht eizen, Uri. Necessity breaks iron." He nodded and may even have understood.

He waited, and said, "We have to go to Moscow," but he understood that Marina, his mother, already knew that.

She said, "Uri, you will have to help pull the spinning wheel. It's not heavy, and Pan Borsuk has found a small cart."

He nodded. Then he sat down on the step-box between her legs and leaned back against her, burying himself in the folds of the rough green wool blanket that was her coat.

PART III

Helen Wakens

WATER, TO HELEN OLIVER, is the water of life. Dumping her nearly breathless body into the bay was like offering ice to a desert traveler dying of thirst and heat. The bay was dark and cold beneath the surface, and it was lovely. The feel of it against her skin brought life back to her from the outside. Vic didn't think twice about it, other than to note that she was much easier to dump than the others, and, he thought, just as dead. And dead wasn't his fault.

Helen floated on her back for an hour, thoughtless and still. She did not chill easily, and did not chill now. In her present state, she had no memory of being teased as a child for swimming in the Dniester River in the dead of winter. The teasing, of course, grew into fear within that small community. She had, they said, descended from a rusalka, and everyone knew it.

The swells pulled her and pushed her. They were like her grandmother; they held her and rocked her. They pulled her down. She came up for air, then returned to the dark, her body moving freely. Her survival was automatic and natural. Hidden by the dark but with her head above the water, she heard the van engine chug, stall, and die. The starter ground again and the engine roared back to life. She heard the car pull off. There was something wrong with the muffler. Vic might have been able to see her as she bobbed nearly twenty feet below the pier road that night, but he didn't look. She seemed dead enough; she certainly dropped like a dead weight. And if she wasn't dead, she soon would be. He thought, she was twice as dead as necessary. He threw her balled-up clothes over after her. Not the shoes. After nearly forgetting it, he stashed her damned purse on his way out and decided he was done with it. The scarf was another afterthought, and he balled it up and threw it over the steel fence in the direction of the purse.

After listening to the van pull off, Helen swam underwater, her body roiling the surface as if she were a large fish. The moonlight caught the roll, shimmering. One good kick in the water landed her on a floating wooden dock, where she sat for hours — it could have been days, it felt like it — her feet and shins soaking in the bay. Though she didn't know it, it was the same burst that landed Rusalka on the rock in front of a horrified, freezing Alexei Basara.

The lights of Sausalito appeared distant to Helen, but so did the lights of San Francisco's tall buildings behind her. The smell of the fish-sauce bay and the color of the Prussian-black water, thick and cold, became her world. There was a candle stub in a tin holder on the floating dock. It wasn't lit. There was a pack of matches beside it and some cigarette butts. The matches were fresh, and for no reason she lit the candle. She was cold now, finally, and the flame was no help. The memory of the little flame on the fiercely weathered planks was Helen's only memory of her survival, and once out of the water for a few minutes, her mind was again gripped by forgetfulness.

She wandered senselessly along the waterfront. She'd been dumped wearing only a slip. She found a blanket. It was folded on a bench, as if waiting for her. No one approached her, no one was near, no one cared. She was now one of the thousands of San Francisco's homeless, one of the lonely, mentally disturbed souls who are, above all, avoided. They are spoken to tersely, or they are ignored. They smelled.

Her beauty was masked by matted hair that covered her face, by mud and dirt, and by a knitted cap she'd picked up, by an old plaid shirt she wrapped around her neck and chin as a scarf. After a few days, she did smell; anyone would have. Out of necessity, she frequented the stench of San Francisco's shadows. She had become an untouchable, and if she wasn't one of the restless dead, she was certainly of the unclean living. Days passed, and she remained incoherent. Her eyes were open, but, really, they might as well not have been ... except that she'd observed an older man who seemed to be watching her. She was incapable of judging that, and she was too mindless to be afraid. Her body, however, did not sense danger. Not from the old man. She trusted her body. He'd left her the blanket. She remembered seeing him but then the thought fled. The blanket was warm.

Days passed in a twilight haze. On Tuesday morning nearly a week after her abduction, Helen found herself on some grass, sitting listlessly at the Greek-styled colonnade of the Palace of Fine Arts not far from Chinatown and not that far from the waterfront. I was talking with William Chu at his cousin's restaurant when she woke. Ruth was engulfed in the records of Helen's ancestors. Mr. Kasparov was meeting with Stepen.

Helen remembered little about the last few days except the candle stub in the tin holder, and nothing from before that. She looked up. Colossal goddesses peered down from those tall tan walls onto a world that was no longer there; they were preoccupied with the past.

The colonnade and the great dome of the palace is all that remains of the 1915 Pan-Pacific Exposition. Helen could see only the backs of the goddesses. They ignored her. She stood and turned and walked from the grass to the colonnade, and then wondered why she was sitting on the steps. She didn't know what day it was, or who was president. She didn't remember riding in the back of a small, battered van to the piers. But vaguely she could recall being rolled off the edge of the asphalt and falling for what seemed like forever until she hit the cold water of the bay, hard. But it was a difficult memory to hold onto; it was like a tree with too many leaves, all of them falling, all of them blown by the wind.

Helen wondered how many days had evaporated, and even as she wondered she realized that she'd stumbled over the first coherent thought to have entered her head. She wanted to mention this realization to someone, though not anyone in particular. She found it difficult to articulate the words. Her stumbling approach to vocalizing her discovery went unnoticed by two tourists, a man and woman, who were walking through the shadowed colonnade, approaching the dome. They were lightly laden with small digital cameras and nylon day packs, and they wore shorts and printed T-shirts that matched. They nearly walked into her. The two paused for a moment, whispered, and then continued their private tour, photographing each other far below the feet of the goddesses who held up the sky. They looked through Helen as if she wasn't there. Was she a ghost?

Then the couple frowned at the poor creature on the steps, which was Helen, and they frowned at the other vagabonds as well, the seemingly infinite number of homeless who had made the couple's visit to the City of Love less than lovely. Angela Merkel, said the man to his wife, would never have allowed such conditions, especially at Germany's most visited and historic sites. The woman nodded, but reminded him of the Syrian refugees at Cologne, and the violence there. She gave one of the homeless men a five-dollar bill, but she ignored Helen, who sat practically in her path. The ragged man with his new wealth got up and left.

Helen looked terrible and she knew it. Still, it was safer that way. Violet-black nestled under her blue-gray eyes, and her languid lids were peach-colored and pink-rimmed, adding the visual symptom of a long and deep illness to her funerary pallor. She looked at her feet. Battered blue Nikes covered them, but there were no shoestrings. She didn't know where she'd picked them up. She had no socks. She had nothing under the slip. She worried, and pulled the blanket closer.

Why couldn't they be red Nikes? She liked red, not blue. She could have used a little red lipstick, that would have helped. She compared herself, briefly, to the goddesses far above her, cast from tinted cement, but found herself to be the opposite of beautiful, and nowhere near as durable.

The other tourists left her alone as well. She wondered if anyone could see her. Was she dead? She'd seen a movie like that once, where the person didn't know they were dead when they really were. She looked up, surprised: Another coherent thought. But she was unaware, after a week wandering in a half-lit world, that the devil's breath was slowly relinquishing its grip on her.

Helen was very tired, but for no reason that she knew. She finally stood up and descended the few steps and walked or floated over to the greensward around the swan pond in front of the dome. The pond was comforting, like something from her childhood, or the childhood of some distant ancestor whose life she could recall as if it were her own inherited experience.

It was late morning, as if that mattered, and sunny, which did. It was wet; it had recently rained. The dampness didn't bother her as she lay in the grass. Unable to fight the fatigue, she closed her eyes and felt as if she were standing, like the weeping women on the wall, looking into a foreign land — a narrow band of existence between her life and the world of the dead. The watery voice of her grandmother caught her ear, and she looked for the voice and for where it was coming from. In a half-dream, she descended from the goddesses' wall and found herself in a world where recent memories might normally abound, but there were none. She found only distant memories, though they were so vivid they might have been yesterday's. They were so much a part of her that they might have been her own. But they weren't, not at first. They belonged to a little girl named Olena Mariya Olenovich, an undersized five-year-old who was, at one time, at some place, the daughter of Leysa, who had died as a young woman, unmarried. And Leysa was the daughter of Klara, whom Helen remembered as Babusya.

Helen's dream was a flood of memories that fell from the dome like rain, sprinkling themselves over the green grass around the pond, at about noon. Still unable to fight the fatigue that had been left in her, she returned to her twilight sleep and found herself living a child's life that had been submerged so far in her mind that she had not remembered it existed. The images were a swirl, like a great wheel spinning. Only the memory of fire seemed to gain substance. The fire, and the attitudes of the Ukrainian village in which she had lived. Were those attitudes any different than those cast at her as she sat homeless in the grass?

The Mayor of Mielnica

August, 1988, Mielnica Podalska, Ternopil Oblast, Ukraine

WHEN KLARA OLENOVICH "RETURNED" to Mielnica from
Moscow with the three-year-old, Olena Mariya, she found
herself in a land she had never actually seen, a town that was both
deeply traditional and somewhat modern. No Basara had set foot in
Mielnica for more than a century and a half ... not since Alexei
packed his young family into a goat cart and fled to Lemberg,
where, he decided, they might blend in a little better.

Olena spent her evenings in their north-side apartment listening to music and news on a tube radio and entranced by the wheel
as her grandmother, Klara, spun flax or wool to sell. Overseeing
them from behind the wheel, on the wall, forever engraved in Olena's memory, was a nineteenth century lubok — a bold woodcut in
an intricate traditional style, hand-colored in bright orange — de-
picting St. Paraskeva Piatnitsa, who was also called St. Friday. She
was not a real saint: Friday was the day set aside ages ago to honor
the goddess.

When Klara taught at one of the local schools during the day, Olena played with the Gypsy children on the poverty-ridden north side where they lived.

Unfortunately, like her antecedents, "those Basaras," Olena's presence in the town made most of the residents uncomfortable. The problem was that Olena's heritage was not her only problem. Compounding things was the absence of the child's mother, who had died. Superstition had not faded quietly away in Mielnica, and people harbored traditional concerns: The death of a mother indicated an evil nature in the child; Olena Mariya was to blame. Secondly, there was no father, and illegitimacy was hardly acceptable.

Third, the girl was unable to speak with any clarity. The lack of speech in her early years was overtly damning. All the people knew well what sort of beings could not speak: rusalkas and golems. Facts are facts. They didn't worry much about the golems because there were almost no Jews after the war. One family, maybe two.

Finally and conclusively, there was the child's birthmark. Klara had been careful to keep it covered, but complete secrecy was impossible — and Olena was nearing school age. She swam with other children in the river. The dark patch on her waxy-light skin was in the shape of a fish and it sat on her left shoulder, toward the back, like a purple burn. It was the very image of Tatyana Basara's mark, but only those who had seen Karel Erben's notebooks would have known that, and no one in Mielnica had seen a folktale collector for generations.

Eventually, the "mayor" of their neighborhood adopted Klara and Olena into his circle of influence. This man was Borys Rybak, a former Olympic swimmer who was famous throughout the oblast. He took on the role of guardian of both Klara and the child for no reason whatever, other than, perhaps, that he came from the same neighborhood originally and had pulled himself up from the poverty and narrow-mindedness common to such places. He considered himself the unelected mayor of Mielnica, and so did everyone else.

In the middle of the night of August 25, 1988, in the north section of old Mielnica, a fire broke out. Klara and Olena escaped with minor complications from inhaling smoke. Both had been asleep during the deep, dark, silent night. Klara bundled up the child amid smoke and flame and ran through the flames to the road.

All that remained of their warm home were scraps of things: the unburned portion of a table leg, or the scorched and tarred metal of cooking pans. The cinderblock side of the building as high as the second floor was still standing. There were blackened cinderblocks and scorched bricks. The stove was black and partly melted from the heat. The oil furnace in the basement had exploded, and the exterior of the next building was completely burned. Four buildings had been engulfed in flame, leaving eighty-six people homeless. The firefight lasted about six hours, but the entire block smoldered for hours longer.

The "mayor," Borys Rybak, was on the scene by dawn, dressed in the clothing he'd worn the day before, but with no socks because he'd been in a hurry. He had already made arrangements for the families in the building, including Klara and Olena: temporary living quarters, clothing, and food. Rybak, a veteran of the Olympics of 1972 (the terrorism in Munich) and 1976, Montreal, was not new to subversive human activity. He summoned enough political pressure to force the local police to investigate the matter as arson, which they had been reticent to do. Without Rybak, the incident would simply have been set aside until it vanished into a dark well of days and weeks and years.

What had not survived the fire, but which left no cindered remains, was the Rusalka Wheel. It wasn't the physical and emotional impact of losing their home that troubled Klara; it was the spiritual and irreplaceable loss of the wheel. It had been the fulcrum of family life, and without it their financial existence would have been skeletal. She returned and searched the rubble for any sign of it. There was none. She was merely one of the dozens of displaced people searching the charred remains of the buildings for what might remain of their lives. But the fire had been voracious.

Having now lost the wheel to the flames and facing the silent but unrelenting hostility of the town, Klara Olenovich took the only path she found open to her. She decided to flee the Soviet Union with her granddaughter. Life for them had never been comfortable there, and all Mielnica (except for the Gypsies) had shunned them … just as their neighbors in Moscow had. They would go to a new world, she decided … somewhere that lacked mythology. America! There were no rusalki in the West.

Klara once again found an unexpected ally in Borys Rybak, and his friendship remained something that she could never understand. Yet it was the mayor of Mielnica who arranged for the papers and the money for the bribes, and it was the mayor who used his political connections to facilitate the physical relocation of the Olenoviches.

Klara, and Olena who was by now six years of age, set foot in America with nothing but a small bundle of clothing that would have barely covered a pair of rats. Rybak had paid $14,000 in July of 1989 for their passage, then celebrated Olena's sixth birthday in August with a foot-tall cake, which he bought, and paid another $8,000 the first week of November to a Russian "businessman" who could guarantee safe passage on a tramp freighter setting out from Odessa on the Black Sea. He never told Klara he was working with the Russian underground; he had no choice because only the mob was strong enough to protect a woman and child on the lawless seas.

Klara and Olena landed in San Francisco on Christmas Day, 1989. Before, Christmas had not been one of Klara's favorite holidays, but that changed … even though Pier 84 on the east side of the peninsula looked like an industrial holocaust.

* * *

HELEN AWOKE ON THE GRASS. Opening her eyes, she realized that she was Olena. She sat up. She remembered coming to America and becoming, with her grandmother, Olivers. It seemed to Helen that she had lived a very long, long life, but really she had not. She sighed. She felt very lonely.

Her memory had begun to return, though she didn't know it because she was inside the change, not outside where she could analyze it. She still wasn't that cold. It was raining lightly. She found a coat and threw it over her shoulders on top of the blanket. The coat was new and she found that strange. No one paid attention to her, she decided, except for the god of coats and blankets. She stood and walked north, not sure why she was leaving the swan pond.

There was an old man watching her. She stared at him, her blue-gray eyes trying decide if he was dangerous. It was the same man who'd been around, here and there, for the last week or so. She blinked, realizing that she'd just wrapped herself around another memory: a week of wandering.

Pier 47

MR. KASPAROV DIDN'T RETURN from his errand. Ruth called me on Wednesday and said she was worried. Visions of Mr. Kasparov, drugged and drowned, flew through my head. I could tell how worried Ruth was simply because she'd picked up the phone. I accepted her concern without question, and after talking with her, I felt certain that wily Mr. Kasparov had somehow, through his sources, discovered the location of the antique store. But I worried that he'd gotten too close to the killers and had been overpowered or simply caught. We could only hope that he was all right. I reminded myself that we were dealing with a serial killer, and there were already three people dead and more missing … which made me worry even more.

I did the only thing a thinking person could do. I decided to stake out the waterfront. Whoever was on their murderous spree would surely return to their favorite place and dump the next body or purse or phone, and I needed to be there. If they did not have Mr. Kasparov, they would lead me to him.

The little information I had indicated that I should set watch near the north end of Leavenworth, a spot where I could monitor everything that occurred on Pier 47. A narrow but deep strip of water lay between me and the pier. I could also watch the warehouse frontage to my right and left.

Unlike much of the city's coastline, the bay front at Pier 47 is neither lovely nor romantic. There's trash everywhere, and plastic sacks and hamburger wrappers are held prisoner by steel fencing and broken wood crates. It smells like diesel fuel and marine waste. The stars don't shine as you look over the water: They seep. If you catch a glimpse of a star here or there where the weave of the fog has thinned, it soon vanishes. The stars must fall, I decided, from salt-rusted nails hammered into the wall of the sky, leaving broken glass everywhere.

The God of San Francisco has abandoned the aging docks and piers in exasperation. By late evening, most of the homeless people have left as well, drifting inland and spreading their cardboard mats and ragged blankets in the doorways of the Financial District. It's too cold to sleep near the water.

But I did not sleep. I pulled a wool blanket tighter around my shoulders as I sat in the gloom. I wore a black watch cap that Ruth had knitted. I hoped I looked rough, and grimaced in the dark. I could have been a murderer, never mind that the cap was cashmere. The air was thick, and humidity muted the sounds of the bay. Silhouetted tankers roamed east and west, moaning at the moon and at Alcatraz and Angel islands on their way to or from the refineries north of Richmond. I tried to get comfortable on a thick stack of cardboard and pulled the blanket up over my head, even though I was wearing the cap. I stared out over the industrial landscape and water, and listened and waited. I was hoping to see a car slow down, pull off, and unload. I was waiting to hear a door or a trunk slam. Whoever I might discover could eventually lead me to the spot where all the murders had taken place: the antique store where the Rusalka Wheel had been pitched on top of a pile of cast-off furniture.

What I really needed was a license plate number I could give to William Chu to trace. I began my surveillance shift at midnight, thinking nothing much would happen until then because of all the wandering tourists; Fishermen's Wharf, which is the city's mini-Disneyland, isn't more than a quarter-mile east. It seemed to me that the best time would be between two and five in the morning — after the tourists thinned and after the homeless bedded down, but before the early morning runners and the fast-walkers with little weights in their hands began their workouts.

I had a small thermos of coffee, which was half-gone by one. I had some cookies, which were gone by two. The silence of the night was broken occasionally by bellowing tankers just inside the Gate. It was interrupted by the distant rattle of shopping carts as homeless insomniacs strayed across the pavement and up the broken sidewalks. But the crashing of a particular cart grew closer, and I turned warily to listen. I could see only shadows, and whoever was pulling it probably could not see much more of me than I of them. I found it unsettling, and my hand searched for a crescent wrench I'd brought, just in case. It grew closer and after what seemed like forever, the person and his caravan were practically in front of me, moving laboriously from right to left on the frontage road.

I didn't move. I preferred the anonymity of the shadows and hoped to be unnoticed. Yet, like a wolf, the intruder must have smelled by presence. The shadow-man was close enough now that I could guess how tall he was. He wasn't tall. He was quite short and didn't move like a man. I felt no better, though, knowing that the poor thing before me was a woman.

I decided the only thing to do was to say something. But what do you say to someone you can hardly see at three or four in the morning on the otherwise silent docks where dead bodies have become common? Have a nice day? How's it going? What do you think of Aristotle? The Niners?

Finally, I said, "If you see a Mr. Kasparov, tell him I'm looking for him."

The short creature in front of me sighed in great relief and said, "Geez, Nat, what're you trying to do, scare the life out of a girl?"

It was Ruth. I said, "You're looking for him, too. You want under the blanket? It's pretty cold. Are you okay?"

"Sure."

"Any trouble?"

"No. It's been okay."

She pushed her cart to the side so it wouldn't block our view and settled onto the cardboard I'd collected. She pulled the blanket over her shoulders.

"Good view from here," she said. "I didn't think about that. You can see the whole area. Any sign of a car dumping bodies or purses?"

She sounded tough, but I knew she wasn't. Yet she was fearless enough to roam the city alone at night.

"I haven't seen anything yet, and the night's almost over," I said.

"How long have you been out here?"

"Since about midnight. But now I'm starting to worry that the killer won't come back because of all the publicity."

"I know," she said.

We were silent for a minute, and she said, "I can't sleep."

"How long have you been out?"

"I don't know. Maybe twelve, twelve-thirty. Methuselah didn't want me out this late alone. He's very possessive." Methuselah is set in his ways. He expects Ruth to be in bed at this hour. "Do you have something with which to protect yourself?" she asked. Somehow, proper English doesn't sound tough.

"I have my lucky wrench," I said. "It was my father's." It made her laugh, but the laughter was swallowed by the bay in front of us.

"I don't know what to do," she said. I was afraid she'd start to cry.

I said, "Wait till dawn, leave, then come back again tomorrow night. The person behind this is crazy enough not to stop. They'll be here eventually. It might be a night or two away." I think I even believed that.

"Do you have a camera?"

"Yes. I just need a good look at their license plate, and then call Bill Chu to trace it to the residence. All I could think of to do was to sit out here and wait."

"I didn't see anything all night," she said. "I'm so upset that I'm losing my balance."

"I have a feeling that they'll be out here again. I'll stay for weeks if I have to."

"I can't believe it."

"What? That serial killers are predictable?"

"No, that you'd stay for weeks. I can't tell you how much it means."

"He's my friend," I said, but I don't think she heard me. She was staring off into the night so I wouldn't see her tears.

"It's more than that for me," she said.

I wasn't quite sure what she was referring to. I nodded anyway. He'd been missing for more than twenty-four hours. Helen Oliver had vanished a week ago. Something had to break soon.

Second Night

I DIDN'T PICK RUTH UP on Thursday. She wanted to rendez-vous sometime after nightfall because her day was disorderly and she couldn't think about trying to be somewhere at a specific time. Neither could she knit because of her state of mind — our preoccupation with the disappearance of Mr. Kasparov. There was nothing I could do to alleviate her terrible stress.

I arrived at our spot overlooking the bay about ten, sure to be there before her and figuring she'd probably arrive sometime around midnight or one. Almost everything was the same: It was cold, damp, dirty, and overcast, but tonight a piece of the moon was trying to swim through the fog. It was golden, and dim as it was, it added to the luminosity of the waterfront. The view across the water to Pier 47 was slightly more visible because of it.

Ruth arrived at eleven thirty and sat down beside me under the blanket. I asked if she had slept during the day. She said she had not, but added that she had rested a little in the middle of the afternoon and that if it was okay she could sleep against me and it would make her feel better.

She rested for about an hour. It was one, but I didn't check my watch. Ruth knitted in the dark after she woke up. I didn't know a person could knit in the dark. I asked what she was working on. She said it was the hat she'd been working on earlier. She'd memorized the pattern, she said, and could tell where she was by feel. It was the same pattern as the one I was wearing, but smaller and a different color. For a long time, we sat quietly as her needles clicked softly.

As I sat in the cold dark, I began to wonder about the strange man we were seeking, Kasparov Uri Kasparov. I realized how little I really knew about the man, other than that he'd been in Ruth's life since she was about ten, and had been a friend, lover, or ... I don't know ... of Mrs. Reynolds. I knew he spoke many languages, made puppets, and loved reading newspapers. I had never seen him unhappy. And I knew he'd fled the USSR in the 1980s after serving an unknown amount of time in one of the gulags. I didn't know what his so-called crime had been. Ruth had mentioned once, in passing, that he had been a minor athlete, practicing, competing, and later coaching judo with the Soviet Olympic team.

The rest of him, the finer points, the little bits of knowledge that help fill out your idea of a person and explain perhaps why you like them so much, were all missing for me. All I knew was that I thought of him as a friend. A close friend. Like family, no questions asked, and none answered.

My voice, even as a whisper, seemed to shock the night fog that surrounded us. It wasn't the only sound, for we could hear distant fog horns, tankers, traffic on the streets behind us, and occasionally, breaking glass. But nothing was close to us or threatening.

I said, "How did Mrs. Reynolds and Mr. Kasparov meet?" It seemed like a reasonable question, appropriate for a night of sitting and waiting and hoping for anything to happen that might lead us to our missing friend.

Ruth turned and looked up into my eyes. Even in the dark, hers were piercing, as if judging whether or not she wanted to part with her thoughts and feelings about the man who had played such an important role in her life.

"Do you have a few minutes?" she asked. She was joking with me, but remained poker-faced.

"Sure. I'll raise my arm if I hear anything … like a car engine on Scoma, or anything that might sound like the killer returning."

"You mean like a splash. Don't be afraid to say it. Do you have your camera?"

"Of course."

"Does it have night vision?"

"I can shoot the car and the license plate. Or a face, even without a streetlight. Even across the water."

"That's what I like about you," she said, "you have a good camera."

"Then it was worth every penny."

Besides my little point-and-shoot, I actually did have a good camera, and I'd brought it with me.

"They met in 1976, the year of the Montreal Games," Ruth said. "Mr. Kasparov was a member of the Soviet judo team. He went to Munich four years earlier, when the Israelis were killed. It shook him up … but that was the last time he could have competed, because of his age. He was one of three stand-ins for his weight class, but he wasn't given the chance. He was coaching in Montreal; I think he was in his late thirties by then. And Mrs. Reynolds was performing with the Montreal Symphony Orchestra in one of the old Expo buildings there."

"She played piano," I said.

"Yes. She was playing Chopin on that tour, but I don't know exactly what."

I waited for further explanation. I could hear the traffic behind us; a truck was crossing Leavenworth about two long blocks away. There was nothing going on in front of us, which was our area of interest.

"Mr. Kasparov and a coach for the Soviet men's swimming team left the Olympics camp and somehow got tickets for her performance. Pretty good seats, too, within eyeshot of the symphony members onstage. Anyway, the story goes, their eyes met and it was love at first sight, for both of them."

What were the chances? A Soviet athlete meeting a world-traveling American musician at a Montreal nexus …

"That sounds romantic," I said. "I assume it all worked out …"

"It didn't."

A sedan scooted up Leavenworth past us, rolling along far faster than was safe. It was a late-model Chrysler of some sort, one of the new muscle cars, glossy black with blackened windows. It spun a few circles, burning its tires on the pavement, and then roared back down the street and was gone. After the sound of its engine blended into the mishmash groan of San Francisco's night, my attention returned to the story of Mr. Kasparov.

"What happened?" I asked.

"Mr. Kasparov asked her out for a light meal after the concert. I don't know how they worked it all out, but she left the Place des Nations with him, much to the surprise of the symphony musicians."

"What about the man who Mr. Kasparov was with? The other coach?"

"I understand he went back to the Olympic village and made all sorts of excuses for him. It was fine until the next day. Everything had been smoothed over on all accounts. But then morning came and Mr. Kasparov wasn't back."

"Was it a day of competition?" The chrome-steel rumble of a shopping cart caught our ears, and we waited in silence as it passed to our right. It was nothing, only the laden goods of one of the street people.

Ruth's attention returned to me, and to her story. "Yes. Some members of the judo team had made the finals, and Mr. Kasparov was AWOL. Worse, so was Mrs. Reynolds. They had to cancel the third and last nights of her concert series. The man who was making excuses for Mr. Kasparov, it was a swim coach, was removed from the team and basically put under guard."

"That seems harsh ..."

"There was a huge concern at the time that Soviet athletes might seek asylum in Canada. And I think the politburo was extremely concerned about bad publicity."

I nodded. The streets remained quiet.

Ruth said, "They were gone for a week, somewhere in the maze of Montreal. It made headlines at the time ... imagine, a missing diva and an AWOL Olympics coach. For a week! It was scandalous, Nat. The tabloids went crazy. Then the Soviet Olympic police finally found them sipping coffee at a cafe. They confined Mr. Kasparov and then sent him back. They sent him to a work camp at Kaisk. They never called it a gulag, but it was. Kaisk was in northern Ukraine I think, and was known for the number of deaths from tuberculosis; it was famous for its graveyard, victims of the lung disease. Hundreds. He was there until about 1980, when he escaped with the help of the same man who covered for him in Montreal. His name was Borys Rybak. They were both from Soviet Ukraine. Mr. Kasparov had spent a lot of time in Kiev and Kharkov, and Mr. Rybak was from south of Lvov, from the countryside. He swam and coached the medleys."

"Were they reunited after his escape? Mrs. Reynolds and Mr. Kasparov?"

"They met first in Istanbul. Mr. Kasparov took the route south through Yugoslavia. It was called the Jewish Railroad because then, in the eighties, a lot of Jewish people were fleeing the USSR. That was where he learned to manipulate marionettes so well ... he was on the road, hiding and running, mostly in Yugoslavia. He lived secretly with several families. Back when there *was* a Yugoslavia. Then afterward they met in France, and then Canada, before he came to the U.S. And I met him here in San Francisco, together with Mrs. Reynolds. So that's their story."

"Was he hurt?" I asked.

"What?"

"Was he hurt, in prison."

"I don't know. He doesn't talk about it. He always just smiles and says he was, quote, 'a prisoner for love.' He said they made chess pieces out of bits of paper wadded into shape with toothpaste and played on a grid scratched on the cement."

The bleating of a small-engine motorcycle tore through the streets to our left. It was nothing. By now it was probably about two in the morning, but I didn't look at my watch. Ruth extracted a steel thermos of tea and two paper cups.

"Nat," she said.

I don't know what I replied.

"My back is getting sore. Can you do something?" She scooted her back toward me. "Lower. Lower, please. I'm not made of glass."

Success

THE RATTLE OF ANOTHER MUFFLER unexpectedly shook us, and Ruth shot up out of the blanket. I was slower getting up. We stood silently for a few seconds, waiting for the vehicle to come into view. The sound was at first behind us, and we caught sight of the car as it headed north to the pier. A beaten-up white minivan crawled north and then turned west onto the dead-end pier road. We were already both making our way there, but we had to take a horseshoe route to skirt the water. Halfway, we could hear the engine running and the snap of one of the van's doors closing. We were close enough to hear the side door roll back.

Finally, we could see it. The headlamps were out, and there was no license plate on the front. Ruth, in old clothes as she played her part, walked slowly, homelessly, toward the van. I, too, was in character, with the blanket still wrapped around my shoulders.

We couldn't see the driver. He was already out of the van, and he'd left the sliding side door open. I could hear him in the fencing and junk on the south side of the road.

I looked in the van as we walked past it. I saw nothing unusual; neither bodies nor personal effects, nothing inside. Ruth was ten yards ahead. We veered into the fenced area. It was too dark to see. Both of us had flashlights, but we didn't turn them on for fear of spooking our prey. I was behind Ruth, which was not where I wanted to be.

We could hear him in front of us. We'd gone maybe fifteen yards in. The fencing and buckets and darkness turned those few yards into an obstacle course. Somehow, the man managed to circle around us and got back to the van while we were still tangled behind the fencing. We heard the door roll shut, and the killer climbed into the driver's seat and revved the engine. It stalled. He cranked the ignition and it fired up again, and he gunned it. We could smell the oil fumes as the engine coughed and finally caught. He was back on the pavement before we could get out of the mess and to the fence.

There was no rear license plate either. Furious at being outmaneuvered, Ruth hurled her metal-housed flashlight at the back of the van as it sped to the corner. The flashlight smacked it hard, and it sounded like she broke one of the taillights.

I was relieved it didn't go through the back window, though I didn't say that.

The driver goosed the engine and was gone.

After two long nights waiting, Ruth's hopes of saving Mr. Kasparov vaporized as we stood there motionless. All we needed was a license plate number. Or the killer. We hadn't planned on him walking out of his dumping ground a different way than he got in. I hadn't thought there'd be no plates.

Ruth just stood there in her rags. Even in the dark, I knew her face was red. I didn't dare shine my flashlight on her. Nothing more than a low moan escaped her lips, and to me, that night, it was the sound I would expect to hear from a mammal, maybe a rabbit or raccoon or badger, who had just come across the bodies of its litter, dead. Her anguish spread across the dock.

"Call 911," she said. Her voice cracked.

I took a deep breath. She didn't carry a phone.

"Where's your phone?" she asked. "Call 911. Do it!" Her voice pierced the air.

"I don't have the phone," I said.

"No, no, no! Why?"

"I left it in the van when we walked by it," I said. "The phone." I felt terrible not having said something, but I couldn't afford to speak for fear that my voice would give us away. "It has a GPS and the phone is on. You have no idea how happy I was that your flashlight didn't hit that back window." Ruth can throw accurately; the tension might have caused her aim to be off. Whatever the cause, I was grateful. "Without a bunch of glass chips back there to clean up, we might have several hours before it's found. I can track it from my netbook. We need to get back to my car. It's in the trunk."

Ruth, who hadn't moved, was utterly silent. She who refuses all phones, knows what a GPS is. She stared at me. I could see her eyes even in the dark. Frankly, even disguised as she was and after her emotional rollercoaster ride, she looked beautiful.

"Thanks," she said softly.

It was 3 a.m.

We checked the grounds with our flashlights before we left. We saw another purse and some clothing. At least there wasn't another body.

PART IV

The Antique Shop

RUTH SPENT THE REST OF THE MORNING with her cat and me, pondering the case of the Rusalka Wheel in her Avaluxe Theater flat as she dressed. I was on the phone trying to reach William Chu. Her air of determination was palpable. We had located the phone, and therefore the van, and through satellite images we found what we believed had to be the shop — from above. It took us until about eight. But Chu was unavailable. His message said he'd been hauled into department meetings all morning, and Ruth was reticent to work with anyone else. I couldn't convince her otherwise, and just kept trying his phone every ten or fifteen minutes, to no avail.

Ruth continued to dress. I'd given up on Chu for the time being. She put her robe on the arm of the sofa and sat for a moment, the chilly air of the flat surrounding her. Despite being up all night, she wasn't tired. She patted Methuselah and scratched his ears and neck. Then she rose and walked bare-footed to her bedroom to choose her costume for the day. She would be wheel shopping. She was on her way to an antique store in Chinatown. By satellite, we could see the building's roof in high definition.

Ruth slid into sequined low-rise boots. The light they caught seemed to reflect her sun-red blouse more than the light of the wider world, and between the two, she glowed. It was, of course, wholly purposeful: There had been only one pair of shoes among the victims that had not been taken by the killers, and that pair was so worn as to be nearly unrecognizable as shoes. Whoever the killer might be, he, or possibly she, had a fetish for shoes. Ruth wore sequined bait.

* * *

WE HAD AGREED that if the shop was open, Ruth would go in alone. I would wait nervously outside, out of sight. If the place was locked, though, we would both break in. She had her lock picking rods in her bag.

We first checked the back side of the alley off Washington and spotted the van. The doors were locked, but I knew my phone was still inside. The engine was cold. The back entrance to the shop was blocked by dumpsters and old steel fencing, and the back door was completely inaccessible, even for purposes of breaking in.

We walked back around the block to Clay Street and Ruth walked down the alley alone, passing the lubok of the orange cat and the window with the glazed ducks. I tried to phone Chu again, and he picked it up on the fifth ring. He said he was on his way. I stayed at the alley intersection, nervously.

Ruth walked down the alley until she faced the antique store window and door, over which hung a sign that said, Sterling's Fine Antiques & Collectibles. It was an homage to the lyric poet of San Francisco's golden age, George Sterling, first among the Bohemians. The small sign was hanging crookedly and nearly invisible beneath the eave and behind a few ill-tended plants in hangers.

There was a closed sign in the small door window. She peered through the large window beside the door, and despite the crust of dust, soot, and spider webs, she could see there were no lights on inside. The place appeared abandoned. Ruth tried the knob. The door was unlocked. There was no alarm.

On the floor inside were a few letters and glossy catalogs. The floor was dusty and there were scuff marks in the dust. Ruth turned and motioned me with her arm, and I jogged up the alley and entered behind her. Our shoes added to the scuff marks. Ruth flicked on the switch near the door, seeking light. It was one of those old ones with a button to push for on, and a separate off button below it. When you push one, the other one pops back out. This switch plate had five pairs and operated all the lights in the room. But no light turned on. There was no sound of a fan or furnace. In fact, the place was very cold. It was silent. If a piece of real estate can be dead, it was.

Narrow aisles meandered toward the back of the shop where there was a glass case, a counter, and the cash register. Behind that was a work area. We could see reasonably well by the light from the front window, but the flashlight I'd brought was useful.

Ruth spotted the Rusalka Wheel within the first few minutes. It was still on top of a pile of furniture. She approached it stealthily and I followed. Both of us felt as if we were being watched, and I found myself looking around and probing the aisles with the flashlight. The place felt wrong; there was something present. But there was no one else there physically, not a soul.

"There's a stairway behind the counter," she whispered. She picked up a walking cane from one of the many racks and piles and made her way to the steps. "I don't like this," she said. We heard a popping sound coming from the floor above, and both of us stopped and cringed, trying to hear more clearly. The sound stopped. Then there was movement that made the floorboards above us creak. "Did you reach Mr. Chu?" she asked.

I looked at my watch. "He said he'd be here. We still have a few minutes. Do you want to wait?"

"No."

"We could wait."

"You wait, I'm going up."

"I'm with you," I said. I picked up an old, dust-covered samu-rai sword that had been standing in an umbrella urn with several umbrellas and canes. The tsuba was bronze but the copper had oxi-dized, and the handle had grit and filth amid the braids. I felt a bit ridiculous, but we were dealing with a serial killer after all, and he might even have Mr. Kasparov in his deadly grips — if we were lucky.

The stairs complained as we climbed. At the top, we came to a foyer from which wide hallways led left and right. Directly in front of us was a small sitting area, like a library or waiting room with several lamps, two cushioned chairs and a television. The walls were bookcases. Down one hallway were bedrooms and a bath-room; down the other was a room to the right that we couldn't see and a kitchen straight ahead that we could see. Window light showed a kitchen that was well equipped for someone very fond of cooking. Ruth sneaked down the hall to check out the room on the right that we couldn't see; it was a living room and, like the rest of the place, was empty of life.

I took the other path toward the bedrooms. Ruth followed. The floor, though solid, groaned lightly under our weight. The first bed-room was empty. The door was open. Ruth inspected the floor. No one had passed that way for months, if one followed the clues, or lack thereof, in the dust. The next room was a small study with a desk and computer. It looked to be the bookkeeping workroom for the business. There were file cabinets, but no life.

Suddenly, there was a thump. It came from the end bedroom, the final room at the end of the hall. The door was closed, whereas all the other doors had been open. I crept up to the door and put my hand on the knob. It was a cast-glass knob set in brass from the ear-ly twentieth century, purple with age. It turned loosely in its fit-tings. But it did not unlatch the door. It just turned one way and then the other with no effect.

"Well," I whispered, "now they know we're here." Ruth shrugged, as if it didn't matter and couldn't be helped. I pulled back and prepared to ram the door with my shoulder. I was sure I could break it in, and pulled my punches so I wouldn't go sailing through and land face-first on the floor.

The door crashed inward. Wood splintered. Ruth followed on my heels with the cane raised. Inside was a tousled bed in a large, wood-paneled room. Along the wall beside the bed was a wide chair and in the chair, in the shadows, sat Mr. Kasparov. He had been tied to the bed with rough twine at the wrists and ankles, but he had worked himself free. He seemed to be sleeping. The smashing of the door hadn't wakened him. The room was dim, but we could see no one else. I quickly checked the closet and a small, open dressing alcove whose window looked out onto a narrow space between this building and the one next to it.

Ruth rushed to Mr. Kasparov, first checking his pulse, then pushing back his eyelids.

"Miss M," said Mr. Kasparov, coming to, "it's so good to see you. I was hoping you could make it, frankly. I am so thirsty I can think of little else." I ran to get a glass of water from the kitchen and returned as quickly as I could. He gulped it down. "I have had strange dreams," he said. "How long have I been here?"

"Two nights and two days," answered Ruth.

"I feel I've been to the ends of the earth," he said, smiling, "or at least all the way to Kharkov. That should count as something. Are they here? Did you see them?"

"More than one?" I said. "It looks as if there's been no one here for quite some time."

"Two nights and two days, perhaps," he said. "Yes, two individuals. A decrepit woman, poor creature, and a gaunt man with facial scarring. I'm afraid I was overpowered."

"It may have been scopolamine, Mr. Kasparov," said Ruth.

Mr. Kasparov paused briefly and then said, "The Russian with the tattoo. The Soviets were very fond of the drug during the Cold

War. I remember an old story about an agent's business card laced with scopolamine. Either an old trick of the KGB, or an exaggerated bit of urban folklore. I have been senseless for several days then?"

"Yes."

"But you found me. How?" He rubbed his ankles, then his wrists.

Ruth explained about the cellphone in the van.

He nodded, approving of my technique. "I'm afraid they were in very much of a hurry, Miss M. It seems that they just got me out of the way as fast as they could. I am lucky, I suppose. I assume they realized they'd been pursued, and escaped with all haste. I'm sorry, I am still a little incoherent, can't think clearly. Do you have a candy bar? I would love a cola. And a shower. Tell me, did you dress to rescue me?" His eyes had settled on Ruth's sequined boots. She nodded and wiped her eyes. His voice trailed off, and I caught the glint of a tear before he blinked it away.

"I do not feel fully recovered, I'm afraid. A bit light-headed and nauseous." He waited a few minutes, drank another glass of water, and said, "I remember nothing after entering the shop and seeing the wheel. But I remember very distinctly the dreams. I recalled some events from my childhood which had been lost to me, and which apply to the spinning wheel. I had seen that wheel before. I knew I had. I believe that I was one of its humans. A piece of its history. I will tell you about that experience sometime, perhaps when I am feeling more like myself."

There was a brief ruckus downstairs. I walked over to the landing and peered down the stairs into the dimness of the antique store. It was Detective Chu and three police officers.

Doc and Helen

A S SHE LEFT THE SWAN POND at the Palace of Fine Arts, Helen Oliver was finally able to piece together most of her life, and it seemed like a necklace of hard brown beads or faded drift seeds polished by dry beach sand. But missing were the beads representing the last few weeks, even the last few days.

She had worked her way back to the waterfront, drawn by a subliminal memory of the antique shop that acted like a magnet.

She did find the shop again. But in Helen's mind, she had never seen it before. She walked carefully down the alley, the lubok of the orange tabby cat seeming to study her as she passed. It was so familiar to her. She wondered, what did it see? So, she looked at her reflection as best she could in an alley shop window, her face next to a red-glazed duck on the other side of the glass. It was not a pleasant combination for Helen, and the person she saw didn't make her any happier. She needed some decent clothes, to begin with. She had never seen such a sorry reflection. And a plate of pancakes or a waffle wouldn't have hurt, either. She had a shirt for a hat. She needed a nice cup of coffee. And something for her face … something major.

"I got a line on some coffee," said Doc, who had agreed to walk with her. He'd kept an eye on her for days, mostly at a distance so as not to bring her discomfort or fuel distrust. He'd tried to introduce himself, but wasn't sure she was tracking. "I'm Doc," he'd said, but she just stared. Still, the trial period was over as far as Doc was concerned. Now, he was all in — a level of commitment he'd pretty much avoided his entire life. Briefly, he wondered what had gotten into him, behaving like this.

"That'll help," he said. "Some coffee. It'll do wonders."

"I need some clothes, Mr. Doc," she said. Doc thought, she really was tracking; she remembered his name. "What I have is very dirty, and this blanket is wet. The water makes it weigh a lot. I have a shirt on my head … it's not my style. Look, I hardly have any real clothes on!" She was very upset. She spread open the blanket, and Doc, surprised, eased her arms down and the blanket back around her. A muslin slip was no way to dress in public.

"Clothes for sure," he said. "Just take it easy." Thank God they were in an alley and not in a park or on a trafficked street.

Doc had tried to get the Chinese cop to pick her up, but when they arrived she wasn't where he'd left her. Old Chu, which is what Doc called the detective because he acted so old for his years, had gone so far as to drive Doc to the piers in an effort to find her. She was gone. Doc didn't see her again until late that evening. He'd been hugely relieved when he found her. But he wasn't relieved at his concern for Helen. It was atypical behavior for him. It was the kind of thing you just don't do … get attached like that. But, aside from the personal perspective, Doc's point was, there was just no telling what evil a person, a woman, could run into in the gut of the city.

"I got some coffee figured out, and look, kid, I got some cash tucked away for clothes, plus I got a good familiarity with St. Vincent's. What'r you doing there anyway?" Her nose was pressed against the window of the antique shop.

"I'm looking in the window, Mr. Doc."

"Just Doc is fine."

"I'm looking in the window, Just Doc."

He looked at her. He figured she was either retarded or had regained a sense of humor.

Then she said, "I'm just kidding."

"Okay, Just Kidding," he said, "what do you see?" Actually, these were the first words the two had exchanged. The previous days had been spent in silence, which had begun to wear on Doc.

"They don't have the lights on. But someone's there, don't you think?"

"How would I know? You know this here is the first intelligent conversation we've had?"

"I just wanted to go in, is all. Somebody's there. I mean, upstairs."

"Why go in?"

"Oh, no reason, really. Curious. I don't know. I feel uncomfortable. I just wanted ..." she tried the door knob, shaking it with a bit more emotional content than Doc considered normal. There was something wrong with the girl, he thought.

"Well they aren't open, Kidding. They're closed. The door's locked. You want some coffee or what?"

"Okay," she said. "Sure. What are you doing, anyway? I mean, following me around."

"Somebody's got to. You're a mess. Besides, it's the other way; you been following me."

"I'm not a mess. And I didn't know I was following you. I'm sorry. Has it been difficult?"

"A mess undone, as the saying goes. We're going to have to get Social involved sometime, you know. I hate to break it to you, Kidding, but you need some help here. I got reasonable friends there. It's that or the cops. I got a friend there, too. A Chinese guy. You'd like him, guaranteed. If there's one thing I know, it's I know you'd like him. Got a heart of gold plate, even if he is a cop."

"I just want to go home."

"Okay, kid. Where's that? Where's home?"

Helen Oliver stared at Doc as they stood in the alley. It was cold there, and shadowed. It was damp, and wet from the morning rain, though the sun had come out afterward.

"If I knew that, I could put on some dry clothes." There were tears in her eyes.

"Stop crying. Any idea where?"

"Well," she said pensively, "maybe. Do you think they'd let us on a bus?"

"No."

"Okay, well, I don't know then."

"Like I say, I got some cash stashed, and some credit at Vincent de Paul. Get some clothes. I could use a new shirt, myself. For when I gotta go plead your case. I'm just saying. Yep. We could get outfitted, then get the bus. But get some coffee first."

"Do you drink?" asked Helen, out of the blue.

"Sure. Been a problem for some, but not me. So what?"

"Have you been drinking while we've been together? All the days? When you've been following me around?"

"You've been following me, kid, and sure, of course. I'm not looking for a morality medal here. So?"

"Well, I just wondered."

"Look, kid, I haven't been drinking for going on one week if you want to know the truth. If you want to know the truth, I been dry as a weed. Been saving up my money. That's how long you've been taggin' around after me. About seven days, give or take. Lucky seven. Been that long. Don't ask me why. I took it on my own self to see you through this, is all, once you started taggin' along. You get home, and I can get back to some decent drinkin'."

"You could stop, too."

"That ain't gonna happen. You kiddin' me? Poor thing. See what I mean, you're all messed up."

"So where is the coffee?"

"Got to buy it. But there's this place I go, you know, to get a good value. Guy I know works there in the afternoons, and I'd say he's getting to work about now. Name is Timmy. He understands."

"I would need half and half in it."

"Well, they got that. Kinda picky, aren't you?"

Helen looked like she was about to start crying again.

"What are you doing that for, kid?"

"I don't know where to go. I don't know what happened ..."

"Look, I don't know what to say," said Doc. "They'll have half and half ..."

"That's not what I mean ..."

"We'll just have a cup of coffee, sit down, reconnoiter. We'll talk about old times, you and me. It's sunny out, everywhere but this damned alley. We'll sit in the sun, have a little coffee, get up and go over to St. Vincent's, set ourselves up, get outfitted, and hop the bus lookin' pretty good. You know which one? Which bus?"

"No."

"Don't matter. Just follow your nose, I guess. Look, we'll do that, and when we come to nothing, you're going to have to get into Social. It just has to be that way. Something's wrong with your memory is all. You're not used to living on the street, and I know that for a fact. You're street-green. You've never been on the street in your life, till now ... Not that you've had you an easy time, that's for sure. I can tell. Don't look at me like that, I know what I see when I see it and bet I know a bit more about you than you do right now. Kid, look, you wasn't raised on Easy Street, let's just say that. Okay? That's clear and visible, anyone bother to look. Hey, someone'll be able to hypnotize your memory back into you, or something. Believe me. They got that kinda thing."

They walked five or six long blocks in the direction of free coffee. Both enjoyed the warmth of the sun that morning. Then they sat down on the sidewalk along the bright, warm side of a building on Columbus with their coffees.

"How long have you been on the street, Mr. Doc?"

"Thirty years, give or take."

"I'm thirty-something."

"As in years old?"

"Yes."

"Where was you born?"

"In Moscow."

"Russia or Idaho?"

"Russia."

"I spent about a year in Idaho one week. Guess being born in Russia makes you a comminist. You should be born in Idaho next time. You'd like it. They don't allow no one to drink liquor on the streets there. Live there long? In Russia?"

"We moved away when I was two or three or something. I don't know, I was really small. Moved to a little town called Mielnitsia. It has different names, depending on who's talking. Mielnica, same thing. It means 'mill.' There was always a grain mill there, with a big stone. It was very famous."

"That in Russia? Part of the Kremlin? You ever see Gorbachev? Got a scar on his face like the one on your back." He sipped his coffee.

"It's in Ukraine, the southwest part. Babusya moved us to here when I was six."

"That's nice of babby-whatever. You mean here, San Francisco?"

"Yes. After they burned us out."

Doc looked over at the woman. "What d'you mean?"

"Burned our house. Our apartment. The whole block. I've never been popular, Mr. Doc," said Helen, attempting humor.

"Who's 'they?'"

"The people. It was a small town, but only one attitude."

"Why?" asked Doc.

"Why what?"

"Why'd they burn you out?"

"Because of my birthmark."

"That fish on your back?"

Helen's brow furrowed. "You've seen it?" She wanted to cover herself up, but she already was.

"Kidding, how could I not see it? I'm the one that got you the blanket, then the coat, then the shirt that you wear like a hat, and a real hat, too. Got you those Nikes ... all you could say is you wanted red ones, which would be the only thing you said to me for days. ... All's you had was that shift underneath. You don't remember. Probably better that you don't. Course I could see it. Don't seem to me much of a reason to burn a person out, though."

"Well, it was."

"Well, if you can remember that, how come you can't remember last week or where you live? What was the big deal about going to that closed-up junk store?"

"I just want to go home."

"To that mill town? Look, girl, if you're cold, we'll be getting some clothes here pretty quick. Soon as we're done sittin'. No need to rush back to a town that burned you out or whatever. Was you hurt?"

"No, I mean home, here. I have an apartment. If I don't think, I might be able to get on the right bus. We'll both go, right? I mean, right?"

"Sure, sure." Doc groaned as he stood.

"I remember where it is," she said.

"Really? Well, that'd be called progress in the right circles. Where is it?"

"Mr. Doc, I can't really tell, but I can get there."

"Okay."

"Doc?"

"Yeah."

"Do you spend a lot of time on the water?"

"Yep."

"Why?"

"I don't know. I like it, I guess. Used to tend crab and halibut boats off Alaska in the summer once."

"Oh." She paused as if soaking it in. "Me, too."

"Worked on a boat?"

"Spend time by the water. Or in it, you know."

"Really? I couldn't tell."

Helen looked directly at the old man. She wondered what it was that connected them. It seemed strange, but for some reason it also seemed very, very normal. She shrugged.

They shopped at St. Vincent de Paul's for more than an hour. It went fairly well. They left their old clothes and wrappings in a dumpster behind the store. Doc and Helen left with clothes for the two of them, and change for the bus, senior rate. It took Helen four hours to navigate the city by bus, in a sort of hit-and-miss path that challenged her to dredge up recent memories. The bus drivers ignored the one-time-only transfers, and let them ride anywhere. By the time they arrived within a block or so of Helen's apartment, she'd regained bits and pieces of the last week. She remembered the spinning wheel, which had been her grandmother's. But she did not remember that it had been at the antique store. Even without full recall, she got off the last bus as a different person. Even Doc could tell. It made him happy. Another strange emotion.

They walked up two flights of stairs to the door of her small apartment. The building was old, and it smelled like mildew. The staircase and hallways were dark. There were rat or mouse droppings along the wall and in the corners of the stairwell.

Helen's apartment door, No. 312, was closed. There was trash piled up on the left side, near the jamb. As Helen approached, she realized the trash was actually her clothing, which had been in her closet. It had been rummaged through, and the pile was strewn over a small area. All the good pieces were gone. She retrieved her emergency key, which was taped just under a flap of old carpeting on the stairwell as it continued to the fourth floor. But when she inserted it into the deadbolt, she couldn't turn it. She tried it in the knob, and although the key slid in, it wouldn't turn.

Helen frowned. She tried the upper deadbolt again, and again couldn't turn the key. She grew exasperated and tried again, as if finding the reality impossible. Doc drew her attention to a paper on the floor. Originally, it had been taped to the door, but someone had pulled it off. "That there is your eviction notice, Helen Oliver," said Doc. "And they gone ahead and changed the locks on you. Look, that's a new one. Still shiny." He pointed to the deadbolt.

She picked up the paper. It looked official; boiler-plate, but legal. It was signed by the building owner and by the super. Helen had never actually seen either of the men. The owner lived in Los Angeles, and the building super had an apartment downstairs. Helen had rented the apartment online, and dropped her monthly rent in the mail slot of the super downstairs.

"This isn't possible," is all she said.

"You've been away," said Doc. "They're a greedy lot, those people."

"But not very long, Mr. Doc. You said it was only a week. Even less. You said it was like seven days or something."

"Helen Oliver, kid," he said, "it was eight days since I saw you roll into the bay. Thursday. This is Friday a week. I didn't know it was you, though. And that van drove off."

She turned. "You saw what happened?"

"I sort of saw all that," said Doc. "I would of pulled you out, but you did it yourself."

"You pulled me out?"

"No, you did. But you just kept swimming for a time like you wanted to stay in there and freeze. Your lips were blue. I gave up after a while, kid. Sat on the dock, and waited. You got your own self out, got a good kick and landed on some floating dock. Other side of where I was sitting."

"You?"

"You're getting your humor back, kid." He had to smile.

She said, "But I had paid the rent. Every month I drop if off to the super."

"I don't know anything about it. You can't get in, though, huh?"

"Oh, I can get in all right," she said, and picked up a small baseball bat that she had kept in her bedroom under the bed, just in case. It was among the apparently less desirable possessions that had been left at her door by the scavengers.

"Look, kid, you need to be careful here. You can't have that. It's against the state weapon law. No, really, I mean it. Here, take this here folding knife. You can have that, but you can't have you a bat. What? Why you looking at me like that? I oughta know, you know. A folding knife is legal; a bat ain't. And I do know. Here, give me that bat. Last thing I need is you getting yourself into jail."

She unhappily relinquished the bat. She didn't take the knife. First, she checked out her possessions that had been tossed into the hallway upon her eviction. There was no telling how many people had rummaged through it, and there was nothing left except the clothing. She was too thin for anyone to get much use out of some of them. Some of her photos were scattered under the clothing, but her pine chest was gone, and the old box that held the photos, and there was no furniture. Maybe the furniture and her little TV were still inside. Helen kicked the wall about six times and tried to rip out the bannister to the next floor. She managed to snap one of the balusters and loosen the newel.

She turned to Doc, breathing hard. "My yarn is missing, Mr. Doc!"

"What?"

"My balls of yarn are missing."

"What?"

"For Christ's sake, my yarn is missing!" she cried. "Can't you hear?!"

"I thought that's what you said. Just didn't make much sense to me is all. Hey, let's buy some new, kid. They got yarn there at Joanne's or the thrift. Lots of colors, kid."

"No, no, no. They're my yarn balls!"

"You're worried about yarn, with all this going on?"

"They were my gran's! They were spun by my great-greats, all the way back. I had seven of them. I had seven balls of yarn that meant everything to me!!" she screamed.

Helen grabbed the bat out of Doc's hands and tromped down the staircase. Doc tried to follow, but she was quick on her feet, as quick as her anger.

The basement floor apartments are numbered with zero: 001, 002; and so on up to fourteen, 014. The super's apartment was number 004.

"You'd never find that in Chinatown," Doc said absently. "Four means death."

"It sure does, Mr. Doc." She knocked on the door, hard. But she held back her fury. There was no answer. She knocked again. Still no answer. She leaned back with the bat and was ready to strike the door above the knob when Doc broke in.

"Hey, just a minute, kid. What'r you doing? Now is not the time to lose it, kid. After all you been through ..."

"Hitting the door!" she said.

"But, look, what if he has a gun? I mean, look, really, what if he has another bat that's bigger'n yours? Or a pistol? You think you can't get hurt?"

"But he has my yarn, Mr. Doc. He has them!"

"Kid, kid, hey," said Doc, "he probably doesn't have them. Someone could have took them from the stuff at your door. Somebody else probably got them ..."

"Oh, he has them, all right."

"But you don't even know who he is. What if his kid answers the door or something? You said you never seen him. What if he has a little boy or a girl?"

"He's in there, you can bet on it. He takes care of his mother. That's what I know. What does it matter that I never saw them? I've only been here a few months! Going on five months is all. I've heard his voice, that's for sure, on the other side of the door. He never answers. I'd know it anywhere."

Her own words made her stop talking. She did remember his voice.

"Never answers the door?" Doc jarred her back into reality.

"No. Never. He comes upstairs to fix something once in a while, like the kitchen faucet once. One time. He never fixed the gas. He came up while I was at work. I never saw him. He takes care of his mother. The faucet was messed up again a day or two later."

"What's, she crippled?"

"An invalid, I guess. I don't know. One of the other tenants told me."

"Who?"

"I don't know, some tenant. A guy with four children and no wife. He has girlfriends. Different one every week."

Helen pulled back with the bat and bashed it into the door, striking it so hard it burst open and then slammed back closed. But neither the lock nor latch kept it closed now. The jamb was trashed.

The ferocity of the blow surprised both Helen and Doc. They stepped back and Helen pushed the door open. It squeaked on its troubled hinges.

They peeked inside. The smell was stale, in a way, and the odor of mice was strong. The smell of mold blended with it. Carefully, Helen went inside. Doc followed.

The apartment was dark and close and damp. She looked for her yarn, or anything that was hers. She found one of her blouses and underclothing. She looked at Doc, as if asking what they should do next. "Sick bastard," she said.

"Next?" he said. "We get out of here, close the door, and don't touch nothing. We go back into town. We never came down here, if you know what I mean."

Helen was crestfallen. "But Doc, I don't want to sleep on the street anymore. I don't want to do it. Where do I go?"

"We get out of here, close the door, walk back to the bus, and get up there to that cop I was telling you about. We're in a desperate situation, Helen Oliver. But I trust him. And that's me saying that. That's all we can do. Social won't do nothing for a week at least. I don't, I can't ..."

"I'm getting a lawyer if it's the last thing I do," she said. She handed Doc the bat; he took it reluctantly and they walked up one flight of stairs and out of the building.

Doc wondered what he could do about Helen. He was homeless himself. It was as simple as that. What could he do to get Helen a place for the night when he'd spent thirty years unable to do it for himself?

"Don't turn me in to the police," she said softly.

"No, he's a personal friend," said Doc.

"He has connections?"

"He knows people."

"He'll arrest me."

"For what? He won't arrest you. But he'll get you the best hot and sour soup in the city. The best duck leg soup if you want."

"Do you have his picture?"

"What?"

"Do you have his picture so I can see what he looks like?"

"Kiddo, I do not go around carrying a photograph of policemen in a wallet that I do not have, under normal circumstances."

"Oh." She shrugged. "I thought I'd ask."

They rode the bus together. Their clothes were new. Well, if not new, they were clean. People thought they were father and daughter. It made Doc feel good. It was a feeling he'd been denied his whole life. He had to smile. And when he did, Helen smiled, too. He didn't feel he deserved this.

She quietly asked, "Why do you think a police officer is going to help us? Me. That would be a first! What is he, some sort of saint?" Images of the lubok of St. Friday from her grandmother's wall in Mielnica flashed before her, and seemed to stick. She realized she wanted to see the orange cat lubok again, in the alley. She wanted to take a photo of it. Then, she realized she no longer had her phone. Someone must have taken it during the twilight sleep. It didn't cost that much, but it took forever to set up the service, and the service wasn't cheap.

"Saint Chu," said Doc.

"Oh, God bless you," said Helen. Doc laughed.

Kirk and Michael

VIC, THE GAUNT MAN, and the hag had vanished. Mr. Kasparov, who had no memory of what had happened to him physically during his imprisonment, was nevertheless able to recall the faces of the perpetrators, the proprietors of the shop. Yet his descriptions led to nothing. My research into similar crimes nationwide for the last ten years was equally fruitless. The killers had materialized and departed like ghosts, and, like ghosts, defied rational explanation. If not for the bodies that lay in their wake, it was as if they had never been.

William Chu was stymied. His work came to an abrupt halt. He had psychological whiplash, but he continued to believe they would be found, probably in some other corner of the country. The reality was this: Yet another of San Francisco's serial killings remained officially unsolved, and the number of deaths would be forever uncertain. The three confirmed fatalities resulted from severe interactions between scopolamine and other medications or the victims' physical condition. The Russian died from an interaction with blood pressure medication, a middle-aged woman died due to scopolamine's impact on her existing liver disease, and the third death, an older man, resulted from the drug's effect on his heart condition.

Though professionally infuriated, Chu took comfort in the fact that Helen Oliver, the first known surviving victim, had been found. She had been found alive. And that was thanks to Doc who did, in the end, trust the detective with his wayward friend, Helen. Chu was grateful.

Occasionally over the next few days, a stupefied victim would turn up, also alive, usually in the Civic Center or in the cold, shadowed recesses of San Francisco where the homeless congregate. The only way anyone knew they might have been victims of the Pier Killer was the red rash on the hand area, or, in several cases, on the neck. In this city, though, no one sorts through the homeless community to find missing people. And no one knows when one of the homeless goes missing because they already are missing in one sense or another. No one cares when they die. Passersby do their best to ignore them, except for, here and there, a pastor or humanitarian of unusual empathy. Maybe St. Friday looks down on them, quietly.

A few victims of the Pier Killer had been discovered purely by chance — the inadvertent show of a reddened wrist to a police officer who had been briefed on what to look for. Those were very slim chances. But once they were identified, they were treated and released to their families, those who had them. Some were not identified, of course, and so they waited for their senses to return. The city's overburdened social services also waited.

Few of the suspected victims had even a trace of the drug scopolamine in their systems by the time they regained consciousness. It had either been eliminated over time or had never been used in the first place. I preferred the idea that the Cold War drug (or, in today's world, the date-rape drug) scopolamine had been purged from their bodies than to believe that macabre ghosts could cast evil spells just as pre-Columbian brujos did. But even the brujos blew jimson-weed powder into the sensitive nasal passages of their victims. Natural scopolamine.

Some of the victims tried to go back to their previous lives, which was not as easy as one might think. Even in the case of the real owners of the antique store, the electricity and gas had finally been turned off by the utility company.

"You know that we located the true proprietors of the antique shop?" said Chu.

"What?" said Ruth, surprised. She'd stopped by his office at the police station after submitting her paperwork in the case.

"The actual proprietors."

"Are they alright?"

"Apparently. The two men who have owned the store for the last thirty years. They turned up in Los Angeles, at a care home. They were lucky. I guess the sister of one of them institutionalized them both, temporarily, after the cops down there found them wandering and stuck them in the county care home."

"Los Angeles. How did that happen?"

"The larger of the two had identification on him, apparently … a receipt in his jacket pocket … making him one of few victims who had any ID at all. We're not sure how they got down to L.A., but I have an officer looking into the buses. The theory goes that someone, maybe a property owner, got tired of the two of them wandering into his yard, and came up with a novel, if unsympathetic, solution: Buy a couple of one-way bus tickets to Los Angeles and herd them onto the bus. Our information so far seems to support that."

Ruth nodded. "Scopolamine poisoning?" she asked.

"Impossible to tell for sure, but I'd say so. It had been so long. The older of the two, the bigger man, Kirk David, has pretty much recovered and is back at their flat above the shop. The other one, Michael Richards, is still only half on his feet, but is expected to be alright in another week or so. He's also back at their flat under Mr. David's care.

"Look, I'm going to stop by their place this afternoon," he said. "I'd like to take another look at the spinning wheel while I'm there, ask them a few questions about it. You're welcome to accompany me."

* * *

C HU AND RUTH ARRIVED ABOUT THREE that afternoon at the alley store. Kirk David answered the door. His skin was pale and so was his hair. He was in his seventies. His shirt was ironed, which said something about his recovery.

They walked through the shop and upstairs to the flat. Kirk said their cleaning crew would straighten things up in a few days. He was apologetic. They sat in the study just off the landing at the top of the stairs. Kirk or Michael had already moved the Rusalka Wheel back upstairs, where it belonged. It was to the side, near the window, where it had always stood.

Kirk was tired. He attributed his pallor not to possible poisoning or attempted murder, but to dealing with Los Angeles human services and then San Francisco's utility company in his efforts to get the heat and light back on. It was, he said, "a nightmare of supreme proportions." He had not lost his sense of the absurd.

Chu showed Kirk Miss Oliver's driver's license to see if it sparked a memory, and Kirk, who said he had never seen her, was genuinely troubled by her kidnapping and narrow escape from death. Surprised, he pointed out the similarity between Helen and the design carved and painted on the spinning wheel, with which he was so familiar. Chu explained to him the provenance of the wheel, which had attracted her to the shop in the first place, noting briefly that Ruth had traced the wheel's ownership forward from the beginning of the nineteenth century, and that it had been in Helen Oliver's family.

"I knew of its past, Detective," said Kirk, glancing over at the wheel. "Angelina unearthed its amazing life story. But we certainly knew nothing of its connection to a living member of the family. I mean … I suppose … Michael and I were very lucky … lucky to be alive."

Kirk was quiet for a while, and took his time bringing fresh iced tea as they made themselves comfortable in the sitting room. Michael Richards then joined them. He was shorter and much thinner than his partner, and paler, for he hadn't yet fully recovered. Though his memory had largely returned, his speech was slow.

"I suppose," Kirk said, "Michael and I will have to consider returning the spinning wheel to its owner. I have always felt, you see, that I was only caring for the wheel on a temporary basis. I never had any interest in selling it. Never, though, did I realize its monetary value. I do believe that Angelina, Mrs. Reynolds, felt the same way. I really had to press for a value … I mean, I did have to insure it, after all. If it were to be sold, I think the only buyer, really, would have been a museum of some sort, and most likely outside the states." A slow minute passed before Kirk made the connection between Ruth and Mrs. Reynolds. He turned to Ruth and said, "You're the child. By God, Michael!" he said, almost shouting, twisting to look at his partner, "we're sitting here with Angelina's little girl! How can I not recognize you, even after all the years!"

Kirk was genuinely happy. And utterly shocked.

"She's been integral to the investigation, Mr. David. I asked for Ruth's help at the outset."

Kirk turned to Michael again, who had sat down on the short sofa beside Kirk, and a knowing glance passed between them. Kirk said, "Ruth M. Miss Ruth, Michael. Angelina's daughter …"

"Yes, Kirk. I'm aware. You're not the only one to have recovered your wits." He sighed. "Yes, of course. You were such a pretty child," he said to Ruth, "Angelina's Ruthie," said Michael. Then he turned back toward Chu. "We saw her only sporadically at such a young age. But we are much more familiar with her work than we are with her. The costuming for the Opera and ACT. It's wonderful work, Ruth. We've been fans for years. You're simply brilliant. Absolutely brilliant. My dear, you are every bit as talented as your dear mother, Angelina."

"Ah, Angelina," said Michael fondly. "The angel."

Kirk said, "As I mentioned, we called on Angelina when the wheel arrived on our doorstep so long ago. I asked her to keep it quiet, you see. I knew the wheel was something special, obviously, and wanted her to look into it."

"How many years ago?" Ruth asked. "I found most of Mrs. Reynolds notes and records, but I'm still uncertain about some of the dates."

"We have been its caretakers, apparently its caretakers, since the summer of 1988," said Kirk. He offered them a plate of cookies, very much welcomed by Chu because he had skipped lunch.

"Since 1988," said Chu. It didn't take any more than that to learn how Kirk David and Michael Richards ended up as guardians of the Rusalka Wheel. Kirk told them, slowly and with deliberation, how they came upon it. Or, more accurately, how the wheel came upon them.

"We were returning from a performance at the opera, Mr. Chu. Detective. I remember distinctly," said Kirk.

He looked at Michael, who nodded, and said, "We have always loved the opera."

Their cab pulled over six blocks from the antique and curio shop that Kirk had recently purchased. They lived in the apartment above the shop. The dusty shelves downstairs were filled with the oddities that Kirk had found several years before he bought Sterling's Antiques; he had traveled mostly in Egypt, Turkey, and Iran.

"I wanted to walk the last half-mile or so home in the fog that night," Kirk said. "It's the city's most defining quality, I think. The fog. The taxi pulled silently away from the curb, leaving us below a street light on Washington. Of course, we were inappropriately dressed in our suits and polished shoes."

Kirk continued, "When we approached the shop, we could see something near the door. It appeared to be wrapped in a blanket. I mean, we had no idea … it could have been a person, perhaps, or, who knew?

"'What's that?' asked Michael, pointing into the blackness ahead of us. I stopped immediately, and Michael ran into me."

Michael, who had been quiet for most of the conversation, interrupted, "I could imagine that it was a human body, wrapped and squatting like a Peruvian mummy. Or a murder victim! Something disemboweled or headless." His recollection sent chills down his back.

Kirk picked up the account again. "There was no traffic in the alley, and only one street lamp at the intersection. The big bulb was dim and needed to be replaced. I remember that well. Michael peered at it through his opera glasses, but it was too dark to see much." Kirk steeled himself and walked up and lifted the blanket, which was damp from the fog, and small droplets of condensation floated on the edges of the exposed fibers. His hand was soaked from touching it. "I had no idea what I might find," he said, "whether a drunk who had passed out, a dead body, or a couple of chairs that someone had discarded."

Kirk threw off the blanket. "I said, 'Quickly, Michael, unlock the bars and the door so we can get it inside.' Some poor soul had discarded a spinning wheel, and even in the dim light I could tell it was obviously old, and my goodness, Detective, it was incredibly beautiful! Striations in the wood caught the light of the streetlamp, and glowed like inlaid garnet."

It smelled of smoke. The stench was strong. They had no idea why. It hadn't been scorched, though, and was perfectly intact. But the blanket had been singed. Once they had it inside, they just stared at it without saying a word. The wheel was beyond comment.

"We knew it wasn't American, and it wasn't English, though it had lines similar to some English turnings of the early nineteenth century. It was neither Belgian nor French … certainly not Danish."

Chu had been listening intently, and so had Ruth. Kirk said, "We carried it inside. And we phoned Angelina the next day. That phone call was the beginning of her odyssey, Miss M, Detective. She left several weeks later for Prague."

"And I was so envious!" said Michael. "Prague!"

Kirk stood and walked over to the wheel. He put his hand on it. "I have always felt it was simply here waiting for something. I never felt it belonged to us. It was just waiting. Perhaps it was waiting for your Miss Oliver."

Ruth said, "You kept it safe all those years."

"Yes," said Michael. "Yes. We felt ... it's hard to say. We felt, as caretakers, that we were just people in its life, and not the other way around."

Mr. Kasparov's Opera

HE IS A VERY SPRY MAN. He's strong. He's funny. Mr. Kasparov's perpetual smile hides nothing: There's no inner soul writhing in existential discomfort. There are no ulterior motives. He is, in short, an individual you could trust with your deepest and perhaps even unsavory secrets, with your shortcomings, with your heart and aspirations. If the man had not exposed his extraordinary intellect in my presence over the last few years, I might think he was simple ... because you don't meet many people who are drenched in the uncomplicated satisfaction of life. It was amazing to see him again as his usual self, after such a trial. It seemed now as if nothing had happened.

Mr. Kasparov, among his many abilities, is mechanically adept. At first, I thought this was just in relation to his car, which is a 1957 Silver Cloud. A Rolls Royce. It's a valuable car that he says he won in a gamble. I believe him, but know nothing more about his amazing acquisition. It runs like a dream, and Mr. Kasparov does all the work on it, from the ball joints and the steering column to regrinding the pistons at a rent-by-the-hour machine shop. I think one of his greatest accomplishments, though, is the reconstruction of the marionette stage track at the Avaluxe Theater, an amazing invention so locked in its own time scape, the 1920s and '30s, that the like will probably never be seen again.

I was lucky enough to arrive at the Avaluxe during one of Mr. Kasparov's work sessions on the stage. No sooner had I greeted Methuselah at the glass doors than Ruth appeared with a rag wrapped around her hair, keeping it in place. With her overalls, she looked like a ship riveter during the war. Her freckled face was smudged with gray-black grease, and she was wearing equally smeared work gloves. Naturally, she gave me a huge, greasy hug. She said she and Mr. Kasparov were working on the stage track. I smiled. I had no idea what that was, but I would soon learn.

The Avaluxe is an anachronism. It caught the tail end of the vaudeville era, which more or less coincided with the end of the traveling Yiddish theater. There were small circuses touring the country at that time as well. Because of that, it has a small stage and performance doors that would accommodate live acting, not merely movies. There was yet another popular form of entertainment during that early age: marionette plays and operas. Not hand puppets, but large stringed and jointed characters manipulated by puppeteers above, and with voices provided by trained actors and singers behind a velvet curtain — men and women who could project their voices in the absence of microphones. Stage marionettes like this are about a foot and a half to two feet tall, and they each have no fewer than eight strings, meaning they take a trained hand to manipulate. Marionette plays involved blocking and lighting just as human plays.

But how would marionettes of this size find a stage appropriate for their plays and operas? The answer is in the Avaluxe's stage track. Basically, part of the regular stage moves forward into the audience on steel rails, lowering slightly so that everyone has sort of a balcony view. It gets narrower and smaller, and catwalks above swing into place through a series of rods, rails, riveted hinges, and drive chains, and they lock in the middle. Amazingly, all this movement is controlled by a large upright gear wheel that a person cranks backstage.

Ruth led me from the lobby into the auditorium, which looked to me like a construction zone.

"They found Helen Oliver," she said. Chu had called me that morning to tell me, as well. He was as elated as the official Detective Chu could be.

"Bill told me," I said.

"He didn't tell me the finer points," said Ruth.

"A friend of his, a homeless man named Doc, contacted him, I guess for the second or third time. This time they were together, Doc and Miss Oliver. Bill arranged a place for her to stay. I think she might have stayed a few nights with his sister. He was a little vague about it. She'd been evicted during the time she was missing. It's hard for me to imagine what it would be like to be drugged senseless, and then to find out you have no home to return to. A nightmare, really."

"Doc?"

"Yes. I know him. He can draw well. I think in this case Doc is the reason that Helen is okay, and I think probably he's the reason she's alive at all, from what Bill said. The doping affected her longer than some of the other victims, partly because of her weight, and maybe it had something to do with her skin, at least that's what the medical examiner was hypothesizing, according to Bill."

"He called yesterday."

"Bill?"

"Detective Chu, yes. Helen will be staying in one of the apartments here at the theater for an indeterminate period. Number 5. It has a small bathroom and a counter by the window that could easily be a kitchenette. It's a little bigger than the others, and has a sitting room, and it connects to No. 4 to make a pretty livable situation."

"Have you met her?"

"Nope. Not yet."

"But you'll live right next to her in your building?"

"Here at the Avaluxe. And apparently your friend the detective has negotiated a permanent home for the Rusalka Wheel. It's going back to the Basara family, namely Helen, who's the eighth generation. The current owners didn't even argue. Mr. David and Mr. Richards. They knew Mrs. Reynolds quite well. They called me this morning. I remember them from my childhood, but our paths haven't crossed in years. Did Mr. Chu give them my number after our visit? It's sort of strange … we've almost run into one another many times over the last ten years, even longer, but never quite hit the target. Of course, I spent a lot of years pursuing my education and so on, away from the city. They invited us to dinner."

"You and Helen?"

"You and me."

"They don't know me," I said.

"Yes …."

"When? Any time definite?"

"Not yet. Soon, though. When Mr. Richards is feeling better. They loved Mrs. Reynolds. I think it's about that. And they invited Helen. They want to host a special welcome back."

"No one's met her but Bill and Doc, then?"

"I have her yarn balls and her family photos, the old ones. And I have the letters between Marek and Hannah. Remember me taking them from her apartment? That was very lucky. Detective Chu told me the rest of her possessions had been hauled out of the apartment when she missed the rent, and everybody had gone through her stuff and most of it was stolen. It's very sad, Nat. All she has left are her photographs, letters, and the yarn balls because I took them for further study."

"What did you find out about the yarn? Anything?"

"Oh, yes. Each of the balls had been spun from flax, with human hair. And each sample of hair was from a different person, I assume all being women because the strands are quite long. Each woman had a slightly different color hair. The oldest sample is more than a hundred and fifty years old. It's very, very slightly green. The next oldest is a light strawberry. I suggest, and not without some evidence, that the oldest sample of hair belonged to Rusalka, or Tatyana, and the reddish one would be Sophiya Basara, the older daughter. Mrs. Reynolds found Sophiya's birth in the municipal records when she was in Europe.

"And so on down the line to Helen's mother. Seven generations, and then Helen. Her name was originally Olena Mariya Olenovich. I think the yarn balls were everything to her. They would have been for me. Those and the spinning wheel."

"She'll be surprised not to have lost them," I said.

"I expect. Detective Chu is going to bring her by."

"When's he doing that?"

"Today."

"I look forward to meeting her, finally."

"So do I. Detective Chu said she spins," said Ruth. "He said that's all she's been talking about."

"I'll bet she does."

"Nat?"

"What?"

"I think your friend is falling for Helen. It's in his voice."

"I see. It's unusual for him to get so emotionally involved in a case."

"I suggested that days ago, when it all started."

"I know."

"Some things we can't control, Nat."

I had to think about that one. She was right, of course.

"Thought you should know ... they're pretty close, I think."

I nodded. "What about the Rusalka Wheel?"

"Today or tomorrow, Mr. Chu said he'd bring it by to leave it with Helen while she's staying here. Mr. David and Mr. Richards are adamant about returning it to her, once it was known that she was still alive. Your friend the detective, you know, the guy with the golden heart? ... made sure Helen got her stolen money back —

reimbursed from what was discovered upstairs at the antique shop. The killers had stashed some money, not much, but, Mr. David said it wasn't his or Mr. Richards. Detective Chu convinced them that if the money was theirs, they could then, perhaps, give it to Helen when the department returned all the evidence to the owners. They saw the wisdom in that."

"That's the Law According to Chu. As you said, some things we can't control. I've found, over the years, that Chu's pursuit of justice is pretty sound."

"No kidding."

"It's a very busy day around here," I said, looking at the mechanical mess.

"We're lubricating all the joints and gears and the link-chains," she said. She started leading me back into the work area. "Mr. Kasparov had to replace one of the chain drives, and shorten the other one … it had stretched from use because it was new, just like a bicycle chain. But it's all working."

"Why are you working on it? Why now?"

"Mr. Kasparov's marionette opera. He's been working on it for a year at least, all the puppets, finding the script (courtesy of Rosemary Monday), going over the lines and the score."

"Anything I might be familiar with?"

"It's Dvorak's *Rusalka*. Rosemary had unearthed it in the Berkeley university library about eight months ago." She waited for my response.

"I'd call that a coincidence …"

She shrugged. "Life can be that way. It took her a couple of years to locate it. It was written about fifteen years after Dvorak's opera, adapted to the outdoor Czech marionette theater. They're about an hour, usually. Sometimes a bit longer, hour and a half."

Obviously, I'd arrived in the middle of things. I asked what I could do to help. She said, "Well, this is pretty close to ready, but we'll be dressing the puppets shortly."

"You made the costumes?" I asked.

"I was working on them long before I was dealing with Rusalka herself!"

"Who will help Mr. Kasparov work the marionettes? Are there a lot of characters?"

"Well, he's rounded up several puppeteers to help, including one who helped him in the past. I got the musicians together."

I looked at the marionette stage. Mr. Kasparov was turning the crank. The regular stage slowly contracted and moved forward toward Ruth and me, and simultaneously grew narrower. Above us, two halves of a catwalk swung to the center from the sides, and locked into position, and a second pair moved forward from behind the rolled-up screen to the front. Black curtains rolled down to hide the puppeteers. There was hardly a sound: They'd done a great job lubricating the monstrosity above and below. We now had a marionette stage.

Though the mechanism was as silent as such a thing can be with all the hinges, chains, and expansion joints moving, one sound caught my attention. A man was standing at the doors that led out to the lobby, and I could see his silhouette. He said, "Anyone home?" It was William Chu. He had two large white plastic sacks in his two hands. He'd arrived with hot and sour soup and the entrees. And, slightly behind him was the willowy silhouette of Helen Oliver. It had to be her. I could tell she was shy. Who wouldn't be, under the circumstances?

Epilogue

ON THE LAST FRIDAY of October, I received a phone call at my desk at the Bulletin at two in the morning. This is when I get off work. It was Ruth. Her use of a phone surprised me. I think she was glad to hear my voice. I was certainly happy to hear hers. Shortly after she and Mr. Kasparov got the stage working, she and Helen Oliver had devoted their time preparing for Mr. Kasparov's marionette opera, which was scheduled for Saturday, tomorrow, coinciding with Halloween and the Days of the Dead. They'd basically gone into seclusion to finish the enormous amount of preparation for such a major production.

We talked for more than an hour, and she discussed her work over the last few weeks. "I still can't link scopolamine with every victim," she said.

I asked how far she got.

She said that she had talked with the medical examiner, Sam Ikawa, about the drug. "He said that when it's combined with several other ingredients, it can be applied to the victim's skin in a strong enough dose to stupefy, but probably not strong enough to kill unless there were extenuating circumstances, like interaction with other drugs or medications. I asked what chemicals would be used. He said one would need an 'enhancer' like alcohol or horse liniment to affect the skin's porosity, and propylene glycol, a 'solvent,' to get it through the stratum corneum. The latter is a common ingredient in soaps and shampoos."

"Stratum what?" I asked.

"The skin. The concoction evaporates on application, creating a supersaturated solution, and the enhancer and solvent allow it to permeate the cells," she said, "like rainwater seeping between bricks."

I pretended to understand completely.

"Frick's Law applies, by the way," she said.

I asked what that was.

"A synergistic effect between the drug, the enhancer, and the solvent that exponentially increases the impact of the drug," she said.

Then I asked about the Russian, who was obviously killed and who had the reddish mark on his wrist.

"Mr. Ikawa said the man died of an interaction between scopolamine and his blood pressure medication, a thiazide diuretic. The lethal interaction is textbook. Did you know that scopolamine, combined with morphine, was used for decades to relieve the pain of childbirth? It produced what was called dammerschlaf, 'the twilight sleep.' The morphine reduces the pain, and the scopolamine induces retrograde amnesia. That's one of the drug's hallmarks: no memory while under its influence. Which is why everyone seemed so disoriented when they returned to normal consciousness."

The twilight sleep sounded sinister, like a "dirt nap" or "cement overcoat." I felt like I was working in a black-and-white noir world of the 1940s, but with a supernatural twist.

Ruth said, "Detective Chu believes it was used on all the victims, applied transdermally ..."

"Did they find any of the chemicals at the shop? In the back where they work on the furniture?"

"No."

"Nothing?"

"Just some acetone that's used to strip varnish. And that was already there."

"But, there should have been something ..." I said.

"Nothing. But Mr. Ikawa said one can purchase scopolamine, ninety-nine percent pure, over the internet. Anyone can get it. He said China produces most of it. And the same goes for the enhancer and solvent — easy access."

"But if there's no trace in the shop. ... Is there an alternative theory to doping?"

"The real devil's breath, I suppose, and not a chemical. An evil spell."

"Very nice," I said. I don't think she was joking.

Ruth was exceptionally chatty that morning. She invited me to the Avaluxe. I said I would love to visit, and asked when would be appropriate. She said tomorrow, Saturday morning, because the marionette opera was scheduled for that evening. I could help with some of the final touches.

Most of the preparations had been made. Mr. Kasparov had sent out personal invitations to *Rusalka*, hand-addressed and including a complimentary ticket. He had made the tickets, using glue and red glitter and hand-scratched images of some of the opera's characters ... the water goblin, the prince and huntsman, Jezibaba the witch, and various interpretations of wood sprites. But most of the attendees received humble tickets from a large roll in the kiosk. Those tickets dated to about the 1950s. Proceeds, he decided, would go to an inner-city humanitarian group that buys homeless people blankets. It seemed appropriate, given Helen Oliver's "twilight sleep."

Word got out. The house was packed, representing a who's who of the city: the mayor, several of the city supervisors, wealthy patrons of the city's Opera and Symphony and members of each, and most of the Acting Conservatory. Someone from each of the city's museums came. William Chu was there. He had an elaborate ticket from Mr. Kasparov. Tony Romano, the patriarch of the Romano family, arrived in a limo. He wore a tux, as did Julie Romano, his extra-large-size cousin. There were four other Romanos. One of the Bulletin's society photographers was milling around, enjoying her work, and most of the other local media were present, too.

The crowd entered and began taking seats. I think Chu had the best seat in the house, just right of center in the first row, with no head in front of him blocking his view. Helen wore a wrist corsage of fragrant white and light green orchids that Chu had brought her.

I looked for Ruth, and finally found her. We sat in the balcony where, throughout the play, we could peer over the black curtains and watch the marionettists at their craft, as well as watch the opera itself. We could see the orchestra pit where musicians played the violin, oboe, cello, flute, various percussion instruments, and a muted trumpet. There was also a harp.

The curtain finally rose, and all Mr. Kasparov's little people sprang into action. The production was elaborate and fast-paced and so thoroughly entertaining that an hour and a half was gone in flash, ending in a standing ovation and an encore of the aria, *Song to the Moon*.

There were refreshments. It took an hour for the crowd to leave; no one really wanted to go and most had a hard time accepting that the opera was over. What was finally left was "family." Then Tony and Julie and the rest of the Romanos said goodnight to all and departed. That left the *Rusalka* troupe (Mr. Kasparov, the puppeteers, and the musicians), Ruth, Rosemary and Miguel, who had driven down from Comptche, William Chu, Helen, and me. We all ended up in the orchestra seating, trying to regain our bearings after such a night. It was nearly eleven by this time, and the outside doors were locked. The auditorium doors were wide open, accepting the light from the lobby as well as a cooling breeze from two small, high lobby windows.

Helen had been talking quietly with Chu. Ruth watched them briefly and smiled. After a few minutes, Helen nodded at something he had said, and, though she seemed hesitant, she stepped up on the stage set and walked to the back, left, where the Rusalka Wheel stood in the thin beam of a single spotlight. It had been present throughout the opera, a prop for Rusalka's world beneath the water. It was unobtrusive. More than a century ago, Yulia Lazarenko had asked librettist Jaroslav Kvapil to keep it out of his story and off the stage. He had. But Mr. Kasparov did not.

Helen's floor-length dress floated with her to the wheel, and she sat on the cushioned stool beside it. For effect, they'd filled the distaff with a veritable cloud of fibrous flax.

Helen started spinning. No one except Chu noticed when she began. Strange reflections emanating from the wheel, however, soon caught all our attention, and we began migrating to the first seats simply to watch.

As it spun, the drive wheel began to flash red and green and blue, catching and amplifying the spotlight with its layers of opal. It seemed to be on fire. As Helen continued to spin, the opal in the wheel changed from fire to ice: The wheel appeared to glow white like the moon. I deduced this was from the blending of the spectral colors at high speed. There was a gold rim edging the wheel, but the rest appeared white. For nearly a minute the wheel appeared regal, as if it were ivory set with garnets and trimmed in gold. It was no wonder Czar Nicholas had coveted it.

She spun a little slower. The thread she was spinning was thin, and in the odd light seemed like spider silk, picking up the light reflected by the wheel. Once the drive wheel had reached a perfectly slow and steady pace, the opal began to glow again. But this time, the light within the wheel was piercing in nature, and beams of red, green, and blue poured across the stage and over the orchestra pit like crazy spider webs. The thin red beams spread between each of us as we sat there, connecting us to one another. Rosemary's ankle was crossed by one red line, and that beam also placed itself across Miguel's ankle, a little higher than where it hit Rosemary. It was wider than the other strips of light, and could easily have been a red cord that tied one to the other. Helen had a broad band of red on her left wrist, lighting up the corsage. As she moved her wrist, the light moved with it, as if she wore a bracelet of red crystal flowers. The same peculiarity held for the rest of the red strands: They were not stationary like reflections of light, but moved as if attached in some way to an arm or leg and when the object moved, so did the strand of light. When any of us moved, the strands moved with us.

Helen kept the drive wheel spinning, and I was left with the distinct impression that the Rusalka Wheel did not cast those strange lights, but rather exposed them as if they were mystical lines that the world didn't want us to see under normal circumstances.

Then she stopped, having spun all the fiber on her distaff. The last of the flax was pulled from her hand and the treadle moved up and down now of its own accord as the wheel spun down. It took an inordinate amount of time for it to stop rotating. Helen sat there smiling. She has a very sincere smile, though I think that up until now she had less reason to be happy in her life. That seemed to have changed; her wheel was now part of her life again. Then, without a word, Rosemary and Miguel left, heading upstairs to the room where they were staying the night. It was No. 3, for guests. The musicians and puppet masters departed. It was close to midnight. Helen also left, kissing William Chu and holding him close, briefly, a little self-consciously, before climbing the wide north staircase to No. 5, where she was now staying.

Ruth left. She was the last one up the staircase.

I continued to sit and stare at the wheel. Mr. Kasparov finally said goodnight, and departed for his apartment, which was only few blocks north. He lives above the garage where he keeps his Silver Cloud.

"You will be here tomorrow?" he said.

I said I would, and congratulated him again on the performance. He smiled, thanked me for attending, and quickly turned to leave. It had been a wonderful night for him. He looked back. To Chu, he said, "Will I be seeing you soon, then?"

"Certainly," said Chu. Mr. Kasparov departed with a wave.

The detective stood, straightened his tie, smoothed his jacket, and left slowly through the auditorium doors and the front glass doors. He stood there beneath the marquee for a moment, a suited silhouette, and then walked off into the night. The mist had settled low along the alleyway.

My exhaustion finally hit me. The day had been long and draining. I continued to sit in the auditorium, and fell asleep. At about two in the morning, I was wakened by Ruth pulling at my arm. She was wearing loose flannel pajamas, the top unbuttoned, and her feet were bare. She whispered, "It would be more comfortable upstairs."

PART V

Appendix I

THE RUSALKA STORIES were collected in the mid-nineteenth century by Karel Erben and Bozena Nemcova, just as the tales of Iron John and Little Red Cap were gathered by Jacob and Wilhelm Grimm. The Eastern European landscape then was mostly encompassed by the Bohemian Empire — made up of the Czech Republic and parts of Ukraine, Austria, Germany, Hungary, Slovakia, and Slovenia. This was the stomping ground of Erben, a Czech historian and folklorist affiliated with the National Museum of Prague for most of that century. His folksong collection, one of his earlier works, was seminal.

The museum dates to 1818, about the time that a man named Alexei Basara came across an unusual woman at a bend in a river in the midst of a forest — a woman who was believed to be a water nymph, a rusalka, according to Erben's nineteenth century tales gathered in the region and stored at the museum.

According to the records that Ruth had found and that Mrs. Reynolds had spent so much time, travel, and energy procuring, Mielnica Podalska had been home to Alexei Basara from the day he was born in the winter of 1775 until he and his family departed in 1823, except for a six-year period from his late teens to early twenties when, traveling, he apprenticed to luthiers in Western Europe. Roughly translated, the place means "Podolian mill," Podolia being the forested valley region in southwest Ukraine on the Dniester River.

Some say the village was named for its windmills, others for the grain mill that had been there for centuries. The big sandstone wheel of the water-powered mill continued to turn, century after century, war after war, as if ignoring the ever-changing political boundaries of little men and the tensions between their little nations. The fact that the millstone was made of the best and hardest sandstone, transported laboriously by wagon from a quarry near Donetsk far to the northeast, is historically and widely documented. It represented, like the upright wheels of the flax and wool spinners of Podolia, the wheel of life.

The regional political center was Borschev, which, like Mielnica, had many names depending on the language. It was much larger than Mielnica, a few hours south-southwest, and was the center of the Borschev administrative district, like a county seat. As with all of Europe, Ukraine's many villages, towns, and cities had a vast, unrecorded library of folk tales. Yet the stories were very much the same.

It was in Borschev that Erben began his research into the rusalka legend, though Rusalka herself had purportedly been found in nearby Mielnica. One did not, at the time, enter Mielnica except by way of Borschev.

In Mrs. Reynold's files, Ruth and I pieced together photocopies of Erben's notebooks, scraps from the municipal archives researched by Jaroslav Kvapil, the librettist, and hand-written translations by Mr. Kasparov and Prof. Zhirin. Combined, they cast a dim but discernable light on Rusalka as she was remembered by villagers several generations after she and Alexei had left Podolia.

* * *

Late April or early May, 1865, Borschev township, Old Ukraine

"EXCUSE ME," SAID KAREL JAROMIR ERBEN, "let us clarify a single point." Old Pavlo Soroka nodded and waited. He smiled. It wasn't every day that one spoke at length about the old events of the villages, and especially to an official — and celebrated — collector of tales with a government position. Erben had already published two collections of stories and an extended collection of folk songs. He'd gained enormous fame in the wake of his work. Even Pavlo had heard about him.

Pavlo was an Old Believer; that is, he had pagan leanings though he counted himself among the Orthodox Christians. The honored Christian saints, several of which were on Pavlo's wall in the form of lubki, were, to Pavlo, nothing more than the old gods disguised in Christian clothing.

Pavlo had never been as important as on the day of his interview. He was under the impression that Erben was a professor, though he was not, and was disappointed that the professor did not wear a uniform of some sort. But, for goodness sake, the man was writing down his every word!

"You say Mr. Basara lived but a few kilometers from here, where we are now talking?" asked Erben of Pavlo. He twisted the end of his gray mustache, and waited.

They sat on either side of a thick oak table near the hearth in Pavlo's small house. His home was disorderly, but clean. There were shelves along the far wall that held the stuff of his long life — tools, oddly shaped pieces of wood, his kobza. The surface of the table wasn't smooth, and that was something that seemed to bother Erben. Pavlo noticed that the professor kept running his hand across it for no particular reason, as if continually surprised at its dips and curved grain.

"Yes," said Pavlo, "that is the case. Alexei Basara's village is south. Please stop that," he said, motioning to Erben's hand.

Erben moved his hand to his lap. "And this was ... how long ago?"

But Pavlo was old and couldn't remember exactly when Alexei Basara might have lived. And, Pavlo's daughter was at the market. She served as his memory these days.

"But you knew him, personally knew the man," said Erben.

"Well, no, I didn't exactly know him," said Pavlo.

"Didn't?"

"Not well, you see. We did meet. The man existed, if that is what you are asking, for I saw him and I indeed spoke with him. Alexei Basara was a man as real as you or me. I would see him on occasion, and speak with him here and there on the market day. I can tell you where he lived with his wife, and I can tell you that she was beautiful, beyond comparison with any other woman in any of the villages, for I had seen her a number of times and spoken with her, of course. Not that she spoke, you see. I can say she was pale like wax and hair flaxen-white in color but the light seemed to cast a bit of green into it, and she was as mute as a fish. She worked the hemp and flax, for it got in her hair and her hair carried a green tint from it, as I said. Some said it was green from the river, but I saw her turning the hemp. They had a daughter whose hair was soft red, and another girl and a boy as well, all very young. Mrs. Basara talked with her hands and formed sounds with her lips that never came out. And I can say without fear of exaggerating, that Mrs. Basara was so in love with Mr. Basara that I never saw either one alone. But they did not paw each other in public, if that is what you are thinking, for they were dignified, not like people today, the young people. They've forgotten the dances. The young people."

"And they are no longer in that house, that village, I take it," said Erben.

"Indeed not, for they left years and years ago, before the heavy winters, with their three children, which would be two girls and a boy, the boy being the youngest, and a goat. They kept a goat."

"A goat."

"A number of goats, they say, but how many, who could know? For cheese and for the hair. Mrs. Basara, that would be Tatyana, her name, was accomplished, you see, like all the women here, making cheese and what the needs of the family might demand. She was very well known for her spinning. She would not slaughter a hog, though, sir, for a fact. She would have nothing to do with it. People didn't like that about the woman. Nor would she wring a chicken's neck! Imagine that! Wouldn't eat a bite of them's what I heard. But when it come to fish, they say she wouldn't cook it! I'm only saying what I heard, then, at the time. But the truth is she wouldn't hurt any animal, just maybe a fish, eat them raw."

Again, Erben asked how long ago that had been, and again Pavlo was unable to get a clear picture of time. But Pavlo's daughter, who was in her late fifties or early sixties, returned from market at that point in the interview and had entered the door in time to hear the question.

She said, "I was eighteen years of age then, sir. We younger folks watched that dear family depart, the mother leading the goats and the father and some other man, some friend, and one white goat, pulling a cart loaded with a few things, her spinning wheel among them, and the young children playing about the cart and in it. That would be forty-odd years ago, I suspect."

"1823 or 24?"

"If that's what I said."

"I have collected any number of histories," said Erben, "and in every case that I have heard about the rusalki, the water folk, they are considered unpleasant and fearsome. In some tales they are quite deadly. And yet, the tale of Mr. Basara is not in this vein at all." He rubbed his chin. "That is to say, the history of it does not correspond to the other circulated tales. Not only that, it is so recent! Stories told for their historic truth most often took place more than a hundred years past, such that no living informant has first-hand knowledge."

"Ar," mumbled Pavlo, who had no idea what an informant was. "You have been talking to the newcomers, then, to think ill of the rusalki. The old folks know what's what! The newcomers don't like women! Women-haters, all. Miss Tatyana was an angel come to earth, though I do agree that the woman was otherworldly. Her eyes! Her hair!"

After several hours, Erben dabbed the ink off his pen on a cotton cloth and carefully licked the back of the golden nib and ran it along the cloth again to remove the remaining ink. He put it down and covered the bottle so it wouldn't dry out or thicken.

"You are not the only villager to remember Alexei Basara and his wife," Erben said to Pavlo. "Yet the others are convinced that Mrs. Basara was, how should I say, malignant? As you might say, as the 'newcomers' see it."

"Malignant? What do you mean by that?" asked Pavlo suspiciously.

"A negative person. They say, some say, she was a soulless rusalka."

"What on earth?!" said Pavlo, now indignant. "Who says such a thing? Soulless? She was the kindest woman I ever met! She was fond of the furred creatures of the forest, killed nary a pig nor hog, wouldn't slaughter a goat, and loved children and not just her own! Indeed, we all felt she was a rusalka, but in the Old Way, in the Old Way! To say she was malignant … indeed!"

Erben leafed through his notes, his pen and ink bottle still on the table. He began to put them and his papers into a leather travel case. He said, "He was a luthier, they say. Alexei Basara."

"Indeed he was," said Pavlo, "and there is not a finer woodworker in the world even today. There on my own wall is one of his kobzas. Shall I play it? You have never heard such a tone …"

"No, no," said Erben. "My time is short. I must be on my way back to Prague at last." But he eyed the instrument carefully. It had a round body, and its neck was long and fretted. The woods, to his eye, appeared to be maple and ash, both of which grew abundantly in that region. The soundboard was surely spruce. Perhaps he could return and take a closer look at the kobza during his next excursion to the countryside. "But tell me," he said, "can you tell me about the spinning wheel? Do you know about that, or had you seen it?"

Pavlo settled back into his chair. A smile crossed his lips as fond memories passed before his old eyes.

"Indeed I can," said Pavlo, "for it was the loveliest of all of Mr. Basara's creations, made with the love that abided between him and her. He made it as a gift, they said. They say that when she spun at night, their little house would glow with light from the spinning wheel, like the aura of a saint. So they say. So they said."

Erben set his case back down and again removed his papers and pen and ink. He smiled, but it was not necessarily a kindly smile. Neither was it the smile of a sensitive friend. It was the smile of a treasure hunter who was unearthing a gemstone only found in the folktales of peasants. "Please," he said, "do tell me about the Rusalka Wheel."

* * *

July 25, 1865, Mielnica Podalska, Old Ukraine

"THEY SAY THAT RUSALKA led her husband, that would be Alexei, Mr. Basara to you, back to the pool where they met on a cold winter's night," said Kristina Tarashenko.

It was by now midsummer, and Karel Erben had returned to Podolia after a few months in Prague. He had just published *One Hundred Slavic Folk Tales In the Original Dialects* and was celebrating his triumph by continuing his collection of tales. What better place than Podolia? He was happy to be back in the field, for his research on the rusalki was incomplete. This time, he ventured at last into the insular village of Mielnica, where Alexei Basara and his wife purportedly had lived.

"Was her name, then, Rusalka? She appears to have been known by Tatyana," said Erben. The very name Rusalka was a corroborating indication that the woman, the wife of Alexei Basara, was considered by the people to be the mythical nymph. The rest of the testimony he'd gathered seemed only to imply that she was; there was no outright acknowledgement, taken as fact, of her otherworldly connection.

Mrs. Tarashenko smiled, her great age showing as either wisdom in her hazel eyes, or mild dissociation. Erben could not be sure which, but he had dutifully spread his pen and papers before him and written down every word. He had to strain to hear the occasionally wheezing voice of Mrs. Tarashenko; it seemed to Erben that her lungs must be very small.

"You've talked to Pavlo!" she said, squinting her left eye as if she'd found him out.

"Pavlo?"

"Pavlo Soroka, of course!"

"Mr. Soroka. Yes. We visited a few months ago, in May, at his home."

"He never lived in this village, sir. He just visited that cousin of his, Mykola. The cousin was from here," she said, "but that Pavlo was an outsider, I don't care what you say. Mykola passed some years ago, may he rest in peace. He was a good worker." Mrs. Tarashenko was, in fact, the only current resident of Mielnica who remembered the Basaras and had dealings with them. She mentioned a birthmark on Tatyana's shoulder, which she had seen personally and which she said looked like a fish. The color was purplish, and she had glimpsed it one day outside. Mrs. Tarashenko was quite heavy and busty, and she noted that Mrs. Basara was exactly the opposite, that she was "slim and flat as a board."

"And you will not find anyone aside from myself who had ever seen that mark," she said proudly.

Erben had Mrs. Tarashenko sketch the outline of the birthmark with his pen in his notebook. He made a few notes near the mark.

The old woman was happy to comply, and, Erben thought, modest-
ly skilled at drawing, though her hand shook. She looked up at Erben as she drew. Realizing that he noted her left-handedness, she
scowled and switched hands.

"I draw better with the left," she said, "but some think that's a
sign of the devil." She finished the drawing and gave Erben back his
notebook.

"Now," she said, "once they were at the pool, there was a certain bit of fear, as you might guess. It is common knowledge herea-
bouts that a rusalka, being one of the uncomfortable dead, is bent
on luring a man to his death. By drowning, sir! Have you found this
to be so? Have you found that, by and by, a person around here believes the water nymph to be deadly? To men, especially?"

"That is the prevalent belief," Erben admitted. "In fact, Mrs.
Tarashenko, I have no accounts that contradict that, except perhaps
from Mr. Soroka."

"Pavlo. Well, my dear professor, you have just been kicked in
the shin by another 'contradictory account,' I can assure you!"

Erben resituated his wire-rimmed glasses on his nose and said,
"Please go on, Mrs. Tarashenko."

"I will indeed. But let us be clear about the Old Ways. The Believers say that the restless spirits cannot so much as pull a hair on a
good man's head. No, that is what they say. The evil spirit, though,
has its ways and has many tools to do the devil's work. They will
drive a sane man or woman to take their own lives, sir. That is what
they do. They will lure, drive, even herd a man off a cliff, but raise
no finger to spill his blood directly. That's a thing they cannot do:
take a life.

"Now, as I say," she continued, resettling herself, "they had
one daughter, a little redhead, about a year old when they set out
for the pool. Took them about a day to walk it. It's where they first
met. They came to the pool, and Mr. Basara was not afraid. He did
not believe that Rusalka could do harm to him and was assured of
her love for him, and so on. It was a hot day, and they had a dip in

the river, Mr. Erben, leaving their clothes on the bank neatly folded. They dove and they swam, and they did other things that are none of your business ..."

"Mrs. Tarashenko," interrupted Erben. "May I ask where you heard this tale? You see, much of my information is very, very old. Very removed. You speak as if you were privy to the events."

"I am privy to nothing, certainly!" said Mrs. Tarashenko, a bit uncertain of what Erben was driving at. "I tell you only what I know for a fact."

"But you could not have been there ..."

"Indeed I was not! I would never burst in upon a person's privacy! You are a fool to think so!"

"I beg your pardon, Mrs. Tarashenko. But how did you learn of this?"

"From herself, from Mrs. Basara."

"She told you."

"Professor, if you are a professor, I have already explained that Mrs. Basara was mute. Do you remember me telling you that ... it was not five minutes ago."

"Yes, yes ..."

"She was a clever woman and in more ways than one," she said, squinting again, weighing whether the professor understood her meaning. She couldn't tell. He seemed a bit slow to her. "She talked to me with pictures and with her hands. And that was enough. She could whisper, somewhat, but only a few words at a time. We drew pictures among ourselves as a way of talking. It may take longer, but nothing is lost."

"You were on a close personal basis with the woman," ventured Erben.

"As I had no children of my own, sir, I felt drawn to Rusalka like a child of mine. She was quite young in age, in her twenties I would say, and so beautiful I simply am at a loss for words. And I was unmarried until late in life and saw myself as her guide and auntie, being good for each other, obviously. And her dear children … for she had two others soon after …"

"And, for the record, what is your age now?" asked Erben.

"That is my business, not yours," she huffed. Once again she squinted, acknowledging the affront to her privacy, but this time her eyes watered slightly because she hadn't yet had tea. She did not tell Erben that she was in her late nineties, or that she was fifty-seven when the Basaras left Mielnica, or that she was a little uncertain of her exact age, though she knew quite well that her birthday was the twenty-ninth of June, recently passed.

She had never talked about her age, in fact, with anyone. Mrs. Tarashenko had far exceeded the life expectancy in that region, and to bring attention to her years could only inflame the superstitions of the villagers: Anyone who lived that long was obviously in league with the devil. Worse, acknowledgement of her age, out loud, would surely attract the wrath of the spirit world, so Mrs. Tarashenko had two entire communities who were uncomfortable with extreme age — the villagers and the spirits.

"I see. But, Mrs. Tarashenko, please continue."

"Mr. Basara had promised to make her a spinning wheel, as he was an accomplished luthier and knew how to work wood. She wanted her spinning wheel to be made of a specific tree or log that had fallen into the river long ago, and she knew of it as it lay down deep in the silt and the dark of the river pool. It was an old maple or may have been a pine of some sort, she said, Rusalka said without words, sir," said Mrs. Tarashenko, now feeling short-tempered. "Said that she used to swim down to see it glowing, as they say, at the river bottom as a youth during the spring. In case you are wondering, it is common knowledge that rusalki inhabit the trees in spring after the cold, dark winter months, but take a morning dip in their pools. Do you understand that, or shall I say it again?"

"I have written it down, every word," said Erben.

"You might learn something here, sir. I was told by Rusalka, who you insist on calling Tatyana Basara, that maple or pine must age six years in the sun, bound by its bark, before it can be slabbed. But this was not the case for that old log. It was ancient, as the story goes, and laced with precious amber and opal. Don't look so confounded, sir. I am telling you what I know and what I have seen, and I have seen that wood personally, and I have seen the very wheel that Mr. Basara made for his loving wife! Seen it! But because it had been under the river so long, it did need to dry out, you see. It turned out that the wood was perfect and straight of grain and also, in places, of a patterned grain that had spread and the gap filled with precious opal. That would be near the base, you see, and would have been the desire of any luthier, which Mr. Basara happened to be anyway."

"Yes, I see."

"And, a very good one at that."

"Yes."

"You don't believe me," she said flatly.

"I believe you, Mrs. Tarashenko. But even if I did not, the mere account of this extraordinary occurrence would be worth saving for posterity. And that is what I do."

"Yes, but you don't believe me."

Erben looked directly into her eyes, and then pushed his glasses up further on his nose. "I will find more proof than just yours, Mrs. Tarashenko. Believe me."

She shrugged and dismissed the comment as hubris. "After they'd pulled it from the river depths, sir, our Mr. Basara hauled it home on a small wheeled cart pulled by two goats, one mottled that gave milk and one white for its hair. Once back at their humble cottage, and believe me it was humble ... the workshop was far larger than the rest of the house ... Mr. Basara set about sawing the log into slabs, and he had the help of dear Rusalka, lovely woman that she was and very attendant to her husband, and then also a young man from the village, and that would have been ... hm, I can't remember his name, though I can see his face as clear as a bell ... he apprenticed to the luthier for some years ... and set about aging the slabs by this means: bound in linen mesh and applying wax, then to place it in a cool dark place for one year, slowly completing the drying process as prescribed by ancient Podolian woodsmen, all this to avoid cracking of the wood along the grain as it dried." She smiled proudly.

"You are quite literate, Mrs. Tarashenko, and very clear in your description."

"Thank you, sir. The pool was not that far, really, a brisk walk of six hours from the cemetery and church. Eight hours if you tarry. I never went there, but I have spoken to those who have, and to Mrs. Basara. But let us say, she also chose the thick trunk of a tremendous, fallen maple tree on the opposite side of the pool to be used for other parts of the spinning wheel, but which never was used, and so became Mr. Basara's stock to make his viols and skrypkas. Two birds with one stone, as you may have heard. And they cut and aged the rest of that wood in a similar fashion and also as prescribed.

"And, you see, it was she, Rusalka, who taught her dear Alexei to age the stock properly by wrapping it in tight-wove linen, waxed, and packing it away from the light for a year. To prevent cracking along the grain. I believe they had their second child before the wood had seasoned. And the little thing looked just like her mother, even as an infant, and she looked just like her sister, Sophiya, as well, but had dark blond hair instead of red. Sophiya means, in our language, wisdom, for I doubt you knew that. I cared for the children at times, as I had no children of my own. The second child's name was Chane, which everyone called Khana as in the Russian and not the Hebrew, and that's a name often used by the Jews, but they weren't Jews to my knowledge. But Mr. Basara was a friend of the Jews, as he was a friend to all, and provided the musical instruments they needed. The boy came along two years after the first and one since Chane.

"Well, you see, he did that, aged the wood, Mr. Basara did, and then began cutting the blanks for all the parts that one turns. He was a good turner, but his specialty was instruments. He made skrypkas and the bows as well, but later he modeled them after the Italian fiddles to sell in the cities. I never did like those Italian things, the way they sound, but Mr. Alexei's were wonderful to gaze on and much in demand. I understood him to be very talented in making those fine Italian-style ones. Anyway, Mr. Alexei called the cut pieces of wood for the wheel 'blanks,' but he meant long cut pieces that were for the legs and uprights and such. Do you have an understanding of turning, sir?"

"Excuse me?" said Erben.

"Turning wood."

"Into what?" he asked.

"Into a frog, sir! Into a mouse! Professor von Dolt, I mean turning wood on a lathe!"

"I see," he said. "No, I am not familiar ..." Erben was taken aback by the insult, but set his anger aside rather than jeopardize the information coming from this rather cross old woman.

"Make a pole lathe by running a strap from a sapling to a pedal, you see. Wrap it once around the end of the blank, which is fixed on the ends so it will rotate like the axle of a hay cart. You *do* understand 'hay cart'? The strap is connected to the pressed pedal and the bending tree. You press and release, so the sapling pulls it back, press again, release, over and over, and you spin the blank first one way and then the other. Then you hold a chisel or whatnot to the blank, and start carving as it spins. You can carve only in one direction, which is obvious if you have been paying attention to what I am saying."

"Oh, yes," said Erben. "I have actually seen that, now that I understand what it was."

"Well, then," said Mrs. Tarashenko, "using his luthier's tools, I suppose, Alexei, Mr. Basara to you, turned the spindles for the wheel, the legs, the uprights, you know, the maidens and the mother-of-all, and he planed flat the table and treadle and so on and so on, and he made all of the parts from heavy opal-streaked maple wood, including the parts for the great wheel and the fly and the bobbins, of which there were many. Bobbins. Many because Rusalka was a very good spinner, and very productive. Sold her flax to the weavers, sold her wool there over the river, far away, for rugs. Rug weavers. Kilim makers. Mr. Alexei carved figures into the wheel, images of the sea. I have never seen the sea, sir, but for Mr. Alexei's carving. I can assure you I am more familiar with it than yourself!"

"Yes. And the great wheel?"

"Sir, I was talking about the great wheel, which may be called the drive wheel because it uses a small belt of hemp to spin the fly. It is called the great wheel or the drive wheel, for it drives the fly and the bobbin. I personally watched the slow progress of that wheel that Alexei Basara made, and I am certainly aware of the opal streaks, which became a sparkling fire when it spun, and the gold leaf and delicate painting he did on the great wheel, pictures of Rusalka and the sea."

"The actual wheel? From, what do we say, before 1830 in any case?"

"Yes. In the twenties. Twenty-two or so. Twenty-one maybe."

"And?"

"The man mixed his stains and paints from the minerals. Lapis for blue, malachite green, cinnabar for red, and an oxide of lead for the yellow. He ground the stones to powder as fine as can be, and added to it the flax oil that I brought him. Mrs. Basara asked for the oil, and, as I worked retting and braking the flax each year, for pay, I saved a portion of the seed and Rusalka extracted the oil for the paint and for the varnish herself. Do you understand that? Yes? Good.

"Mr. Basara, for his part, painted elegant figures of the rusalki and their lives and her loves and her soul — for they do have souls, Mr. Erben, whatever you may say or believe! — and his work was elegant, far and wide, and coveted by many, for he carved it into the wood before he applied the paint! And he gilded the edges of the wheel and the fly and parts of the maidens and uprights. It was remarkable. The angels would have taken it, had they been thieves!"

"My goodness."

Mrs. Tarashenko paused. Her demeanor changed. She grew sullen and her smile turned to a stern, thin-lipped frown. She was very, very old and she was tired of talking. She said, "Do you say that I am lying?" There, the words were out. Her voice was flat.

"No, no," said Erben quickly. "Not at all. I was only expressing my shock that such a thing could truly exist."

"I saw what I saw, professor doctor, and I know what I know. Maybe the fact that a thing of such beauty could exist in this world seems impossible to you. But I tell you this on the shrine of St. Friday, take my soul if it isn't true … Mr. Basara cut and aged and sanded and planed and scraped and carved and painted and varnished and gilded that wheel as testament to his love of Miss Rusalka! Tatyana, as the others called her! No truer love, no truer wheel, for it would spin of its own accord for an hour without pressing one's foot to the treadle but one time alone!" She was shouting, caught herself, and fell silent.

There was a long pause.

"And there is another thing," said Mrs. Tarashenko hesitantly, as if she were uncertain if Erben was worthy to hear.

"What is that, Mrs. Tarashenko?" asked Erben. He was sincere, and Mrs. Tarashenko could tell that. So she continued.

"When dear Rusalka spun her wheel, the drive, and the bobbins as well, would catch the light, and it would begin to reflect, and it would cast threads of red light about the room, such as I have never seen before or since. And, my Mr. Professor, it would do this for not one other person who had the privilege of spinning on that wheel! Only herself. And if I dare say more, I would insist that those red strings of light had a mind of their own, and that they danced of their own accord, and not simply as reflections of the sun or some such thing."

Erben's brow furrowed. "How interesting."

His response upset Mrs. Tarashenko considerably, who interpreted it as disbelief combined with disinterest in the secret she held most dear, that of the red lights. But she wouldn't let it rest there, adding, "The koldun, old Mr. Mazur, said those were the strands that hold the world in place, you fool, the lines that connect the mountains and streams, the trees and the stone, and soul to soul. The living to the dead." She was referring to an older man who had lived nearby at the time and was much sought after then for his curative potions and incantations.

Again, there was a long silence. This had not been an easy interview for Karel Erben. "Mrs. Tarashenko," he said. "Can you tell me again about how long ago that was? You say after their first two children, but when might that have been? Is 1823 correct?"

Mrs. Tarashenko blushed slightly. "Would have been some forty years ago and more, if I measure the days correctly. Forty-two or so. And I will not tell you my age, sir! Though I might have been fifty-something at the time, not marrying until my sixties! And I indeed saw the wheel and I can tell you there was no more beautiful spinning wheel on this earth, not even the jeweled creations of the czars!

"And I know that great wheel was as true as Mary's birth," she said, blushing at her oath. "And to see that dear woman spin ... I will tell you this, sir: She spun as if twisting heaven and earth together. Simple as that. They say that spun fiber connects paradise with us down here, connects life with death, and hers was nothing less than that thread that binds the one to the other. And by St. Friday herself, those red strands of light are that very thread."

"But what happened to the spinning wheel? And to the family Basara?" asked Erben.

"They had to leave, I suppose. In eighteen and twenty-four if we are counting correctly. Folks never trusted her, though she was as true as that luthier's wheel. Their very house was burned to the ground! Oh, yes, one night they set that house in flames and burned them out! Burned them out for fear of the unclean dead, sir!

"But they lived through it, I am happy to say. Lived through it somehow and left with all they had about two days after. Two days but only one night.

"And there was one man behind it all, and he urged the other villagers to set the flame. And he was an evil sort and never set his hand to the torches, just had others do his work. That, my dear sir, is what the evil dead do, the restless spirits, for they have no power to deal out death themselves, only to drive another off a cliff, or to suicide. Yes, suicide!"

She caught her breath and, with her kerchief, dabbed the corner of her mouth.

"And they took that wheel with them, for they had managed to save it somehow, and placed as it was in the cart along with the youngest child, the boy, and the girls walked behind with a few goats, playing and throwing grass grains at one another and laughing, but not the boy because the boy was still toddling. And they had a pair of goats to pull it as well, when they left."

"More than two goats," said Erben, and he jotted down a note.

"And then the folks buried the ashes of the house and the drying shed, and that would be all that I know about that. They were on their way to old Lemberg, where folks are more understanding. And I don't know about them after that, but I do know that they were happy or I would have felt something, for I was that close to Rusalka."

"Who did? Who burned the house?"

"I told you. You don't listen. I will not say the name of the man, for I will not draw the evil toward me. He lived with his crippled mother somewhere in the village, taking care of her for she had a curve in her spine. Do you think me a fool?! So I say again, why, it was the villagers, of course. Burned it to the ground and buried the ashes so as the forest spirits wouldn't infest it later, and also as the Basaras could not return. There's leshiye come in from the wood there and again, they say, and that's a fact that's true. But they wanted that family gone and wanted no memory of them, the villagers, and this I know, for I was there. Then, the same day, a bit later, they burned out the koldun, Mr. Mazur, for it was him that looked into that bowl of water of his and saw what he saw, which was violence coming toward the family Basara, and he told Alexei Basara it would be best for him to take his family away from here before it was too late, and for they might die of the violence in the form of beatings and fire. And they believed Old Mazur about the unrest and they hid the wheel in the forest and some of the tools as well — for the most part it was his tools, the luthier tools. And that was why, when you first sat down, you said you could not find the man's home, though Pavlo Soroka told you exactly where it should have been. Pavlo is an outsider, sir! His memory is better some days than others, as I am sure you know. But I think he forgot the burning, is all. He's not from here, I can tell you that. He's from over the way, over to Borschev. That town is too big!"

Erben had been writing as quickly as he could, but even using his abbreviated method of verbatim notes, he could barely keep up with the talkative Mrs. Tarashenko. He knew she had to be nearly a century old, simple arithmetic.

"Then they left Mielnica for Lemberg in 1823?" he asked.

"I already told you that. Everyone said Lemberg."

Appendix II

A brief chronology of the Rusalka Wheel
and the generations through which it passed:

GEOGRAPHICAL NOTE: Mielnica and Borschev are towns within the Borschev raion, or district, of Ukraine's Ternopil Oblast (or province, which was established in 1939). They are 140 miles from Lemberg. This area is referred to in *The Rusalka Wheel* as Old Ukraine, and through the years was ruled by various nations and commonwealths including the Ottoman Turks, the Polish-Lithuanian Commonwealth, the Kingdom of Galicia, the Austro-Hungarian Empire, Russia, Poland, the USSR, and eventually the nation Ukraine.

1775 (*October*) Alexei Basara is born near Mielnica, to Burian Basara, a tavern keeper and flute-maker (he carved folk sopilkas from local woods such as maple, hornbeam, and birch) and Sasha Basara, a flax spinner.

1817 (*November*) 42-year-old luthier Alexei Basara meets Rusalka at a pool on the Dniester River outside Mielnica.

1820 The red-haired Sophiya Basara is born, first child of Alexei Basara and Rusalka.

1821 Alexei builds the legendary Rusalka Wheel from submerged ancient-growth maple laced with opal deposits, a gift to his love, Rusalka.

1821 and **1822** Chane and Grigory Basara are born to Rusalka and Alexei Basara.

1822 The municipally sanctioned marriage of Alexei Basara and Tatyana (the name adopted by Rusalka), whose surname is illegible, is listed in the official records of Borschev. (*Note: Non-orthodox church and synagogue marriages were not recognized by the state, and the children of such unions were restricted from attending school, etc., essentially forcing compliance with the government. However, the municipal records of state-sanctioned marriages made possible the genealogical research that Jaroslav Kvapil and Mrs. Angelina Reynolds undertook in the 1890s and 1980s*).

1823 After being burned out by townsfolk afraid of having a rusalka in their midst, the Basara family flees Mielnica for Lemberg in a goat cart.

1830 Czar Nicolas I of Russia attempts unsuccessfully to acquire the Rusalka Wheel after a kniaz, or prince, of the House of Galicia informs Nicolas of its existence. The moment was memorialized in an engraving by Ivan Alexeyevich Ivanov (b. 1779 in Moscow), an architect, painter, and printmaker who also illustrated Alexander Sergeyevich Pushkin's* work, including Pushkin's unfinished poem, *Rusalka*.

1840 Sophiya Basara marries Ivan Pipenko.

1842 Anichka Pipenko is born, daughter of Sophiya.

1850 Czech historian and folktale collector (in the vein of the Brothers Grimm of Germany) Karel Erben is named Archival Secretary of the National Museum of Prague at age 39.

1853 Karel Erben publishes *A Bouquet of Folk Legends*, a collection of tales from the Bohemian countryside.

1856 Premiere of *Rusalka*, an opera by the Russian composer Alexander Sergeyevich Dargomyzhsky.* The libretto was adapted from poet/playwright Pushkin's unfinished poem of the same name.

1865 (*April-May*) Karel Erben visits Borschev, recording rusalka lore.

1865 Erben publishes his seminal *One Hundred Slavic Folk Tales and Legends in the Original Dialects*.

1865 (*July*) Erben returns to Borschev district, visiting Mielnica township, further recording rusalka lore.

Kristina Tarashenko, age 93, sketches from memory the Rusalka Wheel in Erben's notebook. She observed the wheel as a close friend of the Basaras in the early 1820s. She also sketched Tatyana Basara's unusual birthmark.

1867 Anichka Pipenko, daughter of Sophiya, marries Vaslav Salenko, a musician.

1871 Yulia Salenko is born, daughter of Anichka. She is mute from birth.

1887 Work begins on restoration of Stryiskyi Park, Lemberg, where Hannah Lazarenko would one day swim.

1889 Yulia Salenko marries Dmytro Lazarenko, a music teacher.

1892 Hannah Lazarenko is born, daughter of Yulia.

1895 (*July*) Czech poet, playwright, and librettist Jaroslav Kvapil visits Yulia Lazarenko in the Lemberg ghetto, and observes the Rusalka Wheel. He then writes his inspired libretto for what would become Antonin Dvorak's most famous opera, *Rusalka*.

1896 Czech composer Dvorak writes his symphonic poems, *The Golden Spinning Wheel* and *The Water Goblin*, foreshadowing his *Rusalka*.

1900 Jaroslav Kvapil is named director, National Theater of Prague, at age 32.

1900 (*April-Nov*) Dvorak composes the score for *Rusalka*.

1901 (*March 31*) Premiere of Dvorak's opera *Rusalka*, libretto by Jaroslav Kvapil, in Prague, with Czech soprano Ruzena Maturova in the title role.

1926 Klara Lazarenko is born, daughter of Hannah.

1941 (*June*) Lvov (Lemberg) falls to the German army; the Rusalka Wheel vanishes. German forces allow Ukrainian nationals to attack Soviets and Jews. Nazi rule of Ukraine begins.

1941 (*October*) Former Ukraine capital Kharkov (before 1934) falls to the Nazi war machine.

1944 The Rusalka Wheel is discovered by Marina Kasparov beside a spring pool outside the besieged city of Kharkov, Ukraine.

1946 (*April*) Hannah Lazarenko is reunited with the Rusalka Wheel among refugees in a forest outside Kharkov, before traveling with daughter Klara, the brothers Bukoski, and Marina and Uri Kasparov to Moscow.

1948 Klara Lazarenko marries Mikhail Olenovich in Moscow.

1949 Leysa Olenovich is born, daughter of Klara.

1983 Olena Mariya Olenovich is born, daughter of Leysa Olenovich, unmarried.

1985 Leysa succumbs to lung disorder, probably tuberculosis.

1986 Klara Olenovich and granddaughter Olena Mariya "return" to Mielnica from Moscow after the death of Leysa.

1988 (*August*) Fire levels the Olenoviches' Mienica apartment; the Rusalka Wheel is thought to have burned.

1988 (*August*) Smelling of smoke, the Rusalka Wheel is discovered at the door of Sterling's Antiques, a collectibles shop in San Francisco's Chinatown.

1989 (*Christmas Day*) Klara and Olena Mariya land by freighter at San Francisco's Pier 80.

---

* Alexander Sergeyevich Pushkin and Alexander Sergeyevich Dargomyzhsky have the same given and middle names.

CPSIA information can be obtained
at www.ICGtesting.com
Printed in the USA
LVOW11s2003280218
568198LV00004B/925/P